God's creation is more wonderous and complex than we know. We live in its silhouette.

Novels by W. F. Rogers

<u>The Mirror and the Prism Series</u>

Silhouette
Point of Refraction

Visit the author's website: https://wfrogers.com

The Mirror and the Prism

Book 1

Silhouette

W. F. Rogers

W&P | WAYRIDGE PRESS

For Paige and Lara, of course

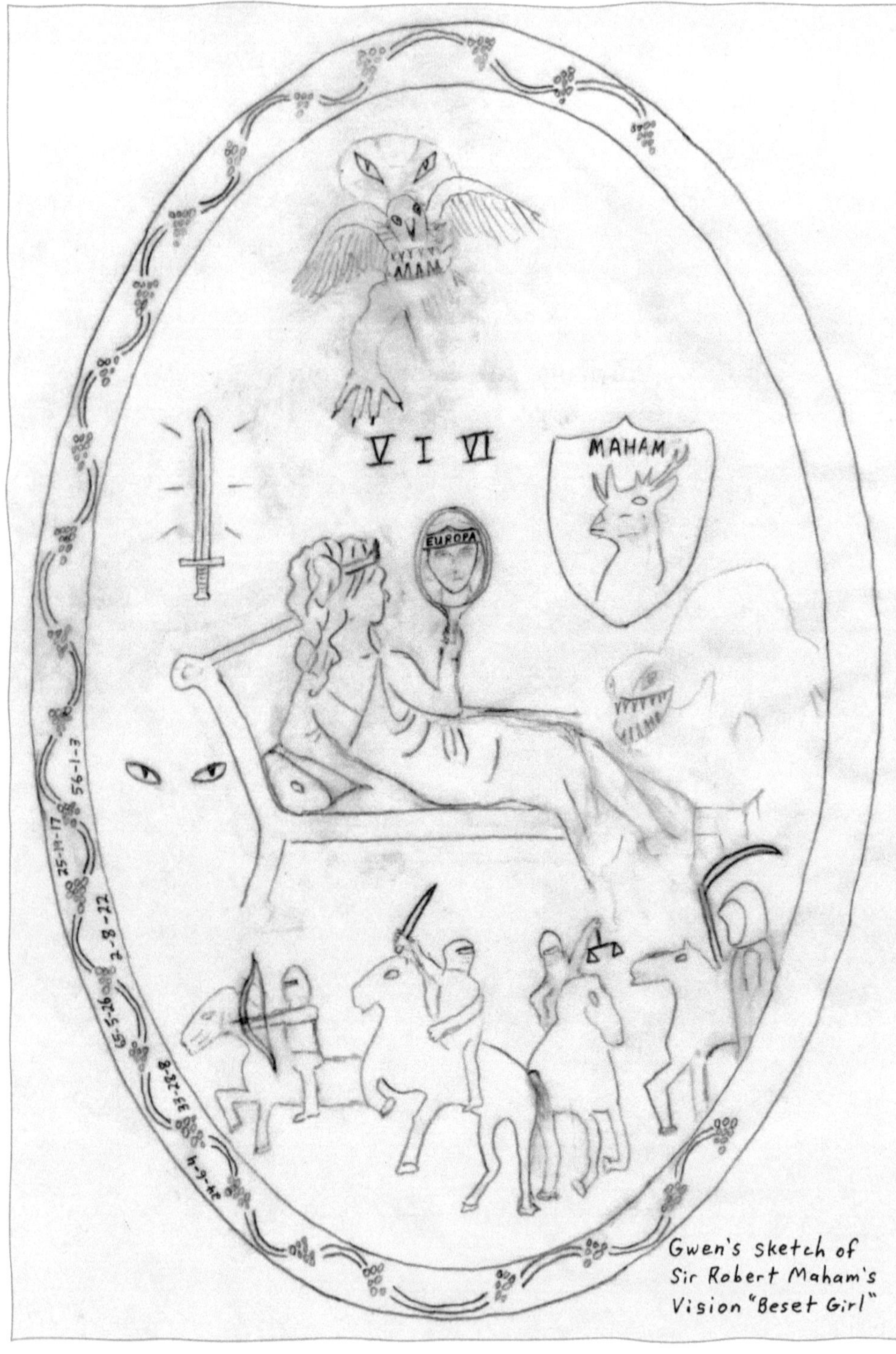

Gwen's sketch of
Sir Robert Maham's
Vision "Beset Girl"

CONTENTS

Hi Paige and Lara,

My English cousins learned I was studying architecture at Trinity College and invited me to spend last weekend at their estate in Devon. I was happy to meet them, and Maham House was amazing. But even more amazing was what I found in the dresser in my bedroom. I accidentally pulled a drawer off its track, and there they were at the bottom of the cabinet—pages from Gwendolyn Maham's 1918 diary.

Ten years ago, my parents took me on vacation to the UK. At a family reunion in London, one of the adults said, "There's one vision left. I wish I knew what happened to Gwendolyn's last diary. If we had it and the prism, we could find Sir Robert's book."

I didn't know what it meant, but it sounded mysterious (and I was scolded for eavesdropping). I never forgot Gwendolyn's name. And there her name was at the top of the pages! I've attached photos of them. You'll see why I say they're amazing. I hope you can read the faded cursive handwriting—I had a lot of trouble.

I'm in Cambridge now but going back to Devon later this month. My cousin William gave me permission to look for the rest of the diary. I've never been so excited. Maybe I should change my major to forensic science!

Best,

Kirk

CHAPTER 1

Night Arrival
24-6-4

Devon, England
March 1918

Gwendolyn Maham was aware she was dreaming. Nevertheless, the dark landscape of the moor was indelibly real and geographically accurate. From a grassy hill a few miles east of her home, she surveyed the breadth and depth of the rolling plain, her eyes lingering on a tor: a pile of granite stacked by elemental powers long before humans arrived in Devonshire. She did not need to touch the rocks to know their cold indifference. Downslope, the bog had a syrupy undertow. The night wind was a shiver; blowing fierce and raw from the North Atlantic, it passed effortlessly through her fluttering nightgown. It swept her frail body upward as carelessly as it might a dry leaf.

Concentrating, Gwen brought herself to a halt in the emptiness between the ground and clouds. She did not like the turn of events. This was a boundary place—neither earth nor firmament. It was a place with more than one nature and yet none of its own, like the line of the horizon or the middle of a crossroads—a place where the fabric of reality was unstable.

The air was thick with scents of rain and ozone. Distant thunder rumbled like an artillery exchange between the Allied and German Armies fighting for the blistered fields of France. Gwen imagined that a dark legion was crashing through a barrier. Then she was seized by an overpowering fear; the storm was coming from the east, *against* the wind, its front roiling like millions of shadows clambering over one another.

"Lord!"

The cry was involuntary. She had not called out to God since the dark night she entangled herself in attempted magic. She could see the jumbled peak of High Tor poking above the horizon. That was where she had estranged herself from Him.

No—their estrangement had begun before that. It had begun when He took Freddie from her. High Tor was a consequence, not the cause. It was *His* fault, not hers.

She felt His presence and wanted to hide.

I'm sending someone to you. Do as he says.

"But—"

But there was no time to ponder. She heard a cantering horse.

She was on the ground now, concealed in a ditch. A man wearing a British officer's greatcoat and cap rode at her from the direction of the storm. When he looked to the sky, she followed his gaze.

Her heart stopped. A winged shadow flew westward toward the manor house in the distance. She could see the creature in spite of the near darkness because it was so very black against the gray-streaked clouds. Its feathers weren't just charcoal-hued; they were voids into which light disappeared. It had the form of a cormorant—a vicious-looking cormorant with a preternaturally long body and wingspan. Only the bird's eyes, glinting maroon fire, were clearly visible.

The cormorant quickly outdistanced the rider, who galloped past Gwen. She caught a glimpse of the man's face and recognized her great-uncle Geoffrey.

She willed herself to the manor and found it all wrong. The house she knew was there, but its floors were fragmented and inserted piecemeal into medieval fortress walls and turrets. That was not unusual—her prophetic dreams often had fantastical as well as real elements. Or rather, they *used* to; she had not had such a dream since the episode on High Tor. She blinked until the fortress walls dissolved and the house was assembled correctly.

The real dwelling was imposing even without phantasmagorical battlements. The southern half of the sprawling great house, dating from the 1880s, was a splendid example of Neo-Renaissance architecture. And the three-hundred-year-old North Wing, though shuttered for half a century and suffering from neglect, was a large and ornate Elizabethan edifice. A visitor once said Maham House had "harmonious dissimilarity in an eclectic sort of way."

Gwen stood on the roof of the Beacon Tower, searching the sky for the cormorant. Blue-gray light flickered within the sullen clouds. On impulse, she turned to her right and looked down through a third-story window.

Inside the bedroom slept a fifteen-year-old girl with pale yellow hair. Her eyes were tightly shut, her mouth a grimace. Gwen had never thought herself pretty. Now, after years of illness, her prominent cheekbones emphasized her gaunt appearance.

She sensed the cormorant's approach. It swooped in a circle and glided over the North Wing before landing on a ledge of the East Tower. For a fraction of a second, it was something other than a bird—something with arms and teeth.

Gwen tried to scream *Wake up!* at herself in the bedroom, but her voice would not work. When she turned back to the cormorant, it was gazing directly into her dream eyes. It knew she could see it. The hair on her neck stood up.

Wind hissed across the roof; heavy raindrops splattered all around. Electric currents condensed and joined. A tremendous lightning arc, brighter and hotter than the sun, shot down from the sky and struck a North Wing chimney.

The thunderclap hammered her room.

Gwen jerked upright in bed, her eyes spectral blue in the lightning light.

"Save us!"

She peered apprehensively at the windows, fearing to see the bird, hoping for some sign of her great-uncle, but it was too black to distinguish anything beyond the panes. She switched on her bedside lamp. It flickered as if modulated by the storm.

A ferocious blast of wind hit the side of the house, and something snapped. The window casements flew open on their hinges and crashed against the wall.

Icy, wet air howled around the room.

Gwen tumbled out of bed and staggered to the gaping window.

The cormorant was perched on the East Tower exactly where she had seen it in her dream.

It dove at her.

Her hand dropped instinctively to her desk and snatched the medieval dagger she used as a letter opener. She thrust its razor-sharp point at the bird.

With an incredible heave of its wings, the animal stopped in midair, narrowly avoiding impalement.

"JACK!" Gwen screamed.

She turned her head to shout toward her bedroom door but was struck dumb when she saw her floor-standing mirror. Reflected in the cheval glass, the creature out the window had leathery skin, fanged jaws, and sinewy hands with clawed fingers.

When she spun around, it was a cormorant again.

She slashed the air in warning. The creature hovered outside, flapping powerfully, flinging rain. Gwen slipped on the wet floor. She grabbed the windowsill to steady herself.

"JACK, HELP!"

The cormorant flew closer. Gwen jabbed at its face, compelling it to retreat. She swung the casements shut but couldn't secure them because the bolt that fastened them to the sill was missing.

The cormorant crashed against the panes, knocking Gwen backward. The creature scrambled onto the windowsill.

"Good Lord!" Jack Maham halted in the doorway. But he hesitated only a second before charging at the bird.

Gwen thought her brother intended to seize it, but he reached for her dagger. He closed his hand around hers, and together they forced the tip of the blade at the cormorant. The thing failed to heed, was pricked in the chest, and recoiled.

It bent its neck to look at its bleeding breast. Then it raised its head and stared fixedly into Gwen's eyes, its own eyes filled with violence and surprise as if it had not foreseen this turn of events.

Then the cormorant uttered a bloodcurdling cry, wheeled, kicked off the windowsill, and flew into the night.

Jack released Gwen's hand and shut the windows against the storm. "That bird was rabid!" He gazed outside. "Can birds be rabid?"

"It wasn't a bird." Gwen breathed hard and sagged against her desk. "At least it hadn't the mind of a bird." She glanced at her mirror. With trembling fingers, she swept dripping strands of hair from her face. Once, her locks had been golden. Now they were a lifeless hue, like the food she was forced to eat.

"Blast!" Jack couldn't secure the window. The latch that fastened the two casements together was sound, but they wouldn't stay shut without the bolt that locked the left one to the sill. He found the missing part on the floor and slipped it into its broken slide. He pushed until the bolt went into the socket in the sill.

Gwen set her dagger on her desk. Then she coughed and collapsed.

Jack helped her to bed. "Are you hurt?"

"No. I—" She shuddered violently.

"Don't worry. The bird's gone."

"No," Gwen said without looking up. "It's still out there."

Jack stepped to the window. "Not anywhere nearby."

In fact, he could not have had any idea what was nearby because nothing could be seen beyond the ribbons of rain streaming down the panes. He touched the cold, quivering glass. "Would you like to spend the night with Christopher and me? You can have my bed. I don't mind sleeping on the floor."

"Perhaps I should."

Jack wiggled the loose bolt in its mangled slide brackets. After some consideration, he slipped Gwen's cross-hilt dagger through the casement handles.

Gwen looked again into her mirror, but all she saw was her own ghostly image. Her skin was very pale, almost translucent. In her white nightgown, she appeared ethereal. Jack, by contrast, was solid. Sixteen years old, he had inherited the athletic Maham build. And his face had acquired a hardness that led people to assume he was several years older than his sister, though their birthdays were barely thirteen months apart.

Of course, almost no one saw Gwen nowadays. Her health had begun to deteriorate when the war started. She had become bedridden after her eldest brother was killed in 1916 in the Battle of the Somme. She had known Freddie was gone the instant he died. He had taught her to read and dance and jump her horse over hedges. She relied on his secret signals to choose the right utensil for each course at dinner—it was a game of theirs. On warm summer days, Freddie, Jack, and Gwen would race around the gardens and woods pretending to be knights and a lady of King Arthur's court, running all the way to the eastern edge of the estate where the narrow River Dartrun splashed its way southward.

Jack put his face to a windowpane. "I wonder if the bird has flown away."

"It hasn't."

Jack tried harder to see. He reached to pull away Gwen's dagger and reopen the windows.

"Don't!" Gwen cried.

He looked at her. "All right."

Gwen swung her legs to the floor. "I think I'll go to the kitchen."

"What do you want? I'll get it for you."

"I want to go downstairs."

"Don't be foolish." Jack spread his arms to block her way to the door.

"I—" Gwen broke into another coughing fit.

He helped her back into bed. "I'll get Mother."

"No, Jack! *Please!*" Gwen begged, clutching her brother's wrist. "She'll give me more of that vile medicine. It doesn't do anything except turn my stomach."

He wavered. "Very well. I'll bring some tea. Or would you prefer milk?"

"Let me go with you."

"Yesterday, you were too sick to continue your Latin lessons, or so you said."

Gwen considered the darkness underneath her dressing table. "There are too many shadows in this room."

Jack looked at the dim recesses in and around the room's Edwardian furnishings. "Why have you fought Mother so hard to stay here?"

"Why do you think?"

Their mother, Lady Buckleigh, wanted to move Gwen to a bedroom near the master suite on the second floor. But Miss Harkless also lived in that part of the house, and Gwen was determined to keep as far from Miss Harkless as possible.

"Lie down and rest."

"Uncle Geoffrey is coming."

Jack stared at her. "When?"

"Tonight."

"No one would travel in this weather."

"He's on the road right now. He was chasing the cormorant."

"Are you sure?"

Rain rattled harder than ever against the window panes.

"Yes."

Jack struck a match and lit the candle in the holder on the butler's table beside Gwen's bed. "I'll get your milk."

"Tea."

"Tea, then." Jack lowered the weather glass around the candle. "You'll be all right?"

She nodded unhappily.

"I'll be back shortly." Jack glanced one more time at the windows, then went out the door.

Gwen stared at the rose-patterned wallpaper in the hallway. It glowed orange for several seconds, then turned gray when Jack's candle was gone.

"The world is so dark," Gwen said. "And empty."

The rambling manor house certainly felt empty. Most of the staff had departed in 1914 with the coming of war—the footmen for the trenches where they were shot or blown up, and the maids to munitions factories where their hands turned yellow. Harrison, the old butler, died quietly in his sleep in 1916. Two women came during the day to clean, and several local boys helped maintain the grounds and stables. But only four full-time servants remained. Mrs. Nellis was now housekeeper and lady's maid as well as cook. Merrill, the chauffeur, had thought of enlisting as a tank driver even though he was forty-five years old but stayed because Lady Buckleigh insisted he was indispensable. Greggs, the gardener, was too ancient for military service and, besides, had a habit of passing afternoons in what Gwen's mother euphemistically called a "dipsomaniacal muddle." That meant idle, mumbling drunk.

Finally, there was Miss Harkless. The children did not know where the nurse had come from nor the circumstances of her hiring in the cheerless winter of 1916. The woman dispensed oily, odd-colored medicines that Christopher, Gwen's younger brother, called potions. A few months after arriving, Miss Harkless unilaterally added *tutor* to her job description and began tormenting Gwen's mind as well as her body.

"I'll be the next to go," Gwen said, coughing weakly. "Won't I, Lord?"

Jack padded down the corridor. The dank air smelled of old fabric and mildew. Why did his sister have to say such troubling things? Was the cormorant really something more than a bird? Gwen had meant what she said—meant it literally. If anyone else had made the claim, Jack would have dismissed it as hysteria. But Gwen knew things that were impossible to know.

The flickering candle cast animated light and dark patterns on the faded wallpaper. Jack passed his bedroom. His ten-year-old brother Christopher was sleeping inside. The chambers on the other side of the corridor were unoccupied. Jack's imagination populated them with phantoms and ghouls.

He veered left, entered the East Tower, and plodded down its stairs.

After reaching the second floor, he allowed himself the comforting thought that his parents were close by. That was quickly followed by the even more comforting thought that Miss Harkless was *not* nearby. She had gone to visit an ailing sister she had never mentioned before.

Continuing his descent, Jack had the distinct impression that he was sinking into a pit. He passed the first floor.

On the ground floor, he came to a heavy, well-padded oak door. The East Tower acted as an amplifying horn. The baize padding on the door kept chatter and clatter in the servants' areas from trumpeting upstairs. But there was no need to close the door tonight, so he left it wide open. He exited the tower and turned right.

The next corridor was as unadorned as those in the main residence were opulent. He walked until he came to the small kitchen. That was what the family called it. It was small only in comparison to the bigger one used to prepare food for banquets; anyone who lived in a normal-size house would have considered it quite large.

He paused inside the door. A knee-deep layer of cold mist floated above the frigid flagstone floor. He had seen something similar on another wet winter night. Knowing that the undulating vapor was only condensation did not make it any less unnerving.

He waded through the clammy mist, thankful that the storm had not cut the house's electric power. The ceiling light came on when he turned the switch.

The kitchen had several modern appliances, including a gas range. He lit a burner and put a kettle on to boil.

A lightning flash illuminated the yard beyond the kitchen windows, catching a beech tree in the middle of shaking its dripping limbs. Animated by the storm, its longest branches scratched and tapped the windowpanes.

"Look alive, men," Jack said, daydreaming of an enemy attack. "The Boche are laying down quite a barrage. The salient is afire with flares and shells. Watch for trench raiders." Two more thunderbolts followed in close succession, adding realism to his fantasy.

"Here I am fighting birds," he said in disgust. "God grant I shall soon be fighting Germans."

He kicked the strange carpet of mist. All he wanted in life was to fight Germans. Well, he also wanted Pamela Hamilton, but his incoherence at their last encounter made Pamela Hamilton an impossible dream.

He placed a cup, saucer, teapot, sugar bowl, and spoon on a tray on the counter near the back door.

The tree continued to tap as if demanding entry.

"You can't come in, old man, so stop your knocking." Jack looked at the window in the back door. He saw only a reflection of himself in the glossy, wet panes.

Then another flash lit the yard, and a grizzled face appeared on the other side of the glass.

Jack jumped backward. His flailing arm swept the counter, and the tea service flew to the floor with a terrific crash and clatter.

The door opened, and in with the gale came a tall, rugged man in a rain-soaked army greatcoat.

"Heavens, Jack!" The deep voice reverberated in composed counterpoint to Jack's fright.

"Uncle Geoff!" Jack gasped, his relief tempered by embarrassment.

Colonel Sir Geoffrey Maham shut the door behind himself. He made no attempt at pleasantries. "Has anything happened just now?" He eyed the mess on the floor. "Apart from the broken china, I mean?"

"No." Jack knelt and foraged in the mist. He put porcelain fragments and silver items on the tray, which he lifted to the counter. He forced a laugh. "Well, a mad bird tried to break into Gwen's bedroom, but—"

The colonel seized the candleholder and headed for the hallway, gazing upward as if peering through the ceiling.

"She wasn't hurt and it's gone," Jack said quickly. "I drove it off."

The colonel paused and stared at his great-nephew. "You drove it off?"

"I stuck it with Gwen's letter opener," Jack explained.

The colonel studied Jack appraisingly.

"Gwen said you were chasing it."

The colonel squinted. "She said *what?*"

Jack bit his lip. He should not have mentioned Gwen's pronouncement. He and Christopher were the only ones who knew about her dreams. But he was saved from his slipup. Mrs. Nellis—hair out of place and dressing gown in disarray—came to investigate the commotion.

"Oh dear…" The housekeeper looked at the colonel, Jack, and the debris on the tray.

Then Jack's parents charged in, looking as flustered as the housekeeper. The earl of Buckleigh had thrown a robe over his pajamas. His wife, Countess Buckleigh, had donned a silk peignoir, but it was askew. Furthermore, her brown hair fell haphazardly about her shoulders, so her appearance at that moment was a far cry from the poised, impeccably dressed and coiffed look she normally presented to the world. And her forehead was tightly crinkled. She did not like disturbance and disorder. She worked hard to keep the family estate operating like clockwork and was quite successful at it. Cecilia Maham, Lady Buckleigh, was a born manager.

Her husband, George Maham, was not. Lord Buckleigh was a scientist first and foremost and had never mastered the art of delegation. Maham, Carter, and Company, Lord Buckleigh's pharmaceutical and chemical manufacturing firm, did not purchase even a test tube without its director's personal approval. But he paid little attention to domestic affairs so long as things ran smoothly.

Right now, things were not running smoothly.

"What's this?" Lord Buckleigh demanded. "What's going on?"

"Good evening," the colonel said.

The earl stared at him. "Heavens! Uncle Geoff! Where on earth did you come from?"

The countess said, "Sir Geoffrey," with a disapproving frown.

Lord Buckleigh ran a hand through his thinning hair. "This is something of a surprise."

"I sent word. Apparently, it didn't reach you." Suddenly aware that his coat was dripping, the colonel unfastened its buttons and shrugged it off.

Lord Buckleigh took the coat and hung it on a hook near the back door. "The telephones have been out."

Lady Buckleigh glanced at the broken china and looked questioningly at her son.

"I was startled," Jack explained. "I was making tea for Gwen."

Mrs. Nellis gathered the porcelain fragments in a rag and took them to the trash bin.

Lord Buckleigh cast his gaze about the mist on the floor. "Where is your luggage, Uncle Geoff?"

"I came on horseback from the railway station in Exeter. My bag will be delivered in the morning." The colonel straightened his uniform and strode to the hallway. "George, I need to speak with you, but first, I must go upstairs. Jack, come with me."

The colonel hurried on his way.

Lady Buckleigh's mouth hung open. "Of all the…!"

The kettle began to whistle.

The countess turned to Mrs. Nellis. "Make tea and take it up to Gwendolyn. Then we'll have to prepare a room for Sir Geoffrey."

The colonel climbed the stairs two at a time. Jack, fifty-five years younger, had trouble keeping up.

"You've seen a lot of action, haven't you?" Jack asked between breaths.

"Let's not talk of that now. War is the devil's business."

"Father won't sign for me, but he can't stop me from joining the army next year. I'm going to machine-gun a hundred Boche for Freddie."

Sir Geoffrey pivoted on the second-floor landing to face his great-nephew. "Killing won't bring your brother back to life. Pray this war ends before you are drawn into it."

Awed as Jack was by the imposing presence of his great-uncle, some inner ember of rebellion sparked his reply. "I pray it will *not* end! Not until I have killed my share."

"Hush! Never say such things. Never think them!" The colonel turned and continued upward.

"Hello, Uncle Geoffrey," Gwen said when her visitor arrived.

"Not surprised to see me?" The colonel regarded his great-niece thoughtfully. "Jack told me about the bird." He went to the jury-rigged window. "This won't do." He rummaged through Gwen's desk drawers, found a ball of twine, and wound it many times through the casement handles to bind them securely together. He left the dagger where it was.

Rain beat against the glazing. The night was as dark as ever.

"Were you at Passchendaele, Uncle Geoff?" Jack asked.

"Yes."

"What was it like?"

"Our lads did their duty." What else could be said about something so far removed from normal human experience? It was a bloody three-month battle mired in mud and fog poisoned with mustard and chlorine gas. Cannon and machine guns had churned the landscape and soldiers into a wasteland of craters and butchered bodies. Hundreds of thousands of names were added to the list of British dead.

The colonel studied Gwen's floor-standing mirror for a long time. "Where is Christopher?"

Jack laughed dryly. "He never woke up. He could sleep through an artillery bombardment. What is it they say about the sleep of the innocent?"

Gwen asked, "Uncle Geoffrey, why do you suppose the"—she did not know the real name of the thing that had attacked her—"the cormorant is trying to get into our house?"

"We will speculate on that in the morning."

Gwen glanced at the window. "At least tell me—" She did not finish the sentence because Mrs. Nells arrived with tea.

"Here we are, m'lady." The housekeeper set the tray on the butler's table beside the bed. "Shall I pour it for you?"

Lady Buckleigh appeared at the door. "Sir Geoffrey, get out this instant. Gwendolyn is ill. Jack, go to your room."

Jack turned to comply.

The colonel did not. "The window lock is broken. I'll sleep here." He pointed at the well-padded armchair next to the butler's table. "That looks quite comfortable."

Jack stopped to watch what would happen.

Lady Buckleigh stared at the colonel. "That won't do at all."

"Please, Mama, let Uncle Geoffrey stay!" Gwen implored.

The wind whistled and moaned eerily. Rain hissed against the windowpanes.

Lady Buckleigh gazed at the quivering casements and frowned. "Perhaps…" She was silent for a time. "Perhaps that would be a good idea after all. Oh, I wish Miss Harkless were here!" She turned on her son. "Jack, go to bed!"

Jack obeyed his mother this time, following Mrs. Nellis out of the room.

Lady Buckleigh fussed over her daughter, arranging the bedclothes. "Keep warm, darling."

After the countess had left, while Gwen was finishing her tea, Sir Geoffrey moved in a slow circuit about the room. He glanced at the desk before ducking briefly into the bathroom and closet. Casually, he leaned to look behind the dressing table. He showed little interest in the small mirror on the table. Nor did he pay much attention to the chest of drawers. He bent to see what was under the butler's table.

Once again, he studied the floor-standing oval mirror.

Then he positioned the armchair beside the window and settled into it. Sighing, he closed his eyes.

Gwen switched off her lamp.

"Don't like storms, do you?" The colonel's words came out of the dark, a murmur amidst the gale.

"No," Gwen said in a small voice.

"You're not going to like the next few days at all."

CHAPTER 2

Prism

33-28-8

Despite what the colonel said, the morning dawned radiant, all of creation washed and sparkling with light refracted through a million raindrops clinging to grass and trees. Even the North Wing was transformed. Gwen was amazed that shabby bricks and ivy could look so cheerful. The sky was cloudless. Mingled scents of the drenched landscape filled her room.

She sat up in bed and stretched, which made her cough. Her chest hurt, as usual. She was alone. Perhaps her great-uncle was in her bathroom. "Uncle Geoffrey?"

There was no answer.

"I guess I don't need guarding anymore."

Christopher shouldered open her bedroom door and carried in a tray with dry toast and watery porridge. "Breakfast," he announced, his usual eager self.

Gwen looked at the colorless food. "I think I'll eat downstairs this morning."

"Mother wouldn't like that."

"Oh, bother Mother!"

The ten-year-old put his tray on the butler's table. "Uncle Geoffrey said he spent the night here."

"Yes, he did." Gwen glanced at the twine and dagger holding the window casements shut. The binding seemed unnecessary now.

She slipped out of bed, pulled on her dressing gown, and went to the oval mirror to brush her hair.

"He brought presents," Christopher reported. "Mine's a big, first-rate pocketknife." He drew the knife from his pocket and pulled out its long, very sharp blade for her to see. "Yours is a tin. Maybe it's chocolates."

"Where would anyone get chocolates these days?"

"Uncle Geoffrey could."

"He's been at the front. All they have there is death. Oh, look." A cardinal had alighted on her windowsill. She saw it in her mirror. The bird's feathers glowed luxurious red.

"Everything appears more magical in a mirror, have you noticed? There's a perspective you don't get otherwise, and colors are somehow brighter and textures deeper."

"In *your* mirror. The glass is very good."

Yes, it was a good mirror. It was also a beautiful piece of furniture, which was why, when she discovered it in one of the attics, she had asked her father if she could have it. Lord Buckleigh had the old cheval glass restored and gave it to Gwen for her ninth birthday.

She ran her hand over the grapevines carved into the mahogany frame, feeling as much as seeing the ridges and grooves.

Colonel Sir Geoffrey strode into the room. "Good morning. Recovered from last night?"

"Yes, thank you."

"Get dressed and come downstairs."

"Yes, sir." Gwen smiled, delighted to have an excuse to disobey Miss Harkless's rules.

"Mother says Gwen must stay in bed," Christopher informed the colonel.

"Fiddlesticks. Come with me, lad, and let your sister dress."

"Well…" Christopher began. But his great-uncle's raised eyebrows discouraged argument. "Yes, sir." When he reached the doorway, he looked back at Gwen. "I'll send Mrs. Nellis to help you."

"No, I can manage by myself." Gwen did not want anything to endanger her prison break—no advance warning in the breakfast room.

The colonel pulled the door closed.

Gwen put on a petticoat and went to her closet. Created from a large space left over when part of the adjacent bedroom was converted into a bathroom, its size emphasized its emptiness. Her meager wardrobe consisted of a single dark green dress. What Gwen had not grown out of, Miss Harkless had taken away, asserting that an invalid girl had little use for clothes. Gwen removed the dress from its hanger.

She dismissed a corset as too uncomfortable for her fragile body. However, there was still the dress to overcome. The seamstress who made it never dreamed a girl would try to fasten it without assistance. Miss Harkless had left it in the closet precisely because she thought Gwen couldn't put it on by herself. The back was closed by a dozen mushroom-shaped buttons, plus a hook-and-eye at the collar. But Gwen had a plan. She secured the unreachable buttons before she slipped the dress over her head.

Her hands found the sleeves and were halfway to the cuffs when things went wrong. She got stuck, her shoulders still inside the narrow, partially buttoned bodice.

She twisted. She squirmed. She nearly said a word Jack once uttered when a boomerang had come back and hit him in the head. Gwen didn't know what the word meant but was fairly certain that girls weren't supposed to use it—or boys, for that matter.

The more she struggled, the worse things became. Her petticoat bunched up. Unable to see and off balance, she toppled over. It wasn't much of a fall, but it triggered a prolonged coughing fit. The heavy wool dress smelled strongly of mothballs, which didn't help. A hairpin poked her scalp.

"Pollywogs!" she bellowed, inventing her own expletive.

Unable to get up, she wriggled on the floor. She began to fear she would have to call for help, but finally got her head past the collar. Lying on the floor, the first thing she beheld was her image in the floor-standing mirror. Oddly, her entire body was deep in shadow. Turning her head, she saw sunbeams streaming through the window. Dust motes drifted in the air, but there was nothing to create a shadow.

She raised herself on an elbow.

Whether it had been an optical illusion or another phenomenon, the shadow vanished. But now she saw words in the mirror. The slanted script could only be seen from one angle near the floor.

> *And the light shineth in darkness; and the*
> *darkness comprehended it not.*

The words must have been inscribed on paper behind the glass. Mysterious, but not mystical.

Gwen extended her arms with all the force she could muster. A button popped off, but her hands made it through the cuffs, and the dress slipped into place.

"Oh, thank goodness!"

Weak from the exertion, she climbed to her feet and stood triumphantly in front of the mirror. Wearing something other than a nightgown excited her. She put her arms behind her back and fastened the remaining buttons.

Down in the breakfast room, Lord Buckleigh scanned his Saturday newspaper. Everything around him glowed in the light pouring through the east-facing windows, but each article put him into a darker and darker mood. By the time he finished his boiled egg, he had read that labor leaders were threatening to strike. The Irish were making trouble over conscription. The treaty of Brest Litovsk had given the Germans control over thirty-four percent of the Russian population. And General Pershing, the obstinate American commander, still refused to integrate his men with English and French forces.

Colonel Sir Geoffrey came in and sat down. "Good morning, George. How are you?"

"As well as can be expected."

The colonel poured himself a cup of tea from the pot on the table.

"Busy at work, I suppose?"

"Quite."

Sir Geoffrey added milk to his tea. "What exactly is wrong with Gwendolyn?"

Just then, Lady Buckleigh entered carrying a rack of toast. She answered the colonel's question before her husband had a chance, saying, "The first diagnosis was pneumonia." She set the toast on the sideboard. "Then it was consumption, and after that, sepsis. We've put Gwendolyn on a soothing diet of porridge, toast, and milk. It's what Miss Harkless recommended." She wiped her hands on a napkin. "What brings you here, Sir Geoffrey?"

The colonel did not say that he was concerned about the special War Cabinet meeting that would be held at Maham House in seven days. Nor did he mention the demon-possessed German prisoner who, beyond bragging about Ludendorff's offensive against Arras and Lens, had inadvertently revealed that a supernatural attack was imminent in southwestern England. Sir Geoffrey did not speak of the dream in which an angel of the Lord had told him to make with haste for Maham House. And he said nothing about the evil being he had spotted above the moor. Lastly, the colonel neglected to disclose that he wanted to examine Sir Robert Maham's illustrations, which were bound in a three-hundred-year-old, one-of-a-kind book hidden in the mansion's library.

Instead, the colonel said, "I was in London to brief Sir Henry"—Sir Henry Wilson, chief of the Imperial General Staff—"and requested a few days leave to see my family."

"It has been some years since you visited. Why now?"

"Frankly? I need a rest." It was true. It was unfortunate that he was not going to get one.

Lady Buckleigh rubbed her forehead as if it hurt. "You are aware that George and I are off to London this afternoon?"

"No, I did not know."

"George has a meeting with Lord Milner tomorrow and insists I be there." The countess glared at her husband. "He seems to have forgotten that Gwendolyn's nurse is away, and we're in the middle of preparations of our own." She turned curtly and left the room.

Sir Geoffrey seized the thread. "George, I heard you've invited the prime minister to hold a meeting here at Maham House."

Lord Buckleigh stiffened. "Well, you know, that's rather hush-hush. Officially, it's a dinner party and weekend stay."

"So I understand." The colonel took a sip of tea. "Sir Henry said you will discuss unconventional means to end the war."

"Yes…hmmm…he told you? That's not public knowledge and not intended to be, if you take my meaning."

Mrs. Nellis brought poached eggs, kippers, a seared tomato, apricot jam, and a dish with a big pat of butter.

"My apologies, Sir Geoffrey, but there isn't any bacon to be had. Everything else should be as you like it, if memory serves."

"Why, Mrs. Nellis, you are a magician! This is wonderful." The colonel perused the items on the housekeeper's sterling silver tray. "Such a lot of butter! I don't want to eat your entire ration."

"We've enough, sir. We have a cow." Mrs. Nellis arrayed the food on the table. "It lives in the stable."

Sir Geoffrey laughed. "Does it? In a thoroughbred's stall?"

The housekeeper checked the level of tea in the pot before taking her leave.

"George, where is Jack right now?" the colonel asked.

"Brushing his horse." Lord Buckleigh folded his newspaper and set it on the table. "We don't have a groom anymore. Shelton enlisted three years ago." The earl touched a fork but didn't pick it up. "Poor fellow was blown to bits at Ypres." He stared out the window. "They'll have Jack in the army in less than two years. Then he'll be dead, like Freddie."

"Perhaps we will win the war this year. Americans are arriving in numbers."

"The Americans may be coming, but the Russians are out, aren't they? How many times have we thought the war was practically over, only to find the situation worse than ever? The Boche—they'll bring all creation to ruin before they stop." Lord Buckleigh picked up the fork after all but didn't do anything with it. "That's why I'm proposing… well…something…to the PM and his cabinet."

Before Colonel Sir Geoffrey could probe the earl's disclosure, coughing drew their attention to the door.

Gwen entered the room hesitantly, pushing off the doorjamb to steady herself.

Lord Buckleigh was astounded. "Gwendolyn! What are you doing down here?"

"I told her to come." The colonel rose and pulled back the chair next to his own. "Have a seat, my dear. Mrs. Nellis has laid out a nice breakfast."

Lord Buckleigh said, "Uncle Geoff! This food's not good for her!"

Gwen eased herself into the chair. "Please, Papa—" She held his eyes. "Can't I have a normal meal for once?"

"Your mother will be cross."

"George, let her eat," the colonel admonished. "She needs something solid."

"Well, I don't know…"

While the earl dithered, Sir Geoffrey took a plate from the sideboard and set it in front of his great-niece.

"Shall I say grace?" The colonel took Gwen by the hand, closed his eyes, and said, "Lord, bless this food for the nutrition of Gwendolyn's body. Give her strength for the days ahead and protect her from harm, that in all things thy will may be done. Bless this family and this house, and drive away the darkness that seeks to enter. These things we pray in the name of our Lord Jesus Christ."

Whether the work of preconscious suggestion or some other device, warmth and relief spread from the center of Gwen's chest out through her arms and legs. Her nausea subsided somewhat. She wanted to eat.

Lord Buckleigh frowned. "That was a bit odd, Uncle Geoff. The thing about darkness, I mean. In a table blessing."

"Habit in these evil times, I suppose."

Gwen took a bite of a tomato and a boiled egg sprinkled with salt, savoring the flavors. The colonel gave her a piece of toast with jam, and she devoured it. She even had one of the kippers.

Then Lady Buckleigh returned. The countess stopped a step inside the door. Her jaw dropped. "What's going on?! Gwen! What do you think you're doing?"

"Mama!"

"Did you eat *that*? Well, you're in for a bad turn, aren't you? Your stomach won't take it." Lady Buckleigh glared at her husband. "George—you know better! How could you?" She motioned for Gwen to stand up. "Come with me. I'm taking you to your room."

"She's comfortable here," the colonel said. "She might as well stay."

"Don't you understand her condition?"

"I have something for her."

Gwen didn't know how the tin box got into her great-uncle's hand, but he held it out to her. She accepted it excitedly and pulled off the lid.

"Nuts," Lord Buckleigh observed, peering from across the table.

"Well, I say..." The countess stared at the assortment of hazelnuts, walnuts, and dried fruits. She pulled the box out of her daughter's hands. "You can't eat any of that."

Christopher came to see what was going on.

"It's a fine day." Sir Geoffrey nudged Gwen toward the door to the East Lobby. "I think I'll take the children for a stroll outside." He motioned for Christopher to follow.

Lady Buckleigh shook her head. "No, that won't do at all. The open air is bad for Gwendolyn."

"Nonsense. It's warm today."

Mrs. Nellis appeared. Perhaps she had heard the raised voices and sensed she was needed.

Lady Buckleigh handed the tin to the housekeeper. "Put this away, please, Mrs. Nellis."

"Yes, m'lady."

"And tell Mr. Merrill we will want the luggage brought down at one o'clock."

"Yes, m'lady."

When the countess turned around, the colonel and her children were gone.

"What on earth?"

Inside the East Tower, Sir Geoffrey descended to the ground floor and opened the door to the cellar. "This way, if you please."

Gwen hesitated. "Where are we going?"

"To the gardens."

Gwen looked into the darkness at the bottom of the stairs. "This isn't the way to the gardens."

"Yes, it is." The colonel turned on a light, ushered the children through the door, and pulled it closed behind them.

Lady Buckleigh entered the East Tower fifteen seconds later. "Sir Geoffrey?" the countess called, looking up the stairs. *"Geoffrey!"* She rushed out of the tower to the French doors that opened onto the terrace.

Seeing no one, she hurried back to the breakfast room. "George! Bring them in."

"Eh? Bring who in from where?"

"Your uncle has disappeared with Gwendolyn. I think he's taken her outside. Go find them!"

"I need to go to my office."

"We're traveling today. You can forget about going to your infernal office. Find your daughter and put her into bed!"

Gwen was wondering what they were up to. "This is the cellar. You said we were going to the gardens."

"And so we are."

The colonel passed the wine racks and went into a storeroom. He made his way between shelves laden with hand tools, hardware, and paint cans. Reaching the far wall, he moved a ladder to get to an iron hook, which he turned.

Cracks formed in the stone block wall. The colonel pushed, and part of the wall swung away from him on stiff, groaning hinges. What had appeared to be sandstone blocks were actually tiles affixed to a camouflaged door that was undetectable when closed.

Musty air wafted into Gwen's face. She was looking into a pitch-black tunnel. "No one knew this was here," she said in wonder.

Christopher danced with excitement. "Uncle Geoffrey knew!" The little boy strained to see inside. "Where does it go?"

The colonel pointed a flashlight into the darkness. "We shall follow it, and you will find out."

"What a smashing secret!" Christopher nudged his way to the front. "I can't wait to tell everyone!"

"Would you like to lead, my lad?"

"Oh yes, please!"

Sir Geoffrey handed him the flashlight. "Don't get too far ahead."

Christopher hastened into the opening. The colonel went next. Gwen followed them into a dim, tight-fitting world: a corridor not much wider than Sir Geoffrey's shoulders. The walls and low, arched ceiling were red brick; however, little illumination reached back to Gwen, so everything appeared charcoal-gray to her. But being at the rear had advantages—those in front swept away the cobwebs. Gwen was not particularly squeamish but didn't like spiders.

Their route sloped downward.

The chill air had been stagnant for years. So had the dust on the floor; it rose and swirled. Gwen fished her handkerchief from her sleeve and held it over her nose and mouth. Twenty steps farther, water dampened the floor, controlling the dust, but Gwen kept using the handkerchief as a filter because the air reeked of mold.

Christopher stopped when he came to a T intersection. The tunnel in each direction had age-blackened walls. "Which do we take?"

The murky darkness to the left filled Gwen with dread. "There's something bad that way."

"To the right," the colonel instructed.

"Where does the other tunnel go?" Christopher asked.

"Beneath the North Wing."

Gwen shivered. "Papa says the cellar under the old house is flooded."

"He's right. A spring opened into it a hundred years ago. The seepage could never be stopped."

They continued quite a distance. Gwen glanced back several times but never saw a living thing. She was relieved when they came to a flight of steps. She gathered her skirt, lifted the hem to her knees, and held the bunched material with one hand. There was no banister, so she pressed her other hand against the wall to steady herself as she climbed. The ascent winded her.

Christopher couldn't budge the eighteen-inch-wide, four-foot-high metal door at the top of the stairs.

"Allow me." The colonel tugged until the little door swung inward.

They were faced with a barricade of boxwoods that had grown flush with the opening. Water splashed somewhere nearby.

The colonel squeezed through the door and forced his way past the shrubbery. He held the boxwoods aside for Christopher and Gwen.

Gwen emerged into a green space. She blinked in the bright sunlight and coughed several times before catching her breath. "We're at the center of the hedge maze in the gardens."

"Correct."

"We came out of the wall behind the fountain," Christopher observed.

The colonel pushed back through the boxwoods to set his flashlight inside the secret passage and close the door.

"We're in the last dead end," Gwen said. She went around the corner to the fountain. There, a curtain of water fell from a scalloped bowl held by three marble Nereids standing in a pool.

Christopher clapped his hands. "Smashing!"

"I'm surprised the gardeners haven't found that door, even though it is well hidden." Gwen considered the tall hedges around her. "The maze pattern is perfectly regular, after all. To get to the fountain, you take two right turns for each left, except for the last. But the entrance to the secret tunnel is the *real* destination. You get there if you take one more right turn."

"Precisely so," the colonel agreed. "Follow me. I want to find Jack."

"May I rest?" Gwen eased herself onto a stone bench.

"Are you all right?"

"I'll be fine in a minute." She coughed to clear congestion and the last of the subterranean air from her lungs. The sunlight was restorative; it warmed her through and through. It wasn't long before she felt strong enough to press on.

The colonel chose direction unerringly, and they emerged from the north side of the maze. Gwen breathed deeply. The air was fresh with shrubbery and grass smells. She was glad to be alive, which was unusual. She couldn't remember having been happy for two years.

Lord Buckleigh stood on the terrace, hand above his eyes to shade them from the glare. He scanned the gardens for signs of movement. It was the second time he had come outside. After failing to spot his children the first time, he had checked their bedrooms.

"Blast it all!"

He charged down the steps and proceeded eastward, taking a gravel avenue bordered with iris, snapdragons, and anemones that weren't yet in bloom. He went one way and then, finding no sign of activity, diverted south of the hedge maze past beds of amaryllis and lilies. After hurrying beneath a white, honeysuckle-entwined pergola, he followed a footpath amidst oak, beech, and maple trees. That took him to a quiet lake with a gazebo at its center. He saw no one there. The only thing beyond the lake was the river that separated the Maham estate from the expanse of Dartmoor.

The earl turned back.

Colonel Sir Geoffrey took Gwen's arm and helped her along. They passed a vegetable garden that Lady Buckleigh kept with Christopher's help.

"Are there any more secret passages?" Christopher inquired.

"There are hidden rooms in the North Wing, but I'm sure your parents have warned you not to go there. The structure is crumbling."

The colonel stopped abruptly. They were near the stables. "What on earth does Jack think he's doing?"

Jack had stuffed a suit of clothes with straw, fixed it to a pole, and topped it with a German helmet. In a rage, he was jabbing the Teutonic scarecrow with a kitchen knife strapped to the muzzle of an old shotgun.

"Haa! Haa!" he yelled as he thrust his mock bayonet. "Boche! Murdering swine!"

Sir Geoffrey walked up behind the young man, who was so preoccupied that he failed to notice. "Stop that!" the colonel ordered.

Startled, Jack whirled around. The kitchen knife slashed within an inch of his great-uncle's cheek.

Sir Geoffrey grabbed the barrel and confiscated the shotgun in a single motion.

"Sorry!" Jack cried. "I'm sorry!"

"Brutality is not honorable."

Jack looked at the ground, ashamed. But then he raised his face, and his expression toughened. "I don't want honor. I want to slaughter the enemy."

"Come with us."

The colonel leaned the shotgun against the stable and led the way back south to a wooded spot. Jack followed meekly.

"I need to rest, Uncle Geoffrey," Gwen said.

"Sit here." He helped her onto a bench and stood with hands clasped behind his back while he waited for her to recover. He gazed for a time at a blue jay perched in an ornamental cherry tree. Then he contemplated his great-niece.

"Gwendolyn Europa Maham. Ever thought about your middle name?"

"What about it?"

"There is no other Europa anywhere in our family tree. I once asked your parents why they chose it. They couldn't say. It was an impulsive decision, apparently."

"Is it important?"

"It's curious."

The colonel surveyed the skies to the east and north, where wispy clouds had appeared. The weather was changing again. "You are under assault."

Gwen didn't know how to reply.

Jack frowned. "Assault? What do you mean, Uncle Geoff? By whom?"

"By beings like the one you stopped last night."

Jack squinted at his great-uncle.

"However, what happened last night was only a probe." Sir Geoffrey looked fixedly at Gwen. "I'm here to protect you, my dear, and I think Jack is meant to help."

Gwen blinked. She believed that peculiar things were afoot and that the cormorant was more than a bird. Still… "I'm sorry, Uncle Geoffrey, but exactly what are you talking about?"

He looked deeply into her eyes. Then Jack's. Then Christopher's. The trees rustled. The blue jay clicked and whistled.

The colonel slipped his hand into his pocket and drew out a prism. He held it so that only Jack could see it.

"What shape is this?"

Jack hesitated. "A rectangle?"

The colonel showed it to Gwen. The glass sparkled.

"Triangle."

"You gave different answers. How can that be?"

"We saw different faces," Gwen said.

"Precisely. A thing can have more than one aspect." The colonel patted Gwen's shoulder. "You are flesh, but you are also spirit. You exist in two worlds, and contrary to what you think, the physical one is less substantial. It is a projection of the other. A silhouette."

He stood so that his shadow lay distinct on the grass. "Christopher—stomp on my shadow."

The boy did as he was told.

"Harder."

Christopher stamped with all his might on the shadow.

"Didn't hurt at all," the colonel declared.

Gwen fidgeted, embarrassed to have discovered that her great-uncle was insane. She toyed with the word *eccentric*—it sounded less harsh.

Sir Geoffrey raised his hand. The prism caught sunlight and cast a vivid spectrum across the walk. When he rotated the glass, the beam changed: purified, intensified.

He aimed the refracted light toward a bed of early-blooming snapdragons. At once, Gwen thought they were the most colorful and intricate flowers she had ever seen, with incredible depth and dimension.

"That's beautiful!"

"Sometimes you must see a thing in true light to know what it really is."

"Is the prism magic?" Christopher asked, awed.

"There is no such thing as magic the way you mean it," the colonel answered. "But there is the power of God."

He spun to face the cherry tree and shouted, "I command you in Jesus's name, do not move!"

With that, the whole area was enveloped in radiance, and all of Gwen's consciousness was drawn to a vile creature squatting near the tree.

Christopher yelped.

Jack squeaked.

Afterward, neither Gwen nor her brothers could accurately describe what they had seen. She recalled a multitude of slimy, grasping arms. Jack remembered black voids: eyes of an inconceivably wicked consciousness. Christopher saw jagged teeth.

When Gwen stared, trying to comprehend what she saw, the thing cursed at her. For a moment, she thought she recognized the words. For that moment, she was back on High Tor, in darkness, on her knees in the rain, in despair.

"Be gone!" Sir Geoffrey commanded.

The thing fled the light so fast it seemed to simply disappear.

Gwen doubled over as if punched in the stomach.

Jack trembled uncontrollably.

"You're in no danger," the colonel told them.

"What was that?" Gwen asked, sounding strangled.

"One of the spirits that rebelled against God. We call them demons."

"And the cormorant?"

"Yes."

"But the cormorant was real."

"So was the being you just saw." The colonel looked from face to frightened face and quickly added, "Christopher couldn't hurt my shadow, remember? We're like shadows to those creatures. They can't touch us, here. Only their deceptions are dangerous."

"The cormorant could have mauled my face," Gwen pointed out. Her great-uncle was omitting important details.

"Yes…an evil spirit can possess an animal. But they'll only do it when forced by a greater sovereignty. It diminishes their reality and restricts them." The colonel slipped the prism back into his pocket. "A type of demon called a taraph joined itself with that cormorant. The possessed creature can bite or scratch you, but not any worse than an ordinary bird."

Gwen frowned. *Not any worse than an ordinary insanely vicious raptor, you mean.*

"Can demons possess *us*?" Jack asked in a thin voice.

"No. No indeed. Have no fear of that. When you have the Holy Spirit in you, no other can enter."

"But a demon *can* possess a man? In the Bible…"

"Only if the person allows it."

"Why would anyone do that?" Christopher made a face. "He would have to be a lunatic!"

"Pride…arrogance…desire. Evil spirits are masters of deception, and their intelligence is mind-boggling. Demons can outwit any human. The only way to outmaneuver one is to avoid its game."

"Geoff! Children!" Lord Buckleigh's distant voice carried over the hedges and through the trees. "Where in blazes are you?"

The colonel looked toward the house. "We had better go meet

your father."

Lord Buckleigh marched toward them like one of Admiral Beatty's battle cruisers at full steam, his breath puffing.

"Here we are, George," Sir Geoffrey called.

"See here, Uncle Geoff. See here. You've created quite a stir…"

Lady Buckleigh opened the top compartment of the icebox so Patrick McCray could load a block. The sixteen-year-old boy was thin, but his ice delivery job had made him strong.

"Thank you for fixing Lord Buckleigh's car, Patrick."

"You're welcome, m'lady. It was the magneto, you know. All I did was rewind the armature."

"Well, Mr. Merrill was quite impressed and much obliged."

The countess made small talk out of habit, keeping her eye on the windows, looking for signs of her children. "You're always tinkering with something, aren't you? Like your father. How is he?"

"Very well, m'lady. He was home on leave in February, you know. He taught me to fly."

"Taught you to fly!"

"I suppose that's an exaggeration. He took me for a ride in an Avro trainer and let me take the controls. It was a grand adventure." Patrick lowered his gaze guiltily. "But he got scolded when the aerodrome commander found out."

"I see. We are looking forward to receiving Major McCray at our upcoming dinner party."

Major McCray, Patrick's father, had demonstrated great valor in combat. After serving two years as a fighter pilot, he had transferred to a bombing squadron. Since then, he had planned and led special missions deep into Germany. Prime Minister David Lloyd George was going to honor the flying ace at the dinner party. That was the acknowledged reason for the major to be there. But Major McCray would also attend a closed-door War Cabinet meeting the following day. Lady Buckleigh did not know the purpose of that meeting. Miss Harkless was not supposed to know but did.

"Yes, ma'am. I'll be happy to see him again." Patrick nodded toward the icebox. "Well, there's your order."

"Thank you. By the way, the telephone in the butler's office is not working. Could you do something about it?"

"I'll have a look."

The boy went across the hallway, up the servants' stairs, and on to the unoccupied butler's rooms. After examining the telephone, he returned to the kitchen.

"It's the microphone," he told Lady Buckleigh. "The diaphragm is loose. I'll mend it this afternoon after I finish my deliveries."

Lord Buckleigh escorted Gwen through the back door and saw Patrick. "Oh—Mr. McCray."

Patrick bowed and tipped his cap awkwardly. "Good morning, m'lord." The boy looked indirectly at Gwen and lowered his eyes.

Gwen stepped beyond her father. "Hello, Patrick."

Patrick touched his cap again. "Good morning, m'lady."

It had been quite a while since Gwen had seen Patrick McCray this close. He had grown taller and more muscular, and his jaw was stronger than before. For some strange reason, at this random moment, the thought popped into Gwen's head that she should have worn her corset after all.

Patrick, suddenly in a great hurry to leave, turned just as Jack came in, and the point of the delivery boy's ice tongs poked the young lord in the derriere.

Jack jumped. *"Ayii!"*

"Pardon, m'lord!" Patrick cried, horrified at what he had done.

"Idiot!"

"I'm terribly sorry!" Patrick bowed deeply in apology.

Lady Buckleigh examined the site of the injury. "Calm down, Jack. You aren't hurt."

"He gored me!"

"It was an accident. Your pants are fine."

"My *pants*! What about my—"

"I should go." Patrick fled through the back door.

"What a nitwit!" Jack hissed. "He's Irish. I expect he's a traitor."

"His father has downed seven German airplanes," Gwen countered.

"He's a dunce. He makes letters backwards."

"At least he didn't get expelled from Eton for fighting, like *someone* we know!"

Jack snarled.

"Stop bickering," Lady Buckleigh commanded. "Someone help Gwen upstairs."

"That was Michael McCray's son," Lord Buckleigh told Sir Geoffrey. "McCray was my chief engineer before the war. Best fluid dynamicist I ever met. Now he's in the Royal Flying Corps. Knows as much about aerial warfare as any man alive, I expect."

Lady Buckleigh faced her husband. "George! *Someone* means *you*. And we have to leave before four o'clock if we're to catch the train. You had better get moving." To herself, the countess said, "Then again, perhaps I should be stalling."

"Yes, yes, I'm going. Come along, Gwen."

Hi Paige and Lara,

I went back to Maham House and found a few more diary pages wedged behind a dresser drawer. And I found corroborating documents and a drawing in other places. I'm sorting through them.

By the way, English titles are confusing. In a note, Gwen mentions that someone incorrectly called Jack "Lord Maham" when he should have been addressed as "Lord Mayfield." Jack's title at that time was Baron Mayfield. In 1918, Gwen and Jack's father, George Maham, was the earl of Buckleigh and called "Lord Buckleigh." But I found a reference to "Baron and Lady Mayfield." It took me days to figure out that the baron and lady were George and Cecilia Maham in 1898. George's father was still alive then, so he, not George, was the earl. George was only a baron in 1898. An earl's eldest son is usually a viscount, but for some reason, the eldest Maham son is a baron.

In a letter she wrote her mother that same year, Cecilia wondered whether she, being the wife of a baron, should be announced at a reception as "Baroness Mayfield" or as "Lady Cecilia." It had to do with her "precedence" being above George's. She was the daughter of a duke, who ranks above an earl, who ranks above a baron. Being announced correctly was apparently of life-or-death importance.

After George's father passed and George became the seventh earl of Buckleigh, Cecilia was called "Lady Buckleigh" or "Countess Buckleigh." (The wife of an earl is a countess.) I'll do my best to get things right.

Here's the table of contents of the Bible in the Maham House library. I added the Roman numerals in square brackets.

Kirk

BOOKS OF THE OLD TESTAMENT

1	Genesis	14	2 Chronicles	27	Daniel
2	Exodus	15	Ezra	28	Hosea
3	Leviticus	16	Nehemiah	29	Joel
4	Numbers	17	Esther	30	Amos
5	Deuteronomy	18	Job	31	Obadiah
6	Joshua	19	Psalms	32	Jonah
7	Judges	20	Proverbs	33	Micah
8	Ruth	21	Ecclesiastes	34	Nahum
9	1 Samuel	22	Song of Solomon	35	Habakkuk
10	2 Samuel	23	Isaiah	36	Zephaniah
11	1 Kings	24	Jeremiah	37	Haggai
12	2 Kings	25	Lamentations	38	Zechariah
13	1 Chronicles	26	Ezekiel	39	Malachi

BOOKS OF THE NEW TESTAMENT

1	Matthew [I]	10	Ephesians	19	Hebrews
2	Mark [II]	11	Philippians	20	James
3	Luke [III]	12	Colossians	21	1 Peter
4	John [IV]	13	1 Thessalonians	22	2 Peter
5	The Acts [V]	14	2 Thessalonians	23	1 John
6	Romans	15	1 Timothy	24	2 John
7	1 Corinthians	16	2 Timothy	25	3 John
8	2 Corinthians	17	Titus	26	Jude
9	Galatians	18	Philemon	27	Revelation

CHAPTER 3

Vision

65-5-26

Up close, the true state of the North Wing became evident. Its facade was worn, stained, and cracked. Some windowpanes were broken. Others had fallen out of their decayed frames. Openings were shuttered or covered with sail canvas.

Jack walked with Colonel Sir Geoffrey to the main entrance.

"In the past, there was another wing." The colonel gestured north and west. "It was demolished when the newer parts of the house were erected thirty years ago." He gazed northward across the grassy hills of Dartmoor. "Five hundred years before that, a Norman stronghold stood on this spot."

He flourished the prism.

As Jack watched, the house bent and twisted like an image distorted by a warped lens, extending and rising. When he looked up, he saw battlements and towers. He stepped back, astonished.

Sir Geoffrey lowered his arm. The fortress walls tilted and withdrew like a translucent photograph being folded and put away.

"Here." He took Jack's hand and carefully put the prism into it. "Try it."

The glass was heavier than Jack expected, and it was warm. He had no idea what he was supposed to do.

"Hold it in the light and focus."

Jack did as he was told, but nothing miraculous happened. He turned the prism, trying every possible angle to the sun, but the glass did not even produce a spectrum. A soap bubble could have done better.

"You must wish to see things as they really are, not as *you* think they are or want them to be," Sir Geoffrey said.

Once again, Jack rotated the prism and wished for the house to change.

"Not your will, but His," the colonel counseled.

Still nothing.

"Saying a name focuses your attention on the person. Try that."

Jack positioned the prism in full sunshine. Remembering what his great-uncle had done in the garden, he said, "Uh…Jesus?"

"Think of him as you speak. You're praying, not casting a spell."

"Am I…am I saying it right?"

"The sound that comes out of your mouth is not important. In fact, he would pronounce his name *Yeshua*. But *Jesus* or any other pronunciation works to concentrate your attention on him."

Jack took a breath. "In *Jesus's* name…"

Nothing happened.

A cloud wandered across the sun.

"Last night, you fought off a demon…" Sir Geoffrey said distractedly as if trying to work out a puzzle. He took the prism back and put it in his pocket. "Ah, well, in time. In time. Come along, if you please."

On the second floor of the library, Gwen walked the length of a shelf of novels, running her finger along the spines. She selected a copy of Sir Walter Scott's *Waverley* and read the first page. She was stalling to extend her time out of bed—and her little brother knew it.

Christopher tapped his foot impatiently. He had promised their father he would take Gwen back to her room once she had chosen something to read. The boy was eager to find Uncle Geoffrey, sure that anything to do with his great-uncle would be an adventure.

As it turned out, Uncle Geoffrey found him.

"Hullo," said the colonel, walking in from the hallway. "A fortunate coincidence that you two are here."

Jack also came in.

"Are you going to show us more secret things?" Christopher asked.

"As a matter of fact, I am. Interested?"

"Yes, sir. Very much!"

"Good! Let's go up."

The circular mahogany-paneled library rose through all levels of the house. First floor shelves were packed with gold-tooled volumes: classical plays, poems, histories, and philosophical works published in Greek and Latin as well as French, German, and English. The Maham family annals—the earliest dating from the eighth century—were also there.

Above a majestically curving staircase, the second level had a wide selection of popular titles by Austen, Dickens, Conan Doyle, Wells, and many others. Overnight guests could find a novel to read in bed—or in the tub, as some preferred.

Climbing to the third floor, an explorer discovered one of the Maham children's favorite places. They liked to look at the books with photographs and drawings of exotic animals and places. And they loved to fiddle with the sextant and other instruments kept in cabinets below the bookshelves. Furthermore, a hatch hidden in the west wall opened into a nook with a view down into the ballroom.

There was one more stair. Its narrow steps spiraled up into a wrought iron and glass dome. The colonel led the Maham children up that stair single file.

Reaching the platform at the top, they crowded around the lectern where stargazers could set sky charts and record their observations. It was where Freddie had taught Gwen about planets, comets, and nebulae.

She sagged against the brass railing, trying not to pant.

"I will show you something, but you must never tell another soul about it. Do you agree to keep it a secret?" The tone of Sir Geoffrey's voice was deadly earnest.

"Yes, of course," Christopher said excitedly.

"I'm serious. This book is important. I do not want it lost or fallen into the wrong hands."

This time, Christopher thought before speaking. "I won't ever tell anyone. On my life. I promise."

"So do I," Jack said.

Gwen nodded. "Agreed."

"Very well."

Prism in hand, the soldier bowed his head and prayed silently. The others found themselves relaxing, as if shielded from something frightening that they had previously sensed but not consciously known was there. The colonel slid a catch underneath the lectern's writing surface, allowing the hinged top to open.

The children bent to peer inside the compartment.

Sir Geoffrey lifted out a cloth-wrapped parcel and lowered the writing surface back into place. Inside the parcel wrappings was a heavy leather-bound book.

"These are the visions of our ancestor Robert Maham." Sir Geoffrey brushed the cover—either a habit or a reverence because there was no dust. He opened the book and carefully turned pages.

Gwen leaned forward. Each vellum page had a drawing. Some were true-to-life tableaus, others highly symbolic. All had numbers arranged in some pattern or other.

The colonel found the one he wanted near the end of the book. "This is *Beset Girl.*"

Inside an oval with a grapevine pattern that reminded Gwen of her mirror's frame, a listless girl lounged on a couch. The girl wore what might have been a Greek tunic or a flowing white nightgown. Her head was turned away, but her wan face was reflected in a mirror she held in her right hand. The name *EUROPA* was etched in a silver diadem on her head. To her left was a gleaming sword. To her right was a shield emblazoned with the name *MAHAM* and the stag from the family coat of arms. Above her were printed the Roman numerals *V I VI.*

The girl was set about by ghostly creatures. She did not appear to be aware of them. Finally, there were four horsemen in the lower third of the picture: a bowman astride a white charger; a swordsman on a red stallion; a man who held balance scales and rode a black horse; and Death, atop a pale greenish horse.

Arabic numbers were printed around the oval:

24-6-4   33-28-8   65-5-26   2-8-22   25-19-17
56-1-3   49-4-19   48-50-6   1-8-44   1-3-16
12-6-12   24-17-14   43-34-4   64-11-28

and

4-1-10   8-2-6   45-7-25   2-8-9   7-6-11
51-3-23   8-4-6   1-16-33   3-12-17   24-16-14
43-18-16   3-7-19   66-22-4   64-17-20

A scrap had been torn from the bottom of the page.

"That's Gwen!" Christopher exclaimed.

The colonel nodded stoically. "I believe it is. It most certainly is not the Europa of Greek mythology."

Jack was skeptical. "When was this drawn?"

"At the dawn of the seventeenth century. Around 1611, give or take."

Gwen looked at the face in the handheld mirror and felt strangely hollow. "What does it mean?"

"Sir Robert's visions pertain to Maham family crises. Often as not, they're linked to happenings in the world at large. Clues in the pictures help us figure out what is going on and what must be done. Notice these?" He tapped the horsemen. "Conquest, War, Famine, and Death. Our time indeed."

Gwen stared. "The Four Horsemen of the Apocalypse?"

"Unquestionably."

"Then this war we're in is the apocalypse?" Jack asked.

"Perhaps not. Creation flows and ripples. You know that many antichrists have come, and will come, before the final one who exactly fulfills scripture. Likewise, I believe the events of our time are portents of even more dire future happenings."

Gwen pointed at the creatures surrounding the girl. "I suppose those are demons." She chewed her lower lip. "They're not merely symbolic, are they?"

"I'm afraid not. But don't be too worried. Remember, demons are created beings. The devil is not his Creator's equal—not remotely. We are on the winning side."

Gwen took a notepad and pencil from a cubbyhole and began sketching the vision.

Sir Geoffrey indicated the Roman numerals in the painting. "These three numbers specify the key book, chapter, and verse." He tapped the leftmost numeral. "V—five—the fifth book of the New Testament, which is Acts." The colonel glanced at the children. "There are twenty-seven books in the King James New Testament. If the first Roman numeral had been higher than twenty-seven, we would have continued with Genesis. However, the first Roman numeral in *Beset Girl* is V, so Acts is the key book.

"There are different editions of the Bible," the colonel continued. "Sir Robert used the ordering of books in the one he owned, which is equivalent to the King James version we have today."

He contemplated the drawing. "The Roman numeral in the middle identifies the chapter, and the numeral on the right indicates the verse. In the case of *Beset Girl*, we see I—chapter one, and VI—verse six."

He pulled a Bible from the bookshelf next to the lectern. "V—Acts…I—chapter one…VI—verse six." He found it and read, "'When they therefore were come together, they asked of him, saying, Lord, wilt thou at this time restore again the kingdom to Israel?'"

Continuing to sketch, Gwen penciled in the face in the hand mirror. Something about "Europa" bothered her.

The colonel swept his fingertip around the Arabic numbers on the oval that looked like the frame of Gwen's mirror. "Each of these three-number sequences also corresponds to a Bible verse. The verses designated by *Arabic* numbers are *not* sequenced from the first book of the New Testament. They are sequenced from the key book. So, for *Beset Girl*, Acts is the starting point. Romans is book two, First Corinthians book three, and so on. Genesis is book twenty-four, and John book sixty-six. Therefore, we can deduce that this cipher at the bottom left of the oval—two, eight, twenty-two—designates Romans, chapter eight, verse twenty-two."

"What does Romans 8:22 say?" Jack asked.

"'For we know that the whole creation groaneth and travaileth in pain together until now.'"

Christopher rubbed his chin, imitating something his father did when thinking. "That must be about the war. What does it mean? What's going to happen?"

"I can't tell you yet." The colonel sighed. "This particular vision has always puzzled me. The verses don't have any common theme or direction. Some of the numbers must be altered. You see this one—thirty-three, twenty-eight, eight—book thirty-three, chapter twenty-eight, verse eight? I believe that what appears to be chapter twenty-*eight* is actually chapter twenty-*three* because Second Samuel, which is book thirty-three in the *Beset Girl* sequence, has only twenty-four chapters. Several others are like that."

Jack folded his arms across his chest. "What's the point of all this? Why are these drawings so important?"

Sir Geoffrey smiled sadly. "Someone in every second or third generation of our family inherits a responsibility and the tasks that go with it." His eyes became distant. "I suspect…my final assignment is to protect Gwendolyn." He looked earnestly at Jack. "I think you, my boy, will be next."

"Not me?" Christopher asked, disappointed.

"It's not necessarily a happy responsibility. I wouldn't wish for it if I were you."

Gwen was sketching a segment of the grapevine that adorned the oval frame in the picture. She paused in her drawing. "If you had to speculate, what would you say is going to happen?"

The colonel shrugged very slightly and shook his head. "Sir Robert's visions are like poetry. They distill the essence of things, not literal facts.

Clearly, you, Gwendolyn, are under attack, and I must do something to keep you safe. Beyond that, I can't discern."

"What do the rest of the Bible verses say?" Christopher asked.

"I could read them to you, but you wouldn't learn much. A verse might be a metaphor like the horsemen. Or it might be a truth that sparks insight and informs decisions and actions. It could be an example to be followed or a call to conviction. Some are charges or commissions. Some are warnings or encouragements. The picture on a jigsaw puzzle becomes clear only after the pieces are put in their proper places."

"So basically, this drawing could mean anything or nothing. What help is that?" Jack wanted to know.

"A prophet isn't a fortune teller. He is a person with the ability to interpret God's word. Each vision is targeted at the individuals who fulfill it. This one *will* become clear soon enough."

Gwen compared her incomplete rough sketch to the original. The demon at the top of the picture had raptor's wings; she had drawn it more substantially and more like a cormorant than had Sir Robert. She turned to her great-uncle and studied the deep lines on his face. "You're more worried than you're saying."

The colonel waved a hand. "It's only a matter of time before I understand the vision."

Gwen put the point of her pencil to the paper to add the next Arabic number—she had copied less than a quarter of them—but suddenly felt faint and stumbled against the railing. "Oh!"

"Jack—don't let her fall!" The colonel rewrapped the book and put it back into the lectern. Then he and Jack helped Gwen down the stairs and took her by third-floor hallways to her room.

The old soldier checked Gwen's pulse and felt her forehead. "Forgive me. I tired you out." He motioned to the boys. "Come, my lads. We'll let Gwendolyn rest."

"Christopher," Gwen said. "Wait. Unfasten my dress."

So the little boy stayed behind and undid the long row of buttons.

Gwen let her dress slide to the floor and tried to step out of the pile of fabric, but it caught her foot and she fell.

"Are you all right?" Christopher helped her to stand.

"I'm fine. Hang my dress up, will you?"

Christopher carried it to the closet.

"Don't tell Mother," Gwen begged.

"You know I won't."

When Christopher was gone, Gwen took off her petticoat and changed into her nightgown. Then she dropped into bed. The sun had climbed high overhead.

"Oh please, keep Mrs. Nellis from bringing lunch," Gwen said out loud. The thought of food nauseated her—and besides, she didn't want her condition reported to her mother.

Her eyes kept wandering to her mirror. She compared its frame to the oval border of Sir Robert's vision. The grapevines were much alike.

Staring at her unfinished copy of the vision, she frowned at the name *MAHAM* on the shield and *EUROPA* in the hand mirror. Why was the girl holding the mirror in her right hand? Gwen favored her left. Something about the key verse numbers *V I VI* bothered her tremendously.

"It's wrong." The picture swam in her head. "It's wrong." Wasn't the shield supposed to be the Maham family crest? The stag's antlers were backward.

Outside on the terrace, the colonel was nearly as frustrated as his student. He leaned forward. "The prism does more than reveal hidden things. It's our most powerful weapon. Don't look *at* it. Look *into* it."

Was there a difference between looking at something and looking into it? Not for the first time, Jack wondered if his great-uncle was merely a hypnotist.

"Red bands," Jack said. "That's all I see." It seemed likely to him that the thing in the garden had been a hallucination. He rotated the prism. A weak spectrum fell on the flagstones.

Christopher watched attentively.

"Deep into it," the colonel said. "Look deep."

Jack pinched the object between his thumb and index finger—and bobbled it.

"No!" the colonel cried.

Jack managed to catch the prism before it hit the stone terrace.

"Be careful!"

"Sorry!"

The colonel reached for the prism but stopped mid-motion. Hesitantly, as if forcing himself, he pulled back. "Look at it again."

Jack held the glass artifact to his eye. The inside was dull red, and it became redder as his exasperation grew.

Mrs. Nellis was checking a pot of soup simmering on the stove when Patrick rapped on the back door. She let him in.

"Hello, Patrick. Come to fix the telephone?"

"Yes, ma'am."

"You're a clever lad."

"It's not very complicated, actually."

"Talking over a wire is a miracle," Mrs. Nellis said as they went to the butler's office. "That's all I know."

Patrick set his toolbox on the desk and took out a bottle of glue. While he disassembled the telephone's mouthpiece and carefully glued two parts together, Mrs. Nellis prattled about Patrick's father and the upcoming dinner party.

"It will take a few hours for the glue to set properly," he said.

Mrs. Nellis had a sudden thought. "Oh, Patrick—Lady Gwendolyn's window latch is broken. Could you look at it while you're here?"

CHAPTER 4

Primary World

2-8-22

Patrick stumbled on the steps. He had been in Maham House many times but never upstairs. Now he was going to Lady Gwendolyn's bedroom. He would be near her personal things. He would be in the place she slept. He wanted to run away. It was no comfort that he had a perfectly legitimate reason to be there. And Lady Gwendolyn would *not* be there, of course.

Mrs. Nellis guided him through a third-floor hallway. Sunlight streamed out of the open door of a west-facing room.

The housekeeper knocked on the door across from the open one.

Patrick's heart nearly stopped. Why would Mrs. Nellis knock?

She took him in.

Patrick halted, unable to move. Lady Gwendolyn was not only there, but she was lying in her bed.

"M'lady, Patrick has come to fix your window."

Gwen rolled over and looked at him. "Oh, can you? Thank you so much, Patrick."

He was unable to reply. If he had been able to think straight, he would have apologized for the intrusion, turned around, and left immediately. Instead, he tipped his cap and plodded woodenly to the window. Gwen pushed herself up, rearranged her pillows, and leaned back against her headboard.

It did not cross Mrs. Nellis's mind that there was anything remarkable about inviting Patrick into Lady Gwendolyn's room. The housekeeper still thought of Gwen as a child. Patrick, if no longer a little boy, was a good soul. She did not notice the perspiration that had broken out on his forehead or the high color of his cheeks and ears.

Gwen noticed it and liked it. She had never made a boy uncomfortable before. She bent forward to watch him, pretending to be interested in his work. She could tell he was trying to avoid looking in her direction. She folded the covers to her waist and fussed with her nightgown.

Metal parts clattered on the floor. Patrick scrambled to gather them up. He was one big self-conscious nerve.

"I need to get back to the kitchen," Mrs. Nellis announced. "Ring if you want anything."

Suddenly, Patrick found himself alone with Lady Gwendolyn Maham in her bedroom. All he could think of was to finish the job as quickly as possible and get out. He removed the remains of the broken bracketry, drilled new holes, and installed a replacement bolt assembly.

Boys were cute when nervous, Gwen decided. Patrick was moving like a machine. She put a hand over her mouth as if to cover a yawn, but really it was to hide a smile.

He accidentally knocked over his toolbox—twice.

Having parked the Rolls Royce near the front door, Merrill was collecting the bags waiting in the Grand Hall. Protocol dictated that luggage be taken through one of the side entrances, but Lady Buckleigh could not have cared less about protocol right then.

She strode in, drawing her husband behind her the way a steamship pulls flotsam in the suction of its screws. "I need Mrs. Nellis *now*! I've got to go over the instructions for Gwen's medicine."

"You've already given them to her twice. For goodness' sake, Ceil!"

Lady Buckleigh turned on her husband. "This is *important*!"

Colonel Sir Geoffrey, Jack, and Christopher came in from the eastern hallway.

"If you're that worried, give them to Uncle Geoff." Lord Buckleigh pointed at the man.

The countess glowered at her husband. Since her sons were present, she suppressed the first reply that came to her mind.

The boys escaped up the grand staircase.

Jack still held the prism. "Uncle Geoff's utterly mad," he declared upon reaching the second landing. He looked at the worthless thing that his great-uncle had said was a weapon.

Christopher hustled to keep up. "He said the more powerful a thing is, the longer it takes to master it. That's why you're having trouble."

"It's a lump of glass," Jack growled.

"Patrick," Gwen said, her mood oscillating between excitement and doubt that any boy could ever be attracted to her. "My electric lamp flickers. Do you think something is wrong with it?"

Against his better judgment, Patrick walked to her bedside and bent down to examine the lamp. Rose scent lingering in the air did something to his balance. Lady Gwendolyn's hair was even more distracting. It glittered like gold. He had never seen it unpinned before.

"Well…" He couldn't stop himself from glancing at her and then couldn't look away. Her eyes were crystalline blue. He felt as if he were falling into them.

"*You!*" Jack shouted from the doorway. "Get away from my sister!"

Patrick jumped.

Gwen started. There had been something deliciously fun about having a boy in her bedroom. Suddenly, it didn't seem like a good idea after all.

"I was—" Patrick gestured dumbly at the lamp.

Jack crossed the floor like a Rottweiler that meant business.

"He's *supposed* to be here!" Gwen cried urgently.

Jack dumped the prism on his sister's writing desk and snatched her dagger.

"Jack!" Christopher gasped.

"I asked him to look at my lamp!" Gwen screamed. She scrambled out of bed and blocked her brother. "See the window? He fixed the latch. What are you thinking?"

Jack stared at the intruder. "Get out of here." His voice was frightening; his eyes burned.

Patrick tried to edge around the bed, but his pants snagged in a fold of the covers and he tripped. He went down, pulling the quilt, blanket, and sheet to the floor.

Jack laughed at the ridiculous sight, his homicidal mood momentarily checked.

Patrick extricated himself from the bedclothes and jumped to his feet.

"Well then…what shall we do here?" Jack pretended to move aside to let the other boy pass but then, without warning, punched him in the stomach.

Patrick grunted and doubled over.

"*Jack*!" Gwen grabbed her brother's arm.

Jack's eyes remained fixed on Patrick. "I saw you leering at my sister. I'm going to give you what for, Irish."

Gwen faced her brother. "Stop it, *now*!"

Her words had no effect. Jack took a step.

"Don't!" Christopher pulled on Jack's shirt, only to be shoved away.

Gwen coughed uncontrollably.

Jack scowled at her. "That's your answer to everything, isn't it? Chores? You're too sick. Schoolwork? Too tired. You just go into one of your coughing fits." He pushed her roughly aside.

She staggered against her desk.

"How can you treat your sister like that?" Patrick knew he shouldn't talk back to someone above his station, but he was getting a little angry himself.

"What? Do you think you're defending her?" Jack lunged with the dagger. It wasn't clear if the move was a feint or if he actually intended to commit murder.

Patrick barely dodged the thrust.

"Stop it!" Gwen needed to do something. "I'm telling you, stop it this instant!" Her thoughts were a whirl. She reached for something to fling at her brother. A hunk of glass on her desk was handy. She scooped it up and cocked her arm to throw it.

She never did. The prism in her hand caught sunbeams slanting through the open door and cast them at every shadow in the room. The faceted glass glinted like a diamond on fire.

Jack gasped, fight instantly forgotten.

Gwen lowered the prism and stared. Even shaded from the sun, it was dazzling. "What on earth?"

"Jack was using it…" Christopher began.

Everyone gazed at the glittering glass.

Then, in a low voice—almost a whisper—Patrick said, "Look at the mirror."

Downstairs, Sir Geoffrey had cornered Lord Buckleigh in the Blue Drawing Room and was learning about the upcoming War Cabinet meeting.

"Don't underestimate the Boche," advised the earl. "The Kaiser and his generals won't stop until every last soldier in Europe is a corpse. We have to make the common German desperate to surrender."

"What are you proposing?"

Lord Buckleigh glanced furtively at the door and windows as if wary of spies. "I've been manufacturing drugs to heal the sick and wounded. But when we got the news about Fredrick, I realized that the only way to save our sons is to kill Germans." His face hardened. "They invented poison gas. Now, everyone is making it by the ton." The earl took a breath. "Well, I've perfected a new composition of mustard gas."

The colonel frowned. "Everyone on both sides carries a mask nowadays. And gas is a fickle weapon. When the wind changes, the infernal stuff floats over your own trenches."

"Not if it's dispersed as a gelatin. It makes a place uninhabitable for weeks—maybe months. And we won't fire it into their trenches. We'll load it into Handley Page bombers and drop it on Berlin, Hamburg, Frankfurt, and every other city. Make them unlivable."

"Are you serious?"

"Deadly serious. Mustard in low concentrations doesn't kill—it blisters." The earl shrugged and looked at the floor. "Infants and the infirm may die. Can't be avoided."

Sir Geoffrey shook his head.

"We'll offer a carrot before the stick," Lord Buckleigh continued.

"What kind of carrot?"

"The literal kind. Miss Harkless gave me the idea. Ship food into Germany. We can do it through neutral Switzerland. She has connections there."

"I don't follow."

"The Germans denounce our naval blockade. Claim it's starving civilians. So we'll feed them to prove we're merciful before we give them the ultimatum."

"My dear fellow, we'd give up our leverage and then maim and kill their babies. They'd be furious. More determined than ever. They'd copy your weapon and use it on us. Instead of forcing a conclusion, you'd open a new phase of war."

Lord Buckleigh fell silent. His eyes wandered to a photograph on a side table—his late son, Lieutenant Fredrick Maham. "Well…"

Sir Geoffrey waited while his nephew pondered.

Then the sun blinked—or so it seemed to the colonel—and the atmosphere of the house changed; the drawing room felt colder. He reached automatically into his pocket. His hand came out empty—the prism wasn't there. "George! I have to go!"

He spun and ran out.

The fluid surface of the mirror made Gwen's head swim. Could the glass really be fluttering?

All at once, she was thrown wildly off balance. Her point of view advanced several feet into the mirror. Or perhaps the mirror had expanded and swept around her.

Then everything was back to normal, as if nothing had happened. She had not moved and was not looking back from a reflection world.

She held onto the footboard of her bed to keep from toppling over. "What do you suppose…?"

Patrick stared out the open window. He said, "There are mountains."

Confused, the others turned to see what he was looking at.

"Those are clouds, dolt." Jack meant to say it with withering scorn, but his voice trailed off. In the distance, rising above the moor, stood a range of snowcapped mountains that no one in the room had ever seen before.

Gwen moved haltingly to the window, fascinated by the sight. When she looked down, however, she gasped and backed away from the sill. Her room was much higher above the ground than it should have been.

All of a sudden, Gwen didn't want the prism. Didn't want it in her hand. Didn't want anything to do with it. She flung it into her armchair. It bounced off the padded back and came to rest in the middle of the seat cushion.

A moment after that, her great-uncle rushed into the room.

"Jack! What have you done? Where's the prism?" the colonel asked.

"There." Jack pointed at the chair.

Sir Geoffrey looked. "Where?"

"Right there," Jack declared, arm and finger rigidly extended.

"*Where?*"

Gwen's heart skipped a beat. The way the glass scintillated—how could her great-uncle not see it? She opened her mouth to ask if he was teasing them.

But before she could speak, she was hit—the jolt was the same as a physical blow—with the utter certainty that something enormously evil was upon them.

"IT'S HERE!" she screamed.

The warning saved her. She would have been killed if Sir Geoffrey had not stepped in front of the thing that burst through the open window.

The colonel grabbed the cormorant by its neck and threw it backward. "God, confound our enemy!" he yelled. It wasn't a curse. It was a prayer.

The cormorant landed on Gwen's desk, caught its balance, and stood on the webbed feet of an ordinary aquatic fowl. That was what the colonel saw. The children saw a mélange of ghoulish humanoid and bird parts standing on long-fingered hands. The creature's beak was a maw filled with jagged teeth. It rose to full height and extended its wings. Sir Geoffrey saw a spread of normal feathers. The children saw plumes stuck to leathery skin. When the monster moved, its overlapping parts shifted and gnashed together.

Jack stood transfixed.

Colonel Sir Geoffrey snatched the dagger from Jack's hand and thrust it at the bird. The thing dodged and hopped sideways, orienting on Gwen. The colonel moved with it, keeping himself between animal and girl.

He pointed the dagger at the cormorant. "In Jesus's name, begone!"

The creature took stock of Sir Geoffrey.

Gwen was mesmerized by sunken ellipsoids of infinite black above and to the sides of the bird's eyes. She saw inside one of those demon eyes and imagined she had been seized and her chest crushed in a vice. The thing hopped to the end of her desk, positioning itself to lunge at her.

Then its roving eyes spied the prism. Its head snapped around and locked rigidly on the object lying unguarded on the chair.

Suffering a tremendous foreboding, Gwen wanted to shout a warning, but she couldn't name the nature of the threat or what anyone should do. The monster hesitated so briefly that she mistook its indecision for clumsiness.

It leapt to the armchair and grabbed the prism with webbed cormorant toes. Then, wheeling, it shoved simultaneously with legs and wings and launched itself out the window.

Gwen tottered against her bed.

"Where's the prism?" the colonel demanded. "Where is it?"

Patrick was the first to recover. "The…whatever it was…took it."

Sir Geoffrey leaned heavily on the windowsill and gazed at the bird streaking into the distance. "Heaven help us!"

Patrick shook his head in disbelief. "What in creation was that?"

Gwen trembled. "A demon."

Jack held his head in his hands.

"It's going to the mountains," Christopher observed.

"Eh? What?" The colonel looked back and forth between the children and the countryside outside the window. "Mountains? You see *mountains*?"

Christopher nodded. They all nodded.

Gwen could not imagine anything scaring her great-uncle, but his face went white. "When did they appear?"

"Right after we went through the mirror," Patrick said.

"Went through the…through the…well, that's done it." The colonel bowed his head and stood very still.

Gwen lay down on her bed and curled into a ball.

"The mirror had nothing to do with your anchoring. It merely allowed you to see what was happening," Sir Geoffrey said absently. He set his jaw. "We'll have to go after the demon."

"How's that?" Jack was not expressing surprise. He was trying to understand words that didn't make sense.

"You're in a bad state now, and the prism is the solitary thing that can set you right. We have to recover it."

"Who is 'we'?"

The colonel swept his arm around the room. "Us."

Jack's eyes went wide. "You can't be serious!"

"Perfectly serious, I'm afraid."

Patrick needed more information. "Sir, you say we're in a bad state. What state are we in?"

Sir Geoffrey looked unhappily out the window and around Gwen's bedroom. Everyone else did the same, wondering what they were supposed to see.

"The world you know is only an aspect of the full reality. A silhouette." The old soldier looked at each of the children. "You have always been fixed—anchored—to the silhouette. You are now anchored instead to the Primary World."

"What does that mean?"

Christopher guessed. He scraped his fingers across a shadow on the wall. "It doesn't hurt if a demon claws your shadow." He repeated the gesture, this time raking his nails from his shoulder to his stomach. "It does if it's your real body."

Sir Geoffrey nodded somberly.

"So," Patrick said, "in the Primary World, demons can claw us?"

"That's one thing they can do." The colonel closed his eyes for several seconds. When he opened them, they were filled with resolve. "Gwendolyn, get dressed."

"Sir—you don't mean to take Lady Gwendolyn with you?" Patrick asked in disbelief.

"I'm afraid so. You and Christopher, as well. For your own safety."

This was too much for Jack. "The putrid thing is halfway across the moor by now. It *flies*! We can't track it, let alone catch it. If we try, *it* will probably catch *us*. And you want to take Gwen? Look at her. She can't walk fifty feet."

"We've no choice," Sir Geoffrey said in a measured tone. "The prism is the only thing that can reanchor you to silhouette." Telling the children that they were exposed, easy prey would have been motivating, but comfort and encouragement were better choices at this juncture. "Jack, you anchored yourself and others to the Primary World. That takes *tremendous* skill. I couldn't do it until I had practiced for almost a year. You'll be able to shift back. I have faith in you."

"I don't think I was the one…" Jack glanced at Gwen. What exactly had happened? Who had done what? He didn't know anything, and he couldn't cope.

The colonel addressed the children. "I don't believe the enemy planned this. The demon merely took advantage of an unexpected opportunity. We have to recover the prism before they can exploit your condition. Gwendolyn, dress in something practical. Nothing too fancy."

She regarded each of the boys in turn, expecting them to offer more resistance. None of them said anything.

In a daze, Gwen went into her closet and slipped her dress off its hanger. She turned and looked at the others.

"What are you waiting for?" the colonel asked.

"Everyone to leave so I can change."

"Ah. Yes, well…" Sir Geoffrey peered into the bathroom. "McCray—see anything unusual in here?"

"Sir?"

"Any gaps in walls or items you wouldn't find in an ordinary bathroom?"

"Uh…no, sir."

"All right, my dear, change in there."

Gwen went in and closed the door.

Sir Geoffrey paced.

A minute later, Gwen called through the door: "Christopher—help me with buttons."

The colonel glanced at his watch a dozen times before the two of them finally emerged from the bathroom.

"Got a bag?" the colonel asked. "Pack a change of clothes and whatever essentials you need for a night or two away from home. Just a few things. We can't be lugging steamer trunks."

"This is the only dress I own."

"Oh? Very good."

Gwen riffled through her chest of drawers and put toiletries and undergarments into a satchel. Patrick stared at a wall in the opposite direction. As an afterthought, Gwen tossed her diary into the bag.

"All right. Let's go to the boys' room," the colonel directed.

Patrick was the first out the door. He stopped so unexpectedly that Jack collided with him.

"Clumsy oaf!" But Jack completely forgot what he was going to say next. The hallway was bizarre. To the south, just beyond his bedroom door, there was a downward-sloping rough stone passageway. "Something has happened to our house," he said dumbly.

The colonel emerged from Gwen's room. "If memory serves, you are looking at a mysterious section of corridor inexplicably spliced into this hallway. It is about thirty feet long and descends five feet. At the end of it, this third-floor Maham House hallway picks up again."

"Yes, sir," Patrick acknowledged. "You cannot see the corridor because you are anchored to silhouette?"

"Correct. What you see is part of a twelfth-century Norman fortification. Bits and pieces of things that have disappeared from our silhouette aspect persist in the Primary World. *Interstices.* Boys, get what you need from your room. Well? Don't just stand there gaping!"

Everyone went into Jack and Christopher's room.

While the brothers put clothes and useful items into a carpetbag, Gwen dropped into a chair and let her body sag.

Patrick examined a toy castle on a table. He studied the shadow it cast. After some thought, he inserted his hand into the castle's courtyard so that its shadow was hidden within the shadow of the walls.

"So," Patrick said, "interstices are places that exist in the Primary World separate from silhouette places."

"Correct, more or less."

"And human beings ordinarily exist in silhouette rather than the Primary World."

"No. We exist in the Primary World, but our presence is *anchored* to its silhouette."

"But we—Lady Gwendolyn, Lord Mayfield, Master Christopher, and I—are now anchored to the Primary World, so demons can physically attack us."

"That is correct."

"I don't understand why they could not have before."

"Creatures of pure spirit—angels and demons—do not cast shadows and therefore do not appear to exist in the silhouette world, though they can move through it. Many people think of spirits as ethereal and insubstantial. The opposite is true. Anchored in silhouette, it is we who are wraithlike. Christopher explained it—will you be hurt if your shadow is attacked?"

"No, but if I've always existed in the Primary World, then demons could always have attacked the real me instead of my shadow."

"It's the anchoring that matters. The analogy of a projected shadow is inadequate and flawed. I sacrificed precision in order to communicate the general concept."

"How did you fight the demon that came through the window?"

"Last night, it was a cormorant," Gwen said.

"It is a bird possessed by a demon. To me, it still looks like a cormorant, albeit a particularly vile one. I can only imagine what the taraph—that kind of demon—looked like to you. It's hampered because it can't leave its host without damaging itself. But it is still immensely dangerous. It must not have realized you were anchored to Primary, or it would have tried harder to kill you."

"We're set," Jack said grimly. "Let's get this over with."

Christopher picked up the carpetbag. Having a last-minute thought, Jack reached under his bed and brought out a saber in a scabbard. It had belonged to an ancestor who had served in the Tenth Royal Hussars.

The colonel approved. "Arming yourselves is a good idea. Here, Mr. McCray, you take Gwendolyn's dagger."

Patrick accepted the weapon. "Wait. Why couldn't you see the prism?"

"That is a good question, and I will answer it later. For now, let's get going." The colonel led his charges out into the hallway. Without pausing, he walked into the interstitial Norman corridor… and vanished.

"Great Scott!" Jack blurted.

It was a moment before Gwen realized her great-uncle was at the far end of the rough stone corridor.

Sir Geoffrey turned, took a single step, and reappeared in front of her. "Since I'm anchored to silhouette, I go right past interstices." Impatience strained his voice. "I could carry you past it one by one, but perhaps you should go through it. Good experience."

Patrick wondered how Sir Geoffrey could carry them past the interstice. What would happen if the colonel, anchored to silhouette, and they, anchored to Primary, were to cross the interstitial threshold together? He studied the boundary. There was a perfect plane of demarcation between the wallpaper, wainscoting, and Turkish carpet of the twentieth-century hallway and the worn gray sandstone blocks of the Norman corridor. However, the sections did not align precisely, and the ancient corridor was narrower.

Seeing no hazard, Patrick stepped cautiously inside the interstice. There was no resistance or barrier of any kind.

"Incidentally, Mr. McCray," Sir Geoffrey said, "I cannot see you now that you are inside the interstice."

"If you put something into a box that doesn't exist in your world, that something seems to disappear," Patrick noted.

"Nor can I hear you," said the colonel as if he had. "Go straight to the Maham House hallway below. Don't dawdle." He went there himself.

The air in the interstitial corridor was cold and stale. Jack and Christopher hurried to the bottom, where the colonel waited. Gwen had difficulty. She took measured steps down the steep incline. Patrick stopped and touched the wall, pretending to study the masonry but actually keeping an eye on her.

She stumbled. "Oh!"

He caught her arm. "M'lady…"

He tried to release her as soon as she had her balance, but she clung to him. He was considering how to assist her without such close contact when he saw, over her shoulder, a set of demonic eyes looming in the air at the far end of the twentieth-century hallway behind them.

"Villains!"

"Excuse me?"

Patrick hooked his arm around Gwen's waist, lifted her, and raced down the incline. Carrying her was easy—she was light as a feather.

"Enemies coming!" he cried when they were out of the interstice.

"Oh, not already!" The colonel pulled Gwen from Patrick. "On your guard! They'll be whip fast."

"What?" Jack looked back the way they had come. "What?"

"They've seen you in an interstice. They know you're anchored to Primary."

Sir Geoffrey scooped Gwen up and ran with her toward the East Tower. "Draw your blades!" he called back to the boys. "Stand your ground!"

"Wait…" Jack looked anxiously up the interstitial Norman corridor.

Clumsily, he unsheathed his saber.

In the East Tower, faster than was safe, the colonel bundled Gwen down the first flight of steps to where the landing between floors would have been if there were not now, in its place, nothing. The stairwell below was a wide, empty, smooth-walled shaft. That was what Gwen saw.

"Stop!" Gwen grabbed at the railing.

"Fear not!"

Sir Geoffrey stepped with his great-niece into space. However, an instant later, they were on the landing thirty feet beneath the dangling upper stairs.

"Another interstice," explained the colonel. "Vertical this time. I've brought you beneath it."

He continued down to the second floor and then, after setting Gwen on her feet, rushed back upstairs. Upon reaching the landing and stepping up, the colonel immediately appeared on the overhanging steps high above. Twenty-five seconds later, he returned with Christopher and deposited the dumbfounded boy beside his sister.

Right after his great-uncle took Gwen, Jack stood on tiptoes to see into the hallway beyond the Norman-era incline. His need to know what was there was at odds with his desire to crouch and hide.

Patrick gripped Gwen's dagger. "What do you suppose is coming?"

Shadows in the upper hallway had depth; Jack had never seen anything like them. They meandered like stalking predators.

"I'll cut you to pieces!" Jack shrieked at the specters, swinging his sword wildly.

Patrick edged backward. "I'll just get out of your way."

That was when Sir Geoffrey took Christopher.

The light in the passageway dimmed as if shutters had been closed, and the stalking shadows melted into the background.

Then bedlam. Two creatures sprang doglike down the ramp. They had teeth and claws and eyes within their eyes. They hopped along the walls to slip around the boys and come at them from behind.

Jack and Patrick spun about and slashed madly with their blades.

When the colonel returned a moment later, the boys were facing in his direction, swinging and stabbing at things he couldn't see. A rip appeared in Jack's jacket, and a streak of blood welled from a gash in Patrick's face.

"Come this way!" Sir Geoffrey commanded.

But the two teenagers were backing away from him. Fighting for their lives, first Jack and then Patrick disappeared from the colonel's sight. The demons had maneuvered them into the interstice and up the ramp.

The colonel shouted, "Boys! Get out of the interstice!"

Jack jabbed and swung instinctively. His rational mind was not involved. He couldn't even categorize what he was fighting. Intermittently, the rangy creatures appeared canine or manlike, but mostly they were bits and pieces flicking here and there.

Patrick was off-balance on the incline, but lunging downslope gave his thrusts extra power. By pure luck, he stuck Gwen's dagger into his opponent's shoulder. The creature recoiled and froze, its wolfish jaw hanging open as if it couldn't believe what had happened. The other demon paused as well. It stared hungrily at its comrade's wound. The injured demon stuck out its dark tongue and licked black fluid oozing from its shoulder.

Abruptly, both demons renewed their assault on the boys.

All was tranquil in the Maham House hallway. Sir Geoffrey could see nothing of what was happening. "Boys…you must come out of the interstice."

"They're in the way!" Jack screamed hysterically from seven feet up the interstitial ramp. His great-uncle was right at the boundary of the interstice. So were the demons.

"Lord, give the boys courage!" the colonel prayed.

"We're here!" Jack shrieked.

Sir Geoffrey bowed his head and raised a hand in supplication. "Father, deliver your servants, in Jesus's name."

The two evil creatures hissed through rippling lips at the speaking of the name.

Jack lost his footing. He tripped down the slope—each unintentional hop, skip, and jerk of his flailing body perfectly timed to evade the demons' clutches. He stumbled out of the interstice and into Sir Geoffrey's arms.

The colonel did not hesitate for a second. He hauled Jack to the East Tower.

One of the demons whirled to go after its escaping quarry. Patrick thrust, and the point of Gwen's dagger went deep into the monster's back. Squealing and spasming like a rat torn by a cat, the thing slammed into the stone wall. Distracted, the other one—the one stabbed earlier—turned to see what had happened. Patrick darted past it.

Carrying his great-nephew over his shoulder in a fireman's carry, the colonel had Jack down nine steps before the boy turned his head and saw the yawning shaft below. But they were on the landing below before Jack could scream.

Patrick pleaded, "God, help me!" He ran through the doorway into the East Tower. The demons were right behind, delayed but not stopped by their injuries.

Patrick charged down the stairs two at a time. He saw the emptiness below, but his brain couldn't accept the reality of the shaft until he was on the last stair step. Panicking, he grabbed the right railing with his left hand because the dagger was in his right. Momentum spun him clockwise; the dagger slashed an arc that sliced through the face of the demon springing at him.

Suddenly Patrick was far below, Sir Geoffrey gripping his arm and pulling him to the next flight of stairs.

"Look out!" Christopher called.

The gored and gashed demons, having pounced on the thin air Patrick had been occupying a split second before they sprang at him, came plummeting down the shaft. They smashed on the landing. They didn't bounce; their impacts made nasty crunching sounds.

Patrick pointed Gwen's dagger at the twitching bodies, ready to continue fighting.

The colonel stayed beside him. "What do you see?"

"Devils on the landing." Patrick stood still and peered intently. He relaxed. "They're dead."

"No," Gwen warned. "They aren't."

She was right. The demons were mangled but not lifeless. Each clutched spasmodically at the other, digging claws into raw flesh, gouging out chunks, and shoving them into their mouths.

Jack, shaking, pressed himself against a wall.

"They're eating each other," Christopher reported, disgusted.

"Good," the colonel said. "It will be a fortnight before the one that wins is a threat. We're leaving. Down."

Jack didn't move. He stared in horror at the feeding demons. Christopher took his hand.

"*Down*," the colonel repeated.

The dazed group descended the next flights of stairs, which were entirely ordinary, all the way to the ground floor. Sir Geoffrey led the way through the baize-padded door to the servants' area. He clapped Patrick on the shoulder. "You did an excellent job, lad."

"McCray was too stupid to be scared." Jack couldn't hold back stinging tears. He was ashamed of his failure and hated Patrick the more for it. He was still so afraid that he lurched side to side, hardly in control of his limbs.

"Be quiet, Jack!" Gwen wanted to hit her brother.

Patrick laughed miserably, the way people do after they've experienced something so horrible they don't have a proper way to express their emotions. "He's not far off. I didn't know what I was doing. It was pure luck."

"God was with you children, and will continue to be." The colonel looked into the kitchen. "Thank goodness no one is here."

The boys set their weapons on a counter. Sir Geoffrey examined the gashes in their arms. "Nothing too serious, but we'll have to watch for infection. Is any of their fluid on you?"

"On our clothes," Patrick said.

"I'm not able to see it. Keep it out of your wounds, if you can. Your shirts are ruined. You'll have to change."

Christopher dug into the carpetbag for replacements.

Jack didn't like the Irish boy wearing his things but was too numb to protest and knew it would be silly if he did.

Gwen dampened towels with warm water.

The colonel found a bottle of iodine in a cabinet. He tore strips from the ruined shirts to use as bandages.

Still mostly in shock, the boys didn't even flinch when the scratches on their arms were cleaned and dressed.

"Why did the devils attack each other?" Christopher asked.

"For power." The colonel dabbed Jack's arm. "God is the source of all existence. Satan and his followers have separated themselves from God. They cannot create reality. They can only take it from others."

"But…they eat their own kind?" Patrick grimaced.

Sir Geoffrey nodded. "They have no love for one another. They don't form bonds of friendship or community. They cooperate only out of common purpose or fear."

Christopher gazed into the hallway outside the kitchen. "Do you suppose the ones that attacked us are dead now?"

"Demons don't die—not even when consumed. They diminish but are not completely destroyed."

"Then we did them no real damage." Patrick said.

"From what you described, Mr. McCray, I suspect the evil spirits you fought will be licking their wounds for some time."

"Literally," Christopher said.

Jack and Patrick put on fresh shirts.

"It would be better," Jack said to his great-uncle, "for us to stay here and protect Gwen while you go after the prism."

"I can't see it. You've affixed it to the Primary frame. An ordinary item casts a shadow regardless of its anchoring, so long as it's not inside an interstice. But the prism isn't an ordinary object. When it transfers, it creates its own interstice and casts no shadow. So *you* have to find it, Jack, and use it to anchor everyone back to silhouette."

Hearing footsteps, everyone hushed and looked toward the hallway.

"Hullo?" Mrs. Nellis appeared at the door. "Oh—Colonel Sir Geoffrey." The housekeeper started when she saw Gwen. "Er...the lord and lady are leaving. They asked to see the boys." She noticed the bloody gash in Patrick's cheek. "Oh dear!"

"He fell," Gwen explained quickly. "Against...something."

Mrs. Nellis looked at the saber and dagger on the counter.

"In a fencing accident."

The colonel motioned. "Jack, Christopher—come say goodbye to your parents." He beckoned to Gwen. "You better come too, my dear." He paused at the door. "Mrs. Nellis, would you be so good as to put a plaster on Mr. McCray's cheek?"

Gwen and Christopher followed their great-uncle upstairs and through hallways. Jack shuffled along behind.

"You may see things that disturb you," the colonel warned as they neared the Grand Hall. "Earlier today, I sensed a type of evil spirit that specializes in secrecy and deception. I couldn't locate it precisely without giving your mother and father cause to question my sanity. There's a good chance it's with them right now. Do *not* react to its presence. There is no way for it to know you are anchored to the Primary World. Don't give it a reason to be suspicious."

"What if the thing *is* suspicious and attacks us?" Jack's voice was an octave higher than usual.

"It's a pseustee—a sneak. It won't attack you physically. Most likely."

They entered the Grand Hall from the archway east of the staircase. The room appeared architecturally as it always had, but Gwen noticed bands of light and shadow that had no apparent source. The parallelogram patterns in the multicolor marble floor looked dizzyingly three-dimensional.

Merrill, the chauffeur, stood by the front door, waiting while Lord and Lady Buckleigh faced off.

"Gwen is draining herself, and no one appears to care," asserted the countess.

The earl refused to give ground. "We are not changing our plans."

"Gwendolyn is fine," Sir Geoffrey declared as they rounded the sweeping curve of the stairs. "As you can see."

Lady Buckleigh twirled around. "What? This is precisely the problem! She *must* stay in bed!" The countess turned to her daughter. "Are you *trying* to kill yourself, Gwen? Are you trying to kill *me*?"

"A good breakfast and walk made me better, not worse, Mama. But I shall obey all instructions to the letter while you are gone. I promise."

"She does seem stronger," noted the earl.

"She's white as a sheet," said someone.

Gwen blinked, neither recognizing the soft, reasonable voice nor discerning its origin.

"She's white as a sheet," echoed Lady Buckleigh.

Gwen had taken the dark swatches on her mother's clothes for shadows. Now she saw the truth, and her blood froze in her veins. A wiry creature with thin, multijointed arms and an elongated, tubelike proboscis was intermingled with Lady Buckleigh's body. Its tiny lips quivered at her ear canal, dripping a syrupy drool. The pseustee was nearly invisible; it wasn't transparent, but its continuously shifting outer layer had confusing hues and patterns.

The demon noticed Gwen's stare. Its eyes narrowed in suspicion.

Christopher pointed at the thing. "Look!"

"Be still," the colonel commanded under his breath.

The pseustee's proboscis dropped in wonder. A great fire lit in its eyes. Its snout curled back to Lady Buckleigh's ear and said, "Geoffrey's got the children all worked up. Christopher is terribly agitated."

Gwen made a spot decision. The spirit could lie, but it couldn't hurt her mother any other way. She would follow Uncle Geoffrey's instructions.

Christopher, however, couldn't control himself. "Get off!" he growled.

The colonel groaned. He closed his eyes.

Shocked, the countess stared at her son. "What did you say, young man?"

Gwen was relieved—her mother didn't think Christopher was seeing things. She thought he was being insolent. Except, upon reflection, that wasn't any better.

The demon laughed raucously.

"Christopher was yelling at the spider." Gwen stepped forward, brushed her hand down Lady Buckleigh's dress, and stepped back before the surprised demon could snap at her.

Lady Buckleigh looked at the floor. So did Gwen, pretending to watch something skitter away.

By a remarkable coincidence, there actually was a spider there: brown and black with a bulbous body and long, thin legs. Gwen had never liked spiders before but was overjoyed to see this one.

The countess lost her train of thought. "Well…I say…"

The demon also appeared to experience a moment of doubt. But the moment passed. The thing drooled into Lady Buckleigh's ear and said, "This is all very odd. Geoffrey's done something to the children."

"This is all very odd," Lady Buckleigh said. "Geoffrey's—"

"Uncle Geoffrey hasn't done anything to us," Gwen interjected.

The countess did not finish what she had intended to say, disrupted by a peculiar, unsettling sensation that her daughter had somehow intruded into her thoughts.

The evil spirit guffawed and giggled, its whole body undulating. "Heh! Made a boo-boo, didn't we, little girl?"

Lady Buckleigh glared at the colonel. "Sir Geoffrey, must you disrupt our lives this way?"

"Gwendolyn looks awful," suggested the pseustee.

"Gwendolyn looks awful," Lady Buckleigh said. "George, I'm staying here."

Gwen acted on impulse. Anger had brought color back into her face and given her energy. She walked to her father and kissed him on the cheek. "Have a good trip, Papa." She bent close to his ear. "Mama is overreacting."

She turned to her mother. "I'm feeling quite well, Mama. Really, I am."

"Why is she dressed if she intends to obey instructions?" the pseustee said.

"That's why I dressed and came to see you off." Gwen's expression was sincere and innocent. "But I promise I'll follow all instructions while you're gone."

Lady Buckleigh continued to look confused.

"Ceil." Lord Buckleigh took his wife's arm. "It's only two days. Mrs. Nellis is here, and Miss Harkless will arrive soon."

That helped.

"And Uncle Geoffrey is here too," Christopher added.

That didn't help. Gwen shot her brother a severe look.

Lord Buckleigh took the handle of his briefcase. "If need be, Mrs. Nellis can have Doctor Foley here in an hour."

"Mama, I'll be fine." Gwen kept her voice even. "Don't worry."

"Very well, then," said the demon with an evil sneer, uncoiling slightly and extending its snout. "Let's have a goodbye kiss."

Gwen stiffened as her mother came toward her. The nasty spirit moved beside Lady Buckleigh's body in a bizarre dance. It was going to bite. Its mouth was small, but its yellow teeth were like needles—and there were plenty of them.

Gwen held steady, determined not to flinch. Where would it strike her? Would it be deadly? Uncle Geoffrey couldn't help her.

Christopher saved the day. He intercepted the countess. "Goodbye, Mother!" In a lightning-quick sleight-of-hand, he sliced the demon's snout clean off with his new pocketknife.

The severed part fell and writhed on the floor like a snake on a sizzling griddle. The pseustee screeched and struck at the boy with the stub of its proboscis. But it had nothing to bite with.

As Christopher stepped up to kiss his mother's cheek, he kicked the demonic snout clear across the room.

The evil spirit scrambled after its lips and teeth.

The situation was as bizarre as it was dreadful. Gwen barely maintained her composure. "I hope you have a good trip," she heard herself say as she kissed her mother.

The pseustee hissed out of the stump of its mouth, sounding like a balloon blabbering air. It gobbled its detached part, dashed into a hallway, and disappeared.

Gwen didn't remember anything her mother or father said after that; her attention was too scattered. She retained the image of her mother looking back from the driveway. That was all.

"The demon's getting away!" Christopher cried when the front door had closed. He darted after the spirit like a dog chasing a cat.

"Come back!" ordered the colonel.

"Everyone has gone mad!" Jack muttered.

It was fortunate that Lady Buckleigh's attention had been on Gwen. If the countess had noticed the ashen color of Jack's skin or the way he trembled, no explanation or assurance would have calmed her. He had not approached his parents to say goodbye. Of course, that was easily explained as English reserve.

"Christopher!" thundered the colonel. "Come here at once!"

The boy returned but protested, "We ought to hunt the demon. It's going to tell its chums about us."

"How can it?" Gwen asked. "You cut its mouth off."

The colonel looked from sister to brother. "He did? Well done, my boy! Well done, indeed! I wondered what that legerdemain with the pocketknife was about. But even so, I doubt you'd be able to find the pseustee. They're hard to spot under the best of circumstances." The colonel frowned. "Unfortunately..."

"Unfortunately what?" Gwen asked.

"Christopher has a point. Pseustees specialize in trickery. They put their being into weaving and whispering lies, not manifesting fierce physical features. So, they need protection. They always work for a master."

"So that thing will tell a worse demon about us?"

"I'm afraid so."

"A pox on spies and liars."

"*You've* been telling lies," Christopher pointed out.

"I have not."

"You told Mrs. Nellis that Patrick fell."

"He *did* fall."

"That's not why he was bleeding."

"I didn't say it was."

"You said there was a fencing accident."

"He was fencing with demons. By accident. It's not my fault that language is imprecise."

The little boy put his hands on his hips. "All right. Are you really going to follow Mother's instructions while she's gone?"

"I said I'd follow instructions," Gwen returned. "I didn't say whose."

"I think that's what pseustees do," Christopher said. "Twist things that are true into deceptions."

Sir Geoffrey hustled the group through the hallways and downstairs to the kitchen, muttering as he went. "How will we convince Mrs. Nellis to let Gwendolyn leave the house?"

Gwen wasn't sure if her great-uncle was asking for suggestions or talking to himself.

"You and McCray go look for the blasted prism, Uncle Geoff," Jack implored. "The rest of us will stay here."

The colonel shook his head. "Didn't you hear me? The pseustee will alert its master. You can't stay here."

Patrick was alone in the kitchen when they arrived.

"Where is Mrs. Nellis?" the colonel asked.

"She was feeling faint and went to her room to lie down."

Sir Geoffrey thought for a few moments before saying, "Gwendolyn, get me a sheet of stationery." He looked about. "Christopher, have you a canteen? Fill it up. Jack, get overcoats. One for each of you."

The children were slow to react. The colonel clapped his hands once, very loudly. "Move!"

"Sir, what would you like me to do?" Patrick asked.

"Collect up everything by the door. Don't forget the dagger and saber. And keep watch for anything untoward. You can see spirits; I can't."

Gwen found a couple of sheets of paper and an envelope in a drawer; she placed them on the counter with a fountain pen. Then she sat on a chair and pulled her knees up to her chin.

Christopher brought two canteens. He gathered bread, cheese, apples, and, after searching through cupboards, Gwen's tin of nuts and dried fruit.

The colonel scribbled a message. He printed *Mrs. Nellis* on the envelope and sealed his note inside. "I wrote that we have all gone to Buckton to consult a friend of mine about Gwendolyn's condition and will be back tomorrow evening. God willing, it is true."

Gwen sat perfectly still in the chair. In her mind, she saw the pseustee intertwined with her mother. The thing was like a giant tumor with penetrating tentacles. "That pseustee possessing Mother…"

Sir Geoffrey held up a hand. "The pseustee did *not* possess your mother. It was influencing her, which is an entirely different thing. Your mother did not invite its presence."

Gwen was not comforted. More than ever, the world was dark and dreadful.

Jack dumped a pile of coats on a chair and hunched over, looking deathly ill. Patrick was in slightly better shape—but only slightly. Gwen could see that he was scared and confused and feeling very much out of place. Ten-year-old Christopher was the only one trying to be optimistic, doing his best to act grown-up.

"Leave me here," Gwen said. "You'll never find the prism if you have to worry about me."

The colonel shook his head. "You wouldn't be safe."

"I'm dying anyway." Gwen stared at her hands. Her great-uncle probably thought she was an innocent girl to be protected. But she was not innocent at all. Not after the rite she had performed on High Tor.

The colonel studied Gwen for a long time. Once again, she had the feeling he was keeping something to himself. Something he knew or at least suspected.

The colonel said, "I'm sorry, but you're coming. We have to trust God." He looked at Christopher's bag. "Good heavens, lad! We're going to Buckton, not Patagonia! We don't need all that." He peered inside. "Well, maybe the nuts and cheese. Hmm. And the apples might be nice." He shrugged. "Oh, bring it all."

"What about Gwen's medicine?"

"I'll punch anyone who tries to give me any," she declared.

"Leave it. Let's be off." The colonel looked out the window. He could not have seen an enemy if there was one. He sighed and opened the door. "Jack, take the lead."

Paige & Lara,

Sorry you were confused. The Primary World = silhouette space + interstitial space. Anchored to silhouette (as you always are), you can't see or enter interstices—you pass by them without knowing they are there. But you could enter interstices if you could anchor yourself to the Primary World.

Suppose you were in a hallway with an interstice like the one near Jack and Christopher's bedroom. Suppose also that you were anchored to silhouette (as usual). Here's what you would see and where you would be after taking seven steps:

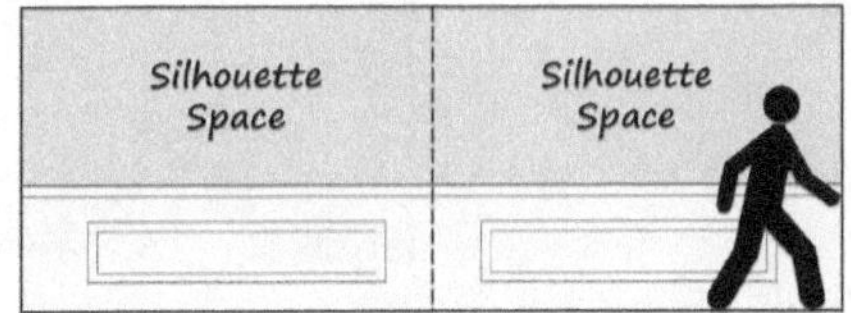

If you were anchored to the Primary World instead, here's what you would see and where you would be after taking seven steps:

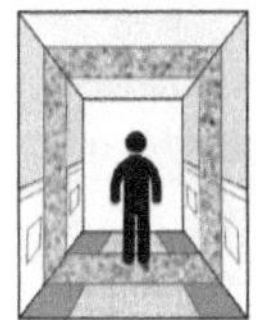

The interstice near Jack and Christopher's bedroom sloped downward and was much longer than the one depicted above, but that was too hard to draw.

Interstitial and silhouette spaces don't always join neatly, but I gather that they do more often than you would expect.

What about vertical interstices?

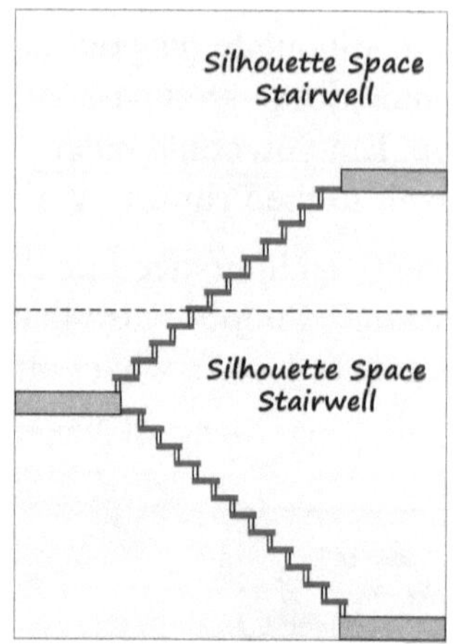

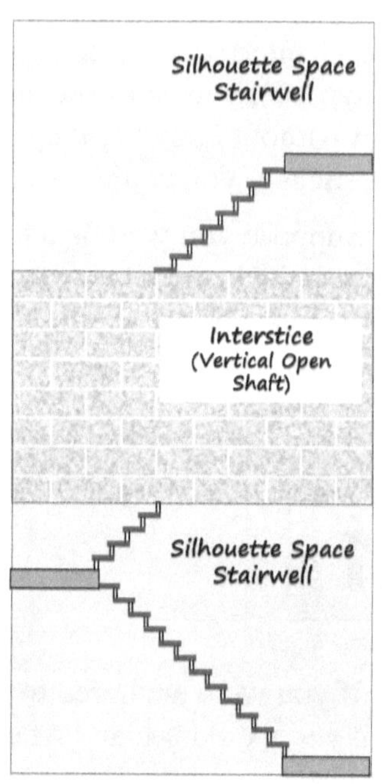

You can see that someone anchored to the Primary World would have trouble with the 9th step from the top.

Now…what would happen if an interstitial wall blocked a corridor? A person anchored to silhouette wouldn't even know the wall was there and could walk freely through the corridor (as in the first figure on the previous page). But a person anchored to the Primary World would be blocked.

So, what if an interstitial mountain ridge ran across a silhouette road? Think about the possibilities.

Kirk

CHAPTER 5

Pursuit Across the Moor

25-19-17

The rhythmic thudding of hooves became splashing and sucking sounds when the three horses of the five riders came to a muddy place in the rutted country road. Colonel Sir Geoffrey was making east-northeast for Buckton, where he intended to stop for the night. Maham House lay a mile behind. Gwen turned and gazed across the open moorland. Her home was now much larger than it was in the real world. She considered. *No—larger than it was in silhouette.* What she saw now was the reality.

Her house and the Norman castle were fused piecemeal. Nineteenth-century builders had unknowingly stacked her bedroom and the rest of the third floor of the east wing atop twelfth-century fortifications. Had circumstances been more favorable, she would have liked to have explored the mysterious place. However, at this particular time, the Frankenstein's monster architecture was disturbing.

She leaned back against Patrick and hugged herself, trapping his arm against her waist. She found the contact comforting.

It had the opposite effect on him.

Sir Geoffrey had put Gwen and Patrick together on May, Gwen's chestnut mare, when Patrick announced that he was not good with horses. The colonel had originally planned to pair Gwen with Jack but wanted a proficient rider on each animal, and Gwen was an excellent horsewoman. Before her illness, she equaled Jack in polo and surpassed him in steeplechase. Sir Geoffrey didn't want to take Gwen himself since he, anchored to silhouette, could not see or fight spirits.

They had to ride horses—a carriage or Patrick's delivery truck would have been a bad idea. Odd things would have happened in interstices.

Sir Geoffrey rarely missed details when making plans; however, he hadn't taken Gwen's dress into account before he and the children were in the stable. The horses were saddled, and he had already put Christopher up behind Jack on Thane, Jack's black gelding, when the colonel realized the problem. Gwen was chewing her lip, looking uncertainly at her horse. He was not about to let her sit sidesaddle. The only option was for her to ride astride May wearing her dress. She had to pull up her skirt.

Once she was in the saddle, the colonel draped a blanket over her exposed legs. Patrick nearly fainted when he was ordered up behind her.

Patrick McCray had been in love with Lady Gwendolyn Maham since he first met her in 1912. His father had taken him on a tour of Maham and Carter's pharmaceutical and chemicals works in Buckton. The McCrays were in the power plant watching a steam engine's oscillating rods and whirling wheels when Lord Buckleigh entered the building. He was accompanied by the most beautiful girl Patrick had ever seen.

Lord Buckleigh and the elder McCray, his chief engineer, struck up a conversation, shouting to be heard above the hissing and thumping machinery. The girl studied Patrick curiously. She was wearing a pure white dress with blue satin trim that matched her eyes. Her golden hair, bound with a ribbon of the same blue, glittered even in the industrial light of the generator room. Patrick couldn't take his eyes from hers. She cocked her head to one side and pursed her lips in a hint of an amused smile, and he was lost.

For two years, he used any and every excuse to go to Maham House, hoping to catch a glimpse of her. He spoke to her on two occasions, succeeding in saying, "Hello, Lady Gwendolyn. How are you?" without his voice cracking. He was not so silly as to believe there was any possibility of a romance between them, but seeing her made him happy.

Right before the war, Patrick's father was asked to a reception at Maham House. The guest list included Nobel laureate Ernest Rutherford, famous for his model of the atom, and several scientists from the Cavendish lab at Cambridge. Lord Buckleigh thought his chief engineer would fit right in. Patrick was invited to accompany his father to a lecture Rutherford gave before the reception. Awed by the distinguished scientists and feeling far, far out of his league both academically and socially, the boy kept to himself. There were other guests his age, including Jack—Mr. John Maham at the time—but Lady Gwendolyn was not there.

Children were not allowed to attend the reception, so Patrick had supper with the servants and then wandered out to explore the estate. The refreshingly cool June evening was scented with honeysuckle and rose.

He came to a large glass building. At first glance, it appeared to be a greenhouse. Instead of plants and flowers, however, the structure housed a sixteen-foot waterwheel turned by a cascade from an overhead trough. The night was clear and the moon full, and silver light saturated the place.

Patrick went inside to study the wheel, which turned an electric generator. A large volume of water rode down in the wheel's buckets and drained into a tile-lined channel. Patrick had just worked out the approximate weight of the water in the buckets and was trying to figure out how to convert that to watts when a motion at the door caught his eye.

Lady Gwendolyn was not quite thirteen, but her evening gown and expertly coiffed hair made her seem very grown-up. Moonlight glistened off her dress, her hair, and the splashing water. She cocked her head and gave him the same wry smile as when they had met at the chemical works two years earlier. "Hello, Mr. McCray. Are you enjoying the evening?"

He was astounded that she remembered his name. Somehow, he

managed to answer, "Yes, very much, thank you, m'lady." He even carried on a coherent conversation as they meandered through the gardens. Since Rutherford was the celebrity of the evening, Patrick held forth on the structure of the atom. In retrospect, he supposed he had been a bore. Lady Gwendolyn had listened and asked questions out of politeness.

Then the war began, and she disappeared. He learned about her illness from Mrs. Nellis.

Jack showed up at Gorton, Patrick's school, in the fall of 1917. Patrick ached to ask about Gwen but could never find a reasonable excuse. Jack was sullen and combative—not approachable at all. It was too bad. Everyone said he had been a good fellow before the war, though not especially outgoing. Anyway, Patrick was more and more occupied with his studies. He hoped to attend university and follow in his father's footsteps as an engineer.

Now, riding to Buckton, he was as close to Lady Gwendolyn Maham as it was possible to be. She turned her head to gaze eastward, and her hair brushed his nose. He looked the other way, back toward Maham House, to avoid breathing in her ear.

When he concentrated, Patrick could separate the manor from the fortress and perceive each building individually. It was like peering at an angle through a windowpane and seeing a reflection mixed with the view out the window. Most people can learn to focus on one image at a time. But Patrick was the only one of the riders who could see silhouette and interstitial matter separately.

The panorama to the north was even more interesting than the house. It wasn't anything like the moor Patrick was used to. The foothills were carpeted in giant ferns and conifers. Behind the forest rose massive mountains.

Patrick watched the sun settle into a notch between two tall peaks. There were many problems with the Primary World. For example, what would happen when the sun went behind the mountains? Those mountains didn't exist in silhouette—they could not block the sunlight shining on the silhouette ground that Patrick was crossing. Would it get dark or not?

Shortly, he had his answer. The sun sank behind the mountains, and the landscape became a patchwork of light and dark. The silhouette terrain around him, his companions, and the horses were still lit. Interstitial topography was in twilight. And everywhere, everything had lost distinctness. There was less sensory information. Before, he had been able to tell a lot about what things were made of and how they were constructed when they had been lit by Primary light. That was no longer the case.

Colors appear gray in semidarkness, Patrick thought. *It's like that.*

He couldn't look at the dazzling spot where the sun had gone, even though it was hidden.

He pondered fluid flow. How did rivers cross interstitial borders? What about the wind? His understanding of the interactions of matter and energy in the Primary World was hopeless. Colonel Sir Geoffrey had said that the shadow analogy was an oversimplification. It was a *colossal* oversimplification.

Just when Patrick thought he was on the verge of a breakthrough, the blanket on Lady Gwendolyn's lap shifted, exposing her left leg to her thigh. It was simultaneously the most exciting and alarming thing that had ever happened to him. She casually pulled the blanket back into place as though it were nothing.

Patrick was ashamed of himself but couldn't help thinking about Lady Gwendolyn's body. It was far too thin, but he still desired her. When setting out from the stables on May, she had insisted that he put an arm around her waist, detecting his unsteadiness on the horse. But almost immediately, he was the one doing the supporting. She slumped against him, coughing weakly now and again, trembling with fatigue.

Patrick looked at Colonel Sir Geoffrey and pointed northward. "That mountain we just passed seems miles distant, yet we rode by it in ten minutes. Could it be smaller and closer than it looks?"

"Your brain is used to receiving two-dimensional images and interpreting depth," the colonel explained. "Now you are anchored in higher-order space and can't process its geometry. That mountain range is many miles from us and covers an area as large as all of Devonshire. The present-day moor is what's left after eons of shaping."

"We're seeing back in time?"

"Not back. *Independent* would be a better way of putting it."

Sir Geoffrey squinted northward as if hoping to see the highlands himself. "Time is merely a property of our universe. Either a thing exists in creation, or it does not, whether past, present, or future."

"Human beings have immortal souls," Christopher said.

The colonel chuckled. "You make seemingly random but surprisingly relevant statements, don't you, my lad? Yes, we have immortal souls. Our existence in eternity is different from that of inanimate objects."

"Can we travel in time?" Gwen asked. "See ancient Athens or Jerusalem?"

"I did not say time was an illusion." But the colonel's brow furrowed. "I wonder."

Christopher announced, "I want to see a dinosaur."

"An ill-considered wish. You would not enjoy meeting a giant flesh-eating beast any more than you have enjoyed your encounters with demons."

"Listen…is that thunder?" Gwen asked.

Jack nodded toward an ugly squall on the southern horizon. "That wasn't there when we set out."

Sir Geoffrey scrutinized the black clouds. "No…but we should make Buckton before the storm arrives."

The travelers and their horses cast long afternoon shadows. Patrick gazed at the line of cold mountain peaks, dark against the western sky. He tried to remember exactly what the panorama looked like in silhouette.

Gwen sensed that her riding companion was curious about something and followed his gaze. "Look!" She pointed at a peculiar streak in the sky. "The demon left a trail!"

The colonel looked where Gwen pointed. "What's that? What do you see?"

"There's something like a ship's wake, gray with yellow-brown smudges and flecks of red. It runs from our house to the mountains."

"Do you mean the clouds?" Jack asked.

"No. That straight line."

The colonel called a halt. "I can't see it. Where does it lead?"

"There." Gwen pointed north.

Sir Geoffrey contemplated the distant mound of rocks. "High Tor." Gwen stiffened.

"Well. I wanted a sign. It seems we've been given one." Sir Geoffrey hoped he sounded more cheerful than he felt. His prayers had not been answered. The prism was entirely beyond his reach. It would be up to Jack and Patrick to retrieve it. He wasn't sure the boys could handle the taraph, let alone the other horrors that infested the place. He could get them within a thousand yards, perhaps, but after that they would be on their own.

At least his instinct to make for Anne Holliwell's house had been good. She could keep Gwendolyn and Christopher safe in Buckton. Anne had been a member of his team since they were teenagers.

"It's gray, you say?" Patrick asked. "I see a wisp, like a cirrus cloud in the sunset...."

"No, no—that gash in the firmament."

Christopher looked back and forth between his sister and the sky. He didn't know what she was talking about.

Sir Geoffrey nudged Ramillies, his horse. "Let's pick up the pace."

A minute later, cresting a hill, the colonel sighted the smokestacks of Buckton.

The children, anchored to the Primary World, saw something entirely different. They were confronted with an almost vertical wall of rock. Deep in shadow, rising like an ocean wave about to break, an eight-hundred-foot-high ridge ran across the road. It extended for miles in both directions.

Jack gaped. "There's a cliff in our way!"

Though he couldn't see it, the colonel remembered the feature from previous forays into the Primary World. "That's why you're riding horses." He thought the statement self-explanatory. It was, more or less, to Patrick—but not at all to the others.

"Our horses can't climb that. We'll have to go around," Jack said despondently. He looked at the oncoming storm. "We should have taken Patrick's lorry."

"Quick lesson." The colonel glanced at the threatening weather and decided to make it even quicker.

"Inanimate objects can be anchored to *either* the Primary World *or* its silhouette. Pure spirits—angels and demons—are unable to handle objects anchored to silhouette. But mortals can handle interstitial objects even though they cannot enter interstitial spaces—*ordinarily*. Under special circumstances, human beings can become anchored to the Primary World, as you have unfortunately found out. So…

"Axiom One: Inanimate objects bind to human beings in the Primary frame. What does that mean? That you, anchored in the Primary World, can interact with things in *both* frames, and when you do, those things will stay with you. Do you understand?"

Patrick nodded. "Yes, sir."

No, thought Jack, Gwen, and Christopher.

Patrick said, "It's why we're still wearing our clothes."

Sir Geoffrey burst out laughing. "Yes, Mr. McCray, quite correct."

"You carried us down the stairs. How did that work?" Patrick wanted to confirm his hypothesis.

"Axiom Two: Mortal creatures temporarily bind to each other when in contact. And…

"Axiom Three: For mortal creatures, the silhouette frame takes precedence over the Primary."

"Which is why you wanted us on horses." Patrick nodded again. The others were baffled.

"Correct. The horses are firmly anchored to the silhouette frame. *You* go with *them* rather than the other way around, just as you went with me on the stairs back at the house."

"But if we were in my lorry…"

"The lorry, being inanimate, would bind strongly to you instead of me in accordance with Axiom One. So when we came to an interstice, the lorry would disappear into it, leaving me quite uncomfortable in midair."

"I see."

"I don't," Gwen complained. "How are we going to get past the ridge?" Her great-uncle was leading them toward it as if it were imaginary, and she was experiencing an unpleasant sense of urgency.

"Don't you see—" Patrick began, but his explanation was interrupted by a deep, discordant vibration that was not thunder.

Gwen's stomach knotted. She looked over her shoulder. The boys also looked, ears perked, bodies rigid.

"What's the matter?" the colonel asked.

"Something is…growling," Gwen stammered. A strange scent on the wind made the hairs on the back of her neck stand on end.

Jack rose up in his stirrups. "It's on the road behind us. Coming fast."

The colonel turned his horse to look. "I don't see anything, but my eyes aren't what they used to be. Are you sure it's not a vehicle?"

Jack stared without answering.

Patrick said, "No. It's an animal of some sort. It's still far away…"

"Stay calm. Describe it for me."

"A horseman, I think."

"It's the pseustee." Gwen was gazing down at May's twitching mane. She didn't need her eyes to know what was coming. "Riding another demon."

The colonel pulled his mount around. "We had better make a run for it."

Patrick didn't hesitate. He kicked and sent May galloping toward the vertical face of the interstitial mountain ridge.

Jack spurred Thane after May, panic overruling the part of his mind protesting that he was charging into a dead end.

"Stay on the road," commanded Sir Geoffrey.

The horses ran as if stampeded, either reacting to their riders' fear or driven by intuition. Thane was faster than May; Jack and Christopher took the lead.

The demons gained at a frightening rate. Even so, all would have been well had Jack not turned his horse off the road to avoid the rock wall. Thane galloped into a drainage ditch, up the other side, and into brambles.

"Come back!" Sir Geoffrey yelled at Jack.

He waved Patrick and Gwen onward. "You two keep going!" Then he went after Jack and Christopher.

Patrick obeyed the order.

"What are you doing?" Gwen tried to take control of her horse, but Patrick wouldn't let her have the reins. He cantered May at the rock wall.

"Stop! Stop!" Gwen screamed.

"Don't you see…" Patrick began.

They went right into the wall without slowing.

Thane was mired in gorse. The ground was uneven, and the animal couldn't get his footing. He reared up and sideways. Christopher lost his balance and slipped, pulling Jack with him.

The colonel came alongside and shoved them up in the saddle, saving the boys from falling. He grabbed Thane's bridle and yanked the gelding back toward the road.

The evil spirits were nearly on them. The pseustee appeared to Christopher to have been grafted onto the front of the other demon, creating what looked like a grossly deformed centaur. Describing evil spirits was nearly impossible. Their physical forms registered in the mind as macabre impressions rather than concrete images.

Colonel Sir Geoffrey got Thane onto the road and slapped the animal's hindquarters, launching horse and passengers straight at the interstitial wall. Just before reaching it himself, he wheeled, raised a hand, and shouted at the demons he couldn't see, "Stop, in Jesus's name!"

In the confusion, the monsters leapt at the colonel rather than at

Jack and Christopher. Thane and the boys riding him went through the cliff as if it were no more than a curtain of vapor. The demons, being spirits, shot right through the colonel and smashed into the very solid Primary granite wall, knocking themselves silly.

The children had stopped and were looking back the way they had come.

"The ridge is interstitial," Patrick explained. "The horses carried us beyond it the same way your great-uncle took us down the stairs."

Ramillies and the colonel materialized before them.

"Mr. McCray is correct." Sir Geoffrey rode up and nodded eastward. "Buckton is a mile from here. I can see its chimneys."

The others couldn't see any chimneys. They saw a desolate hillside. A low roar like that of crashing waves came from somewhere beyond.

"We need to keep going," Sir Geoffrey said. "The demons will get over the ridge soon enough." He gestured down the road. "There's one more interstitial barrier to cross. Once we're past it, your pursuers will fall many hours behind."

"The weather's closing in," Gwen murmured. She was exhausted. Even her coughs lacked strength. The adrenaline that had sustained her during the mad escape from the demons was now spent. She would have fallen out of the saddle if Patrick were not holding her.

Right then, a dense mass of cold air slid down the mountain slope, and the riders were hit by a driving wind. A thunderbolt cracked and reverberated like the discharge of a massive weapon.

"Stay with me," Sir Geoffrey ordered, kicking his horse to trot.

But the road was a vague surface in the low light. Ramillies stepped into a hole and stumbled.

"Blast!" The colonel dismounted and, after a quick examination of his horse's leg, announced, "He's not going to be able to carry me."

Gwen tightened her arms around Patrick's. "What do we do?"

"Well…" Sir Geoffrey looked into the blackness ahead. "You children go on without me." He sighed. "Stay on the road. Buckton isn't far. In about half a mile, you'll come to an interstice. You can't miss it—it's quite wide and filled with water. The horses will carry you past it. I'll join you at Mrs. Holliwell's house as soon as I'm able."

"Can't you walk with us?" Jack asked plaintively.

"You need to get to the interstice faster than I can walk."

"Why?"

A bloodcurdling howl answered the question.

"Jack, *lead*! Remain calm and, above all, stay on the road."

Jack hesitated for several seconds but then, without saying anything, turned his horse around and proceeded into the night. He barely knew what he was doing or where he was going. The world had closed around him, activating, amplifying, and exposing his character flaws. Men should maintain cheerful nonchalance when in peril. English storybooks were full of characters that fought with a stiff upper lip against impossible odds, quipping about the Reaper's unwieldy scythe and impractically long robe. Jack fell far short of his own expectations. In fact, he was a coward. Compelled to confront his failings, his emotional defenses were breaking down. He was nearly paralyzed. His great-uncle had been his only rock in this strange and terrible reality.

Being put in charge forced him to focus on his responsibility instead of the monsters, and that steadied him a little. But the storm intensified. Branched lightning spread across the sky.

They made steady progress for two minutes. Then Jack sensed that demons had spotted them. He spurred Thane into a full gallop.

"The road!" Gwen wanted to yell, but she didn't have the strength. Her voice was lost in the wind. "We're off the road!"

The others realized it independently.

Jack reined in his horse and circled, looking for signs of a path. He couldn't tell where they were. He couldn't even tell what direction they had come from.

"Follow me," he ordered, proceeding downwind.

"The interstice is that way." Gwen pointed to the right.

Jack lost all control. "You don't know any better than the rest of us!" The viciousness of his voice cut through the wind.

Gwen scowled. Not bothering to reply, she turned May to the

right and tapped her heels to trot.

Furious as he was, Jack followed, terrified of being separated.

The roaring sound increased until its source was right in front of them. Still, they saw nothing. Cold, humid air blew from changing points of the compass like snow leopards circling their prey. Everyone felt it—dreadful things were closing on them. Frigid raindrops stung their faces. There was no sign of the road.

"Stay together," Jack shouted. He kept randomly touching his face, rubbing his saddle's pommel, patting Thane's neck, and gesturing this way and that.

The rain became a downpour.

"I'm sorry, but I'm terribly scared," Patrick whispered.

Gwen glanced over her shoulder. He had spoken with such innocence. Did he think he was the only one? "The demons are coming. More than just the two."

"What do you suppose Sir Geoffrey would do?"

Gwen didn't have an answer.

Her brothers came alongside. She was appalled at Jack's face. Even in the semidarkness, it was obvious there was no color in his skin. His staring eyes seemed to have sunken into his head. His lips were drawn back, and his teeth were chattering.

Gwen looked and saw, lit by a lightning flash, a blood-red animal shape no more than a thousand yards away. "Jack—!"

The alarm in her warbling voice set Jack off. He kicked Thane hard. The gelding leaped forward. But Jack stopped his horse after covering fewer than fifty feet, yanking with such force that Thane's head swung up and around. The animal stumbled to a halt.

Gwen stopped barely in time to avoid a collision.

They were at the brink of a sheer-sided cliff. Lightning revealed a churning sea far below. The roar they had been hearing was the wild surf breaking against rocks. The dark sea might have been a finger thrusting up from the Atlantic Ocean, a vast loch, or a wide channel between islands. Miles of phosphorescent, foam-streaked water lay between the riders and the other side, which they could not see.

"It's the interstice Uncle Geoffrey told us about." Gwen steered May toward the edge. The horse resisted and pranced, frightened by the storm, her riders' anxiety, or something underfoot.

"Stop!" Jack screamed. "We have to find the road!"

"Don't be stupid, Jack. May and Thane will carry us over."

"No," Patrick said. "He's right."

Gwen stiffened. "What?"

"There's a gully or ditch bordering the interstice. See the seam? The horses will stumble, and we'll be thrown. We'll lose our anchor to silhouette and fall into the sea."

"We don't have time to look for the road," Gwen yelled. "The demons are almost here!"

Jack steered his mount southward, seeking an escape. Thane shied from the gully.

Panic gripped them all. Even Christopher had reached the end of his normally inexhaustible good cheer. But suddenly he shouted, "Jump the ditch! We've ridden this part of the moor a hundred times. There aren't any ditches between our house and Buckton that Thane and May can't jump."

Patrick tried to think it through. "Uh…"

Jack was beyond thinking. He trotted Thane a dozen yards back from the ditch, turned him, and kicked.

"*Yhaaaa!*" he yelled and kept on yelling.

Horse and riders lunged up and vanished.

"Did they make it?" Patrick asked. "I couldn't tell."

Gwen saw no point in answering. She positioned May and kicked the horse's flanks to command her to canter. At just the right moment, Gwen went up in the stirrups and May jumped.

Gwen didn't think. Despite having ridden through a solid stone ridge only minutes earlier, she didn't believe she would survive the next few seconds. It was just that falling into a raging ocean was better than being torn to pieces by demons.

She and Patrick were in the air for no more than a few heartbeats but traversed miles. She screwed her eyes shut.

They came down on grassy turf. Gwen wasn't ready for the landing and had the breath knocked out of her.

But they were across a barrier their pursuers could not quickly pass.

CHAPTER 6

Jonah

56-1-3

Once the horses had been stabled and the children given dry clothes, Mrs. Holliwell replaced the dressings on Jack's and Patrick's wounds. The good woman's husband had practiced medicine in the little town for fifty years before his death in 1912, and the surgery at the back of the house was well-equipped.

"There's no sign of infection," she announced. "I'll check you again tomorrow."

The colonel had led his limping horse the last half-mile to Buckton through the driving rain. Mrs. Holliwell eyed his damp clothes. "Sir Geoffrey—go stand by the fire in the parlor and get dry, or you'll catch your death."

The slight, white-haired woman served her guests a supper of soup, sausage, and cabbage. They ate without appetite. After the meal, the company went to the parlor, where Sir Geoffrey added coal to the fire and poked until it burned brightly. Jack prowled around the chintz-covered chairs like a caged tiger. The others sat quietly. Mrs. Holliwell brought tea.

"Now that we're fed and warm," Sir Geoffrey said, "it's time to talk about tomorrow."

Jack stopped pacing and stared at the floor. Gwen slumped in her seat.

The colonel drew a chair close to the fire and sat down. "I believe I know how to find the prism." He crossed his legs. "This is not the first time a devil has gotten its hands on a human artifact, and the streak Gwendolyn saw in the sky pointed toward some of their hiding places." He thought for a while. "Two of the spots are a stone's throw from silhouette terrain. That's important because the taraph can't get into interstices; it's paired with a flesh and blood cormorant."

Jack was dubious. "How can you be sure the taraph didn't give the prism to another demon?"

"I doubt any of its pure spirit cohorts could handle the prism without great cost to themselves."

Patrick leaned forward in his chair. "Sir, how is the taraph able to see it? You can't."

"The taraph is anchored to silhouette by proxy. It's not anchored to silhouette intrinsically."

Patrick thought about that. "I'm able to see the Primary World landscape even when riding a horse."

"Precisely. Your circumstances and the taraph's have parallels."

"Aren't there other possessed animals? Or people? Couldn't they take it?" Jack asked.

"Few demons will have been told that the prism was stolen, and fewer still where it is hidden. Knowledge is power, and no devil willingly gives up power. Power is the basis of all demonic interactions—the goal, the means, and the currency."

Sir Geoffrey rose from his chair, detached the poker from the brass stand on the hearth, and contemplated the fire. He prodded the coal. "Greater spirits have no more consideration of weaker ones than you or I do of washrags. They use them as disposable tools. Or eat them."

Gwen was exhausted and sore all over. She sipped her tea. Despite knowing she should be paying attention, she watched Patrick over the rim of her cup. He noticed her gaze and returned it.

The colonel arranged the coal efficiently. The flames danced cheerily.

Patrick marveled that Lady Gwendolyn's eyes held him so tightly when his every reflex was to shear away.

"What's their objective?" Jack asked. "What are they trying to do?"

The colonel replaced the poker in the equipment stand. "To find a source of reality apart from God."

He turned, clasped his hands behind his back, and stood like a teacher in front of his class. "Lucifer was the greatest of the angels, and in his pride, he believed he could be equal to his creator. He persuaded a third of the heavenly host to rebel against God. Demons possess frightful intellect—far superior to that of any man or woman—but they aren't omniscient. They have blind spots and no power to change reality. When they rebelled, they thought they would become masters of creation. But they discovered they could not exist isolated from their maker. At best, they could temporarily sustain themselves by consuming the substance of others."

"But they're still rebelling," Jack said.

"They made their choice. They, unlike men, do not change."

"Even so, why do they bother?"

The colonel looked into the fire. "They believe they can win. They think they've found a loophole."

"What is the loophole?" Jack asked.

"Human beings." The colonel sighed. "God made us in His image. That is, He made us creative, and He gave us the ability to love—so He also had to give us free will. Anything manufactured or coerced is not love. Without choice, what may appear to be love is only following instructions."

Sir Geoffrey picked up the poker again. "But free will only exists when decisions have consequences. Therefore, we humans can do what demons cannot: alter God's creation in ways He never wanted or intended." The colonel prodded the fire. "Sin."

A shower of sparks swirled up the flue.

"Just as a diamond has weak points and will fracture if struck precisely so, creation has weak points. Pivotal junctures where individuals either do what God intends or sin. Sometimes the junctures are associated with well-known historical events. For example, four years ago, Gavrilo Princip chose to pull the trigger to shoot the bullet that killed Archduke Franz Ferdinand, setting off the horrific war we're fighting. But just as often, the weak point is a small, private choice that no one ever knows about."

"How does that help demons?" Jack asked.

"They have assessed the structure of God's creation and mapped its fracture points. They believe that if they can tempt mortals into causing enough damage, the whole thing will collapse from end to end—that they will gain substance independent of God by contriving a reality of their own making, even if it doesn't involve actual creation. In their favor, humans are weak and easily persuaded to sin."

Gwen wondered idly whether Patrick was courting a girl. She doubted it.

Sir Geoffrey sat down and returned to the matter of finding the prism. He described the geography of the mountains. Gwen wasn't listening.

"The prism is likely in a hollow below the eastern pinnacle," the colonel concluded. "My friends and I call it The Cache. You've seen the silhouette of the nearby western summit—High Tor."

Gwen's attention snapped back.

Released from the spell, Patrick asked, "Sir, what is the prism, exactly?"

The colonel poured himself another cup of tea. "It refracts Primary light, revealing true reality. It can also diffract, allowing us to interact with interstitial matter and enter interstitial space, as you have found out."

"What is the taraph going to do with it?"

Sir Geoffrey shrugged slightly. "It isn't of any use to demons, as far as I know. They merely want to keep it from us."

"Then why doesn't the taraph destroy it?"

"I don't believe an evil spirit can destroy it. As I mentioned, the prism has a unique anchoring; it retains a sort of inertia from the silhouette frame even when carried into an interstice."

Patrick pondered that information. "Sir, where did the prism come from?"

"It was made by my ancestor, John Maham, two hundred and twenty years ago."

"Was he an alchemist?" Christopher asked, using a word he had learned recently.

"A physician and amateur physicist." The colonel set his cup on its saucer. "Mr. McCray will next ask how the good doctor made it. The answer is, I have no idea."

None of this addressed what Jack wanted to know. "If the demon flung the prism into an interstice, how will you get to it?"

"I won't. You and Patrick will. I thought I had made that clear."

Jack became very still.

Sir Geoffrey summarized his plan. He, Jack, and Patrick would ride to High Tor. The boys would dismount and continue into the interstice on their own. The job might have been a Sunday jaunt, the way the colonel described it. There were obstacles and enemies to be dealt with, but he would guide the boys. God would be with them, and their prayers would be answered. All their problems would be solved once they recovered the prism and Jack reanchored everyone to silhouette.

The room became very quiet. Even the fire was subdued.

The old soldier went to the window by the front door. He cupped his hands against a pane and peered into the night. The storm had subsided. The cobbled street was dotted with puddles, but the wind was down. "I need to run an errand. Jack, I would like to borrow Thane."

Gwen sat up. "You're going somewhere *tonight*?"

"Yes. To Exeter. I want to consult friends about the verses in Sir Robert's vision. I'll be back first thing in the morning." The colonel lifted his greatcoat from the stand by the door.

Jack was taken aback. "Who will protect us during the night?"

"Don't worry." Sir Geoffrey donned his coat and did up the buttons. "Anne, would you please work with the children? Teach them a bit?"

"Of course."

Jack looked uncertainly at the elderly woman. She smiled back pleasantly.

The colonel turned suddenly to Gwen.

"You mustn't die."

She gazed at him. Did she have a choice?

He looked deep into her eyes. "Don't be deceived. Be strong in your faith."

And then, without another word, he opened the door and stepped into the night.

The sight and sound of the front door shutting stunned Gwen. The click of the latch was like the snap of a trap.

Jack crossed the room and stopped only when he came to the closed door. He put his hands to his head and shut his eyes. He pivoted and looked at Mrs. Holliwell. "Can demons get into this house?"

The woman shrugged. "They can squeeze in, yes. But they won't. You heard what Colonel Sir Geoffrey said. They hate and fear one another. Their coalitions are complex, and they share information only when it is to their advantage. It will take time for word of your predicament to spread."

Patrick looked at Mrs. Holliwell. "What can we do to protect ourselves?"

"Well, dear, you can pray."

"Pray?" Jack snorted. "Yes, I suppose that's the only thing we can do."

"It's quite effective against evil spirits, you know. It muddles them."

"How is that, ma'am?" Patrick asked.

"Blinds and slows them. It allows God to repair us and the damage we've caused to His creation, counter to their actions."

"Colonel Sir Geoffrey commanded the demons that attacked us," Patrick remembered.

"But it didn't work," Jack said.

Patrick considered. "I think it did. Each time, things went wrong for them."

"Ask for strength," advised Mrs. Holliwell. "Ask for peace of mind. Above all, ask for faith. Try it now."

The children glanced uncertainly at one another.

Christopher was first to bow his head. Patrick followed his example. Jack sat down and did the same, but somewhat skeptically.

Gwen hesitated. She did not want to talk with the Lord. But she also did not want Mrs. Holliwell to think her contrary. Self-consciously, she closed her eyes.

The boys began with dry words silently thought, mechanically following Mrs. Holliwell's directions. They became aware of the hissing, popping fire and the water slowly dripping from the roof outside. The ticktock of the clock on the mantel grew louder and louder. But indeed, such was their need that they began to feel God's presence. Soon, instead of repeating the same introspective wishes over and over, they let themselves be guided.

Patrick asked for discernment and wisdom.

Christopher wanted the ability to help find the prism.

Jack begged for courage. His breathing slowed, and he relaxed for the first time since becoming anchored to the freakish Primary World.

Gwen was in a face-off. She and the Lord regarded one another through an opaque barrier. After a few minutes, she realized that she was the one regarding; He was calling. However, that didn't change anything.

"When you ask for something in prayer, learn to concentrate on God rather than your request," Mrs. Holliwell said. "He already knows your need better than you do yourself. Once you are able to focus, let Him lead you: not your will, but His. Demons do not want to be where God is working, so your ultimate goal is to disappear—in your prayer, that is, not in life. You will be more yourself, more the individual He created you to be, not less."

A few minutes later, she said, "Now *I* shall pray."

Hands lifted, face tilted upward, the woman praised the Lord, gave thanks, and asked out loud for the children's enemies to be confused, scattered, and powerless to do harm. She appealed for guidance and concluded, "We pray these things in the name of our Savior, Christ Jesus."

Jack thought about what his great-uncle had told him—that saying

Jesus's name would help him focus on the person of God. Jack still wasn't sure how he was supposed to apply that guidance. "Why do we pray in Jesus's name?"

"Because we, his followers, have been given authority. When we pray or command spirits in His name, we are acting on God's behalf with His power, so long as what we ask is in accordance with His will."

Gwen stared at Mrs. Holliwell. A minute ago, while the woman was praying, a diffuse white radiance had saturated the room, pushing back the shadows. "That light…what was that?"

The boys wondered what Gwen was talking about.

Mrs. Holliwell seemed equally confused by Gwen's statement. "When we pray, we allow God to change us. The world around us becomes richer as a result. Perhaps you sensed that."

"Are you going to pray all night?"

"I shall watch and pray, but not all night. God knows your need." Mrs. Holliwell rose slowly and stiffly from her chair. She collected cups and saucers and placed them on a tray. "And I'm afraid I don't have the energy for a protracted vigil."

She went off to the kitchen, politely declining Patrick's offer to help with the dishwashing, saying she had her routine.

There was a long silence. Jack stood and began pacing again.

Patrick needed more information. "Colonel Sir Geoffrey said he was going to consult someone about a vision. What did he mean?"

"There's a sketch of it in my satchel." Gwen waved at the luggage.

Patrick went and looked inside. Blushing, he brought Gwen her bag. "Perhaps you should get it."

She pushed aside undergarments, extracted her rough, half-finished copy of the vision, and offered it to Patrick.

He smoothed the paper and studied the illustration.

"That's Gwen." Christopher pointed at the girl. "You can tell in the original. Our great-great-great-great-great-something-or-other, Sir Robert, drew it three hundred years ago."

"I suppose these are the horsemen of the apocalypse?" Patrick put his finger on the figures. "And this is your coat of arms?"

Gwen nodded. "Yes."

"What are the numbers?"

"Bible verses."

Patrick touched the Arabic number at the bottom left of the oval. "Then, this would be the twenty-fourth book of the Bible, chapter six, verse four?"

"No." Jack indicated the Roman numerals *V I VI*. "This is the key verse. The first numeral designates the book, counted from Matthew. You find all the other verses by counting from the key."

Patrick studied the Roman numerals. "Four, one, five."

Jack was too fatigued to manage more than token scorn. "No. Five, one, six. You read them backwards."

"Well, you see, it's a reflection."

Jack looked dumbly at the drawing.

"This is the mirror in Lady Gwendolyn's bedroom, isn't it?" Patrick said. "The image inside the oval is a reflection."

The others bent to look.

Jack shook his head. "Then the rest of the writing would be backward, and it's not. See here?" He pointed to the name "*Europa*" on the girl's diadem seen in her hand mirror.

"That's reflected in two mirrors, so it's corrected back to normal."

Jack frowned. "This one isn't." He tapped his finger on "*MAHAM*."

"But your name is a palindrome. It's the same backward as forward, so it looks normal even in a mirror."

"I *knew* something was wrong!" Gwen turned to Christopher and pointed at a Bible in the bookcase across from her chair. "Get that, will you?"

"Matthew, Mark, Luke, John," Patrick said. "If it's sequenced from Matthew, then the fourth book is the Gospel of John. The key verse is John chapter one, verse five."

"Uncle Geoff said it was Acts one, six—and he knows a lot more about these things than you do." But Jack sounded uncertain.

Gwen paged through the Bible. She sat up straight and exclaimed, "Patrick is right!"

"How can you be sure?"

"'And the light shineth in darkness; and the darkness comprehended it not.' That's written in my mirror!"

"In your mirror?"

"Yes. If you're down on the floor, you see those words behind the glass. It has to be the key verse!"

"Then all the other numbers are wrong," Jack said slowly.

"The first number on the oval frame is twenty-four, six, four." Gwen looked at the Bible's table of contents and counted from John. "Book twenty-four is Revelation." She found the chapter and verse.

"'And there went out another horse that was red: and power was given to him that sat thereon to take peace from the earth, and that they should kill one another: and there was given unto him a great sword.'"

"It's this bloody war." Now even Jack was convinced. "What's the next one?"

"Thirty-three…First Samuel…twenty-eight, eight." Gwen leafed through the book. "'And Saul disguised himself, and put on other raiment, and he went, and two men with him, and they came to the woman by night: and he said, I pray thee, divine unto me by—'"

Gwen went silent and read on without speaking, the blood draining from her face.

"What's wrong?" Christopher tried to look over his sister's shoulder to read the rest of the passage.

She clutched the Bible to herself and wouldn't let anyone take it.

"What does it say?" Jack demanded. "It's no use trying to hide it. We'll find another Bible."

"It's the Witch of Endor…" Gwen whispered, eyes downcast.

Christopher looked from face to face. "Who is the Witch of Endor?"

Gwen blinked hot tears. "I am."

"I don't understand," Patrick said.

Jack tried to shrug it off. "Uncle Geoff said Sir Robert selected verses for any number of reasons. They're rarely literal or direct."

Christopher waved his arms impatiently. "Would someone please tell me what this is all about?"

Jack turned on him. "King Saul asked the Witch of Endor to bring up the spirit of the dead prophet Samuel. It didn't go well."

Patrick squinted. "How does that story apply to Lady Gwendolyn?"

"She tried to bring Freddie back from the dead." Jack stared at the table. "Out on High Tor." He threw up his hands in exasperation. "It was pretend nonsense."

"Miss Harkless has books of spells," Gwen said woodenly. "I—I tried to cast one."

Jack scowled. "Even *if* the verse is about you, figuratively, what does it matter?"

"We…the cottontail…" Gwen's voice trailed off.

"It's nothing to be proud of," Jack said, "but so what?"

"Something came." Gwen shivered violently. "It was *in* me for a moment. I let it in."

Patrick stared. Yesterday, he would have been embarrassed for Lady Gwendolyn, believing her insane. But today he had spent an afternoon fleeing from demons, and her statement did not sound crazy. It sounded ominous.

"I was angry with God, and I told Him to get away from me."

Jack started to shrug, but he ended up with his shoulders hunched. "Something did happen. It was hard to breathe."

"All right, even if it *is* about you, what's the point of it?" Patrick asked.

"I'm condemned."

"I don't think….well…what's the next verse?"

Christopher leaned to look at the drawing. "Sixty-five, five, twenty-six."

Gwen did not move. Jack took the Bible and roughly turned pages.

"Mark 5:26. It's about the woman who had been sick for years: 'And had suffered many things of many physicians, and had spent all that she had, and was nothing bettered, but rather grew worse.'"

Patrick thought for a moment. "Jesus healed her. It's hopeful."

"He didn't intend to heal her," Gwen said softly. "It was by accident."

"I don't think God does anything by accident."

Christopher said, "Next is two, eight, twenty-two."

Jack turned pages. "Acts of the Apostles. 'Repent therefore of this thy wickedness, and pray God, if perhaps the thought of thine heart may be forgiven thee.'"

"You've already done that, haven't you?" Christopher asked Gwen.

Gwen squirmed. "I was sorry, yes."

"You see?" Patrick brightened up. "Whatever you did on High Tor, you've been forgiven."

She was sorry that she hadn't succeeded in bringing Freddie back from the dead. And she still wanted nothing to do with God.

"Twenty-five, nineteen, seventeen is next," Christopher declared.

"Genesis 19:17," Jack said. "'And it came to pass, when they had brought them forth abroad, that he said, Escape for thy life; look not behind thee, neither stay thou in all the plain; escape to the mountain, lest thou be consumed.'"

Jack read back for the context. "It's about Lot escaping from Sodom."

"Mountain..." Patrick sighed. "I think Colonel Sir Geoffrey was right. We have to go to the mountain. The place he called The Cache. So you can reanchor us to silhouette, m'lord."

"But Lot said he would die if he went into the mountains." Jack read ahead and summarized what happened: "He asked if he could go to a nearby town instead and was allowed to do it."

"Sir Robert's vision didn't include those other verses." It didn't make Patrick happy, but he felt compelled to point out the problem.

The idea of anyone going into the mountains scared Gwen. She supported Jack's interpretation. "It was a warning that we would be running from demons. We've come to the nearby town. This is where we'll be safe. We should stay here while Uncle Geoffrey goes after the prism. It will be someplace he can get to...even though he doesn't think so."

Everyone was silent for a minute. Jack went and poked the fire.

"It's unclear," Gwen muttered. "That's all."

"What's this?" Mrs. Holliwell asked, rejoining them.

Christopher jumped up. "Patrick decoded Sir Robert's vision! Uncle Geoffrey had the wrong key! It's a mirror image!"

Mrs. Holliwell was familiar with Sir Robert's visions and knew of Colonel Sir Geoffrey's frustration with *Beset Girl*. "Slow down, dear. Start at the beginning. Tell me what you've discovered."

Jack explained the mistake and read the correct verses. Gwen hung her head and was glad no one told Mrs. Holliwell what she had done on High Tor. When Jack came to the passage in Genesis about Lot, Patrick summarized the debate.

Mrs. Holliwell was thoughtful. "Was that the final verse?"

Gwen shook her head. "I didn't have time to copy all the numbers."

Christopher checked the sketch. "The last one we have is fifty-six, one, three."

Jack picked up the Bible. "Jonah."

He found the reference.

"'But Jonah rose up to flee unto Tarshish from the presence of the Lord, and went down to Joppa.'" Jack paused before reading on. "'And he found a ship going to Tarshish: so he paid the fare thereof, and went down into it, to go with them unto Tarshish from the presence of the Lord.'" He frowned. "Do you think we're supposed to take a boat somewhere?"

Gwen felt herself being swallowed already.

Patrick had a notion. He got up and went to the bookcase. He pulled out the Oxford unabridged dictionary and looked up *tarsia* to confirm that the word meant what he thought it did. *Tarsia* sounded like *Tarshish*—a little. Was he making an association out of nothing?

Mrs. Holliwell asked, "How many more verses were there?"

"More than twenty," Jack guessed. "We've only got a quarter of them. Even if they provided clear direction—which they don't—the ones we have won't help us find the prism. And does anyone really think we can survive in a demon-infested interstice? We can't go blundering around those bizarre mountains on a wild goose chase. That's *off*. I doubt we could even get to the mountains in the first place."

Patrick said, "I have an airplane."

Everyone stared at him, puzzled.

"An F.B.5 Gunbus. A trainee crashed it a couple of years ago."

Jack did not know what to do with this information.

"It's an obsolescent type, and the RFC didn't want it anymore, you know?" Patrick kept on as if he were reporting something perfectly topical. "I repaired it. It should fly."

Before Gwen could scold Patrick for boasting pertinent to nothing, Jack said, "We have to sail to America."

Mrs. Holliwell could only respond to these declarations by suggesting they all go to bed. "We'll give Sir Geoffrey the correct verses when he returns in the morning."

She would not allow Patrick to leave. His mother had died in 1905, and his father was away at war, so he lived alone at home. Even if he had lived in the Gorton dormitory, there was little anyone there could do to protect him.

Her grown children, David and Charlotte, lived in Portsmouth and London, respectively. Their bedrooms were available.

Jack was not particularly happy sharing a room with Patrick. He thought the Irish-born commoner should be put in either the kitchen or Dr. Holliwell's surgery; however, he decided there was comfort in numbers and withheld protest. So Patrick got one of the twin beds in David's room.

Christopher wrapped himself in blankets and lay down on a rug. He was apparently under the impression that anyone on a holy quest should sleep on the ground.

Another thunderstorm rolled in after they put out the light.

Jack lay awake. He tossed, tormented by vivid memories of demons. Priding himself a modern, rational man, he had believed evil spirits to be no more than fantasies of superstitious, prescientific peoples. The reality was much stranger and more terrible than he could have imagined.

In the dark, every sound seemed to portend danger. Jack did not know if Mrs. Holliwell's house always moaned and creaked in a high wind or if he was hearing spectral assassins forcing their way inside. The woman had said they did not need to keep watch. He questioned her judgment. He had his saber beside him in bed; he hugged the scabbard and clenched the hilt.

Nor could Patrick sleep. Eyes open or shut, he saw Lady Gwendolyn. He felt her leaning against him on her horse. His memories were infused with the scents of her skin and hair: an alluring mélange of linen, wood, musk, and rose. The shock and guilty thrill of seeing her bare leg was even stronger than when the blanket had slipped and exposed it. Lady Gwendolyn had been entirely unconcerned about being pressed against him. Had she, socially isolated, never lost the innocence of childhood?

During the ride across the moor, his emotions had been stabilized by the necessity of concentrating on the situation at hand. Now, with nothing requiring attention, the day's events seemed more substantial and real than when they were occurring.

Alone in Charlotte's room, Gwen slept in a nightgown that Mrs. Holliwell's granddaughter Jane used when she visited. The furnishings and decorations were feminine and cozy, but the room couldn't have felt bleaker. Gwen longed for the familiarity of her bedroom in Maham House. Then again, that place was riddled with interstices.

She listened to the storm. She wanted things the way they were before the war. She wanted Freddie back. She wanted to be sitting with her mother beside a cheery fire.

I must be strong, she thought. *I must be strong. Patrick is strong. He is solid.*

Her swirling thoughts orbited multiple centers: family, God, demons, and the clever Irish boy.

Restless as she was, she lay inert. She didn't have the strength to squirm. Every part of her body ached. Jack's opposition to hunting down the prism encouraged her. How could he and Patrick ever manage to recover the thing? It was hopeless. She feared for them.

And the verse from Jonah nagged her. A Jonah was a person who brought bad luck. She was the Jonah.

The more she thought about it, the more convinced she was that she should slip away and die by herself. Yes…she was nothing but a burden and a jinx. Uncle Geoffrey was wrong. It was time for her to go. Her eyes shifted now and again to the door, half expecting Death to steal in to conduct her to the place of the dead. Would the route be more direct than usual, starting from within the Primary World?

She reviewed in her mind the events that had brought her here. But in the middle of her ponderings, she felt a presence and was afraid.

"Get up."

"Uncle Geoffrey?" Her eyes searched for him in the darkness.

"Come with me."

"Where are you?"

"Up the stairs."

She slipped out of bed and walked barefoot out of the room to the stairs at the end of the hallway. She climbed the cold wooden steps.

Coming to the attic, she pushed into the wind blowing through a wide-open dormer window and leaned outside.

Dark clouds ringed the house. Two great armies clashed in the breaks between thunderheads: one all-absorbing darkness, the other dazzling light. She grabbed onto the sill to steady herself.

"Don't be afraid."

The man standing next to her was wearing an English army officer's uniform, but she realized with a shock that he was not her great-uncle.

"Who are you?" she asked. Someone who could end her life with no effort at all—she was sure of it. She would have shrunk back had there been any space to move.

"Look at the mountains."

She did as she was told. Although the craggy peaks were many miles away, she saw them in great detail, able to fix on individual gullies, trees, and boulders as easily as on the entire range.

"The prism is there, as Sir Geoffrey believes, but not in The Cache. It is below the rim of the Defile of Ash. Do you see the place?" The officer pointed to a feature like an amphitheater on the side of a prominence that extended into a very dark, steep-walled valley. The Defile of Ash had an acrid smell. "Retrieve your prism while our forces have the taraph trapped."

Gwen stared at the man. "You've captured the demon?"

"No, but he can't get through our lines."

"Can Jack and Patrick get to the prism unopposed?"

"God is with you."

That didn't answer her question.

"Those are your orders. Don't delay."

Gwen looked with dread at the Defile of Ash and felt herself falling. What did the officer mean by "*Your* orders?" *You* was ambiguous. She wanted to believe he meant *your group*. But she had an uneasy feeling that someone expected her to play a physical role in the search. If that were the case, someone had made a grave mistake.

She turned to ask for clarification, but the soldier was gone. Her muscles went limp. She closed her eyes, and the world dissolved to black.

Seven hours later, Gwen woke up in bed, sore and numb. It was still dark. She listened to the slow, steady rain. She had not forgotten her dream. Was it something more? Had she been visited by an angel? Or a demon trying to trick her?

Shortly, the rain tapered off, and a corner of the window lightened. By the time Mrs. Holliwell came to check on Gwen, everything in the room was sunlit.

"Good morning, dear."

"Good morning. Is Uncle Geoffrey here?"

"No. Not yet."

The older woman uncovered coals in the bedroom fireplace, exposing them to air. She added kindling and two small logs. Flames spread until all the wood was alight.

Gwen forced her body to move. Rising and putting her feet on the floor got her blood flowing, but her limbs were horribly stiff.

Mrs. Holliwell glanced at the wardrobe where Gwen's dress had been hung. But she went to the dresser. She poked into drawers and removed a neatly folded skirt and blouse. "These are my granddaughter's. They'll be more convenient than that dress of yours." She handed them over. "You'll find cardigans in the wardrobe. Do you need help with anything?"

Gwen inspected the skirt. It fastened on the side, and there were only four buttons. "No, ma'am. I can manage." She was pleased. The trim, navy blue wool skirt and lacy white cotton blouse looked smart together.

Mrs. Holliwell left to fix breakfast.

Gwen took off the borrowed nightgown. Exposing her skin to the air was like diving into a cold river.

She put on a fresh chemise and knickers, then petticoat, stockings, skirt, and blouse. She shivered until she had the buttons done up. Only after standing close to the fire for several minutes did she feel warm.

She sat at the dressing table and brushed her hair, having about the same luck untangling the knots as she did sorting out the threads of her thoughts. She wanted to know whether the person in her dream was a messenger sent by God or a random character invented by her frazzled, dreaming brain. Surely God would not send children to a place called Defile of Ash? And what role would she play in the operation, exactly? Perhaps she was to lure away the taraph, sacrificing herself like a chess piece so the boys could get to the prism. If so, there was no need to find a place to die—it was assigned.

Until now, she would have accepted that fate calmly, even with contentment. At least her death would serve a purpose. But all of a sudden, the thought of having no future upset her. She couldn't say why, other than the change of heart was somehow Patrick's fault. As a result, she was rather cross with him.

She wove her hair in plaits, tucked the ends under, pinned it, and went to the kitchen.

Everyone was out of sorts that morning. Sleep had not made anything better. Not that Jack or Patrick had slept much. Even Mrs.

Holliwell was uneasy. No one mentioned it, but Colonel Sir Geoffrey's absence was like a hole in the air.

At breakfast, when asked what they should do if the colonel did not come back soon, Mrs. Holliwell dumbfounded Jack by replying, "Go to church."

"What?"

The white-haired woman set fried eggs and toast on the table. "It's Sunday morning."

"But…evil things are searching for us," Jack stammered.

"My house is not a hiding place. Nor is it a refuge. They will eventually track you here."

Jack drew a breath. He didn't want to be out in the open. And he didn't want to be seen in the company of commoners. "We aren't dressed for church."

"Mr. McCray can lend you something appropriate. We will stop at his house."

Before Jack could think of a suitable reply, Gwen asked, "Mrs. Holliwell, what do angels look like?"

"Well, dear, pretty much anything you like."

"How is that?"

"We can't see an angel's true self, not even in Primary light. We don't have the senses. Instead, we see an interpretation of our own making. Sometimes, they appear as men. Sometimes, beautiful winged women because we've seen them portrayed that way in paintings and sculptures. Occasionally, they are optical metaphors. Remember Ezekiel's visions?"

"Could an angel appear to be an English soldier?"

"To us at this time? Quite likely."

"Could a demon?"

"Yes, but to a believing Christian, a corrupted soldier."

"How do you mean?"

"When working deceptions, demons present themselves to our subconscious minds as beautiful, wise, and noble. But in reality, they are twisted. If one trusts in the Lord, one perceives the distortion—feels that something is wrong."

Breakfast was finished and dishes cleared, but Colonel Sir Geoffrey had not returned. Up to that point, Jack had been silently rehearsing arguments to convince his great-uncle to call off the expedition to the mountains. But when Mrs. Holliwell said they must depart for church, his fears slid sideways. Had demons found a way to capture or kill his guardian?

Numbly, he followed the others out the front door.

The party went north. They passed a thatched cottage, came to High Street, and walked toward the center of town. Buckton was dreary that morning. The gray stone row houses, damp and dripping, melted forlorn and impersonal into the misty background. Thin, irregular patches of black-green moss on north-facing walls and roofs gave the homes a shabby cast. Since the Middle Ages, Buckton's fortunes had risen and fallen with the tin trade, and by 1918, most of the mines on Dartmoor had closed. The town's life had become tied instead to Maham, Carter, and Company and to Gorton College, a well-respected though not prestigious boys' high school. Both Jack and Patrick went to Gorton. Jack chafed at attending a second-tier institution, but his father had given him no choice after his expulsion from Eton.

The McCrays' house was on the northwest side of town, not far from the Gorton campus. One of Major McCray's suits should fit Jack if the trousers were pinned. Christopher could borrow Sunday clothes that Patrick had outgrown but never handed down.

The spire of the church appeared above row houses on their right. Shortly afterward, they passed a derelict interstitial building. Gwen glimpsed an indescribable supernatural being slinking through an alleyway. She saw another standing like a sentry on a rooftop. Mrs. Holliwell warned the children to ignore spirits.

"There's a demon walking with Mr. Horner," Patrick said under his breath, looking straight ahead to avoid eye contact with the thing. "I thought Mr. Horner was a God-fearing man."

Mrs. Holliwell carefully negotiated a stretch of rough pavement. "Demons harass Christians to make us stumble and fall away—or at least make us cynical and cross. It makes us look bad. Actions speak louder than words, as the saying goes."

"They aren't bothering you," Christopher observed.

The good woman smiled dryly. "They can't endure anyone who prays continually. I'm mindful when they're near and keep the Lord always in my thoughts. Still, they attack me sometimes, and it's a trial."

"Are you praying now?"

"Fervently."

Gwen asked, "Have you ever been anchored to the Primary World, Mrs. Holliwell?"

"Oh yes, many times. But never trapped there. Your great-uncle is very protective of his people."

Gwen considered the statement. "What is it that you...people... do?"

Mrs. Holliwell scanned the street ahead. "Gather information and fix what we can. Do what God asks." She smiled sadly. "But we're all getting old."

Patrick drifted left to avoid an interstitial corridor running alongside the sidewalk. The buildings to his right were farther away in the Primary World than in silhouette. No more than fifteen to twenty feet wide, the weedy interstitial trail cut northwest through town. He said, "Someone who served as a gunner in my airplane mounted a tarsia in the forward cockpit."

No one had any idea what that meant.

"Tars—where Jonah wanted to go?" Christopher asked.

"Jonah was bound for Tarshish. A tarsia is a wooden mosaic," Patrick said. "But tarsia and Tarshish sound similar, don't they? So I've been wondering. The tarsia in my airplane has symbols. One is the fish that first-century Christians used to identify themselves to fellow believers. There's also a thistle and red carnation within a holly wreath."

"And you are mentioning this precisely why?" Jack had Gwen's dagger in a makeshift sheath concealed under his jacket; it poked his hip annoyingly. He wished he could have brought his saber. Almost as much, he wished he was not near the Gorton campus. He prayed they would not encounter anyone he knew.

"I've been wondering if the tarsia is a message for us."

Mrs. Holliwell thought for a while. "Thistle symbolizes sin and sorrow. A carnation signifies pure love. Holly represents the crucifixion and resurrection of Christ in the Passion."

Gwen frowned.

Jack shook his head. "I don't see what that has to do with—" He stopped dead. A short distance ahead, High Street curved, but the interstitial trail continued straight on, paralleling the Gorton campus wall. Ordinarily, in silhouette, the six-foot-high brick wall of the dormitory yard was hidden behind a hedge of bushy hawthorn trees. The interstitial trail, however, separated hedge and wall so that, in the Primary World, there was a twenty-foot-wide lane between them.

Mrs. Holliwell, anchored to silhouette, could not see the wall because the thick trees were in the way. Jack, anchored to the Primary World and looking down the interstitial lane, had a fine view of the wall. He also had a fine view of the backs of three boys sitting atop the wall: Gideon Moran, Harold Sutton, and Tommy Carson.

Jack got along even worse with his schoolmates at Gorton than those at Eton. He was glum, detached, and cold, and they responded in kind. Moran hated "Baron Mayhem." Jack called his enemy "Giddy Moron." On occasion, they came to blows. Jack always lost—Moran was the captain of the boxing team.

Anchored to silhouette and facing the dormitory, Moran and his pals could not see Jack—the hawthorn hedge blocked their view. Jack, however, would soon pass the trees and be exposed. His first thought was to tell Mrs. Holliwell they must detour to the west. But then inspiration struck.

Jack darted into the interstitial lane before the others knew what he was doing. He ran at his enemy and, coming out of the interstice behind Moran, shoved the unsuspecting boy with both hands.

The boxer tumbled into the schoolyard. Neither he nor his friends had seen Jack.

Moran scrambled to his feet, howling mad. "Whoever you are…"

He vaulted the wall and landed in a fighting stance. "I'm going to knock you—" But there was no one to fight—only hawthorn trees.

Jack, back in the interstice, laughed so hard he doubled over.

Gwen and Patrick were dumbfounded.

"Where did Jack go?" Mrs. Holliwell demanded.

Gwen rushed into the interstice.

Mrs. Holliwell groaned at the second disappearance. "Oh, not another one!"

"Jack," Gwen growled in a voice that would have impressed a drill sergeant, "come here, *now*!"

Moran's anger turned to dismay and then apprehension. Gideon Moran was superstitious, and the church graveyard was only a short way down the road. "Who's there? Who's there?" he hollered.

Jack flung a pebble out of the interstice. It struck Moran's forehead. The boy yelped and jumped backward into the wall, knocking the wind out of himself.

Sutton and Carson gaped at their comrade, perplexed and alarmed.

Moran scrambled madly back over the wall and ran for the dormitory, yelling, "Ghost! Ghost!"

Jack couldn't stop laughing.

Gwen grabbed her brother's arm. "Jack, there are *eyes*!"

Jack went quiet and followed her line of sight. A sinewy, multi-armed, apelike thing crouching on the dormitory roof was staring at them.

"We're in an interstice," Gwen hissed. "It *knows*!"

The demon raised its face to the sky and howled an eerie, warbling cry. The piercing call terrified Patrick and the Mahams; Mrs. Holliwell heard only a crow cawing into a chimney.

"We have to get out of here!" Gwen said shrilly.

Patrick and Christopher gazed south. A hellish man-shaped shadow had emerged from an alley down the street. The two boys shrank backward, inadvertently stepping into the interstice with Gwen and Jack.

Mrs. Holliwell was alone. "Dears," she said with all the calm she could muster. "Come out of the interstice."

Instead, Jack bolted north. "Run!"

The others followed him like herd animals in flight. Gwen found strength she didn't know she had.

The interstitial lane pierced a block of row houses. The fugitives were through the gap before they knew what they were doing.

Remarkably, Jack had a plan. It wasn't necessarily a bad one, despite being the product of panic, but it could not succeed without luck. An enormous amount of luck. His idea was to find animals and ride back across the interstitial sea. That had saved them before; it could save them again. "We need horses!"

In a flash, Patrick knew exactly what was going to happen—every detail—as clearly as if it were a recent memory. Part of his mind observed with analytical detachment while other parts reacted to the unfolding events. "My house—follow me."

It wasn't far. Patrick turned a corner and ran to a street on the edge of town. "Here." The McCrays had five acres of land with a house and a barn.

Jack sprinted to the barn, assuming the horses were stabled there.

He opened a side door and stopped, dismayed. The space was filled with machines. "Where are the horses?"

Patrick pointed north. "Neighbors."

Jack stared. He could see three horses—but they were in a paddock on the other side of a wide field. "We'll never make it. We'll be caught."

Patrick waited.

"We need a diversion," Jack's gaze fell on an odd-looking contraption parked outside the barn doors. "What's that?"

"A Vickers F.B.5 Gunbus."

To put it in other terms, a tandem cockpit pusher biplane. An underpowered, ungainly, pusher biplane. It had a stubby, bathtub-shaped fuselage with a rotary engine bolted to the back. Behind the propeller, the tail was stuck on booms extending from the upper and lower wood-ribbed canvas wings. Wires and struts held it all together. The F.B.5 had been a frontline British fighter in 1915, but by 1918 was hopelessly outdated. This one, as Patrick had explained, had crashed and been junked.

He had replaced ribs and spars, overhauled the engine, restrung brace wires, and reworked control pulleys and bell cranks. He had meticulously stretched, stitched, and doped the canvas until it was taut and stiff. He had even repaired the Lewis machine gun in the forward position, though that was because he wanted to find out how the mechanism operated.

"Does it run?"

Patrick had not tested his airplane yet, but he said, "Yes. It's fueled and ready to fly."

"We'll use it as a diversion. Start it and send it that way." Jack pointed in the opposite direction of the neighbors' paddock. "We'll run for the horses while the demons chase the machine."

Patrick felt calm in spite of his racing pulse. "Without someone controlling it, it'll turn sideways or flip over."

Gwen said. "Demons are coming."

"I'll do it," Patrick said. "I'll control it."

"Listen…" Jack didn't care for Patrick. Still, he didn't want to abandon him. But Jack had no idea what else to do. He was aware that he was a terrible leader. "All right. Drive it around to give us time. Then head to the paddock. We'll leave a horse ready for you. It's not far to the sea."

"That's no good," Gwen said. "He'll be caught."

Patrick knew what he was meant to do. More than that, he knew he would do it. He knew the alternatives he would choose and what would result. His actions were certain—as unchangeable as if the events had happened in the past. Did that mean he had no choice? No free will? It did not. The decisions were his and his alone.

He verified that the magneto switch was off. Then he ducked under the tail booms to get to the propeller. He pulled it around a few times to prepare the engine.

"You'll have to swing the propeller to start the motor," he told Jack. "Do you know how to do it?"

Just then, they all heard shuffling and low, unintelligible speech coming from the other side of the barn. They held their breaths.

Christopher dropped to his knees, clasped his hands together, and closed his eyes tightly. "Please, God," he begged very, very softly, "please save us."

Gwen felt the effect. It was halting and weak compared with what Uncle Geoffrey or Mrs. Holliwell had achieved, but the noises moved away.

Patrick looked at Jack. "Get ready."

"Stop!" Gwen said. "You want a distraction? I'll go back to Mrs. Holliwell's house. The demons will come after me, and you'll get away."

Jack stared at her. "That's suicide."

"I'm dying anyway."

Jack shook his head. "We're not giving you up to those things."

"Why not? You're ready to give Patrick to them, aren't you? *I'm* dying. He's hale and hearty. He's the one who should live."

Patrick climbed into the F.B.5's rear cockpit. He was mildly surprised to see Christopher scramble into the gunner's cockpit in front of him, which was in itself surprising because he had known that it would happen. He donned the leather flying helmet and gloves his father had given him as Christmas presents.

Christopher examined the machine gun and asked, "Will this work on demons?"

"End of discussion," Jack told Gwen. He stepped between the tail booms.

Patrick adjusted his goggles and took a deep breath. "There are chocks under the left wheel," he told Jack. "Pull their lanyards after the engine starts."

This was one of the decision points.

Christopher looked around, suddenly aware that things were happening behind him.

"Switch is on," Patrick announced.

Jack grasped the propeller as if it were an armed bomb. In fact, it was a little like that. On occasion, Merrill had let Jack crank the family's

Rolls Royce. Once, the car had backfired and nearly broken Jack's wrist. He could be cut to pieces if he made a mistake with the propeller. He nerved himself and shoved the propeller blade down.

The engine sputtered but failed to start.

Jack tried again, ignoring his sister's angry cries. This time, the engine coughed and surged to full power. The noise was deafening. A nauseating cloud of dust, gasoline, and castor oil enveloped the airplane.

Patrick adjusted the mixture; the roar smoothed but remained as loud as ever. The Gnome engine had only two throttle settings: off and full power.

Gwen, horrified that Patrick was going through with Jack's plan, became even more horrified when she realized that her little brother was onboard. She jumped onto one of the undercarriage skids, reached up, and seized Christopher's arm.

Simultaneously, Jack yanked away the chocks. He saw an instant too late that his sister was holding on to the other side of the airplane.

The wheels started to roll. Panicking, Jack swung under the nose, meaning to pull Gwen off. He hopped and skipped sideways to keep his balance in front of the accelerating machine.

The situation was perilous. The airplane had no brakes. A blip switch allowed the pilot to cut the ignition. Patrick was tempted to press it before they crossed the shallow ditch between the barnyard and the open field. It was odd knowing that he would nearly do one thing but ultimately do another. Once again, the detached part of his mind pondered the riddle: There were no choices that he *wanted* to make—all had consequences—but he was going to make choices.

The wheels dropped down into the ditch, then bounced up. The starboard wing smacked Jack just below the waist and scooped him up. He would have slid back into the whirling propeller and been shredded if he had not caught hold of the strut by Patrick's right shoulder.

The same motion tossed Gwen into the air. She didn't pull Christopher out of the airplane; he pulled her in—headfirst. It was a very unladylike moment.

Patrick watched in fascination as these events unfolded in perfect precision. He eased the control stick forward to lift the tail and reduce the drag. Jack clung to the strut for dear life as the plane bounced across the rough ground.

The neighbors' stable was still three hundred yards away when the pack of demons appeared, racing after the airplane. Patrick already knew the demons would be there. However, he did not know about the one directly behind them—precognition was not clairvoyance.

Christopher and Gwen, struggling to arrange themselves, also saw the pack. Christopher swiveled the Lewis gun, but it wouldn't turn nearly far enough to aim backward. Anyway, he didn't know how to fire it.

All Jack wanted was to get to the horses and jump on one. He fixed his thoughts on that hope. With every jostling bounce, he was in danger of being tossed off the wing into the propeller behind the fuselage, but the demons terrified him even more. He screamed for Patrick to steer to the right. The engine noise completely drowned out his words.

As it turned out, Patrick was already doing his best to veer right—but for a different reason. He was trying to point his airplane into the wind. He looked back at the sprinting demons. They were no longer gaining; if anything, the plane was outdistancing them. But the children would not reach the paddock more than a few seconds ahead of the pack—not nearly enough time to saddle or even bridle horses. In any event, they were meant to go another way.

The F.B.5 had sufficient speed. Only one decision remained.

Patrick took a deep breath, verified that Jack was holding on tightly, took a second breath, and, as he already knew he would, pulled back on the control stick. The noise and vibration continued unabated, but the bouncing suddenly ceased as the airplane lifted into the air.

Patrick watched the paddock pass below. He tried not to look at Jack's shocked face. It was harder to ignore Gwen's wide eyes staring at him from less than three feet in front of him. There were no good options, but it didn't matter now. It was all decided. He dipped the left wing and steadied his course.

Gwen's heart sank. Ahead lay the interstitial sea and, beyond that, high in the cloud-wreathed mountains, the Defile of Ash.

Hi Paige and Lara,

I found the rest of the diary! And other things. Here are sketches of a Vickers F.B.5 Gunbus. I've also attached a map I discovered in a beat-up briefcase in a Maham House attic. I don't know who drew the map (possibly Sir Geoffrey with compass directions added by Patrick) or if it's accurate (I suspect it's notional rather than realistic), but it's consistent with other information I have. I added the dashed lines.

Kirk

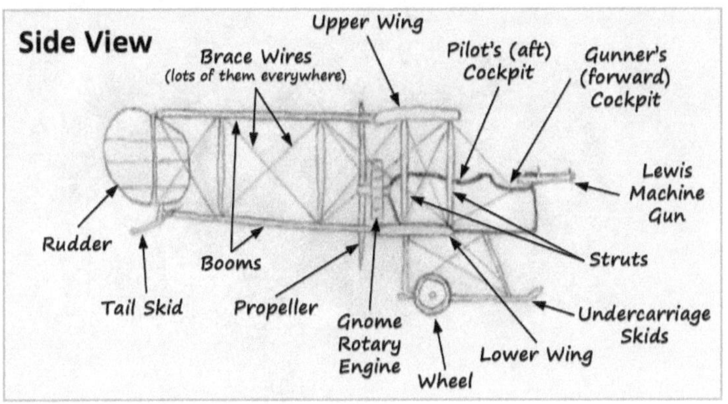

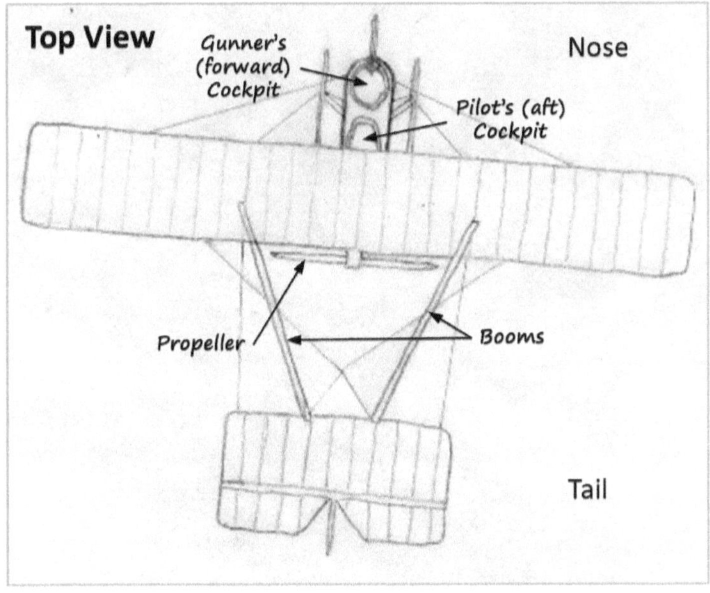

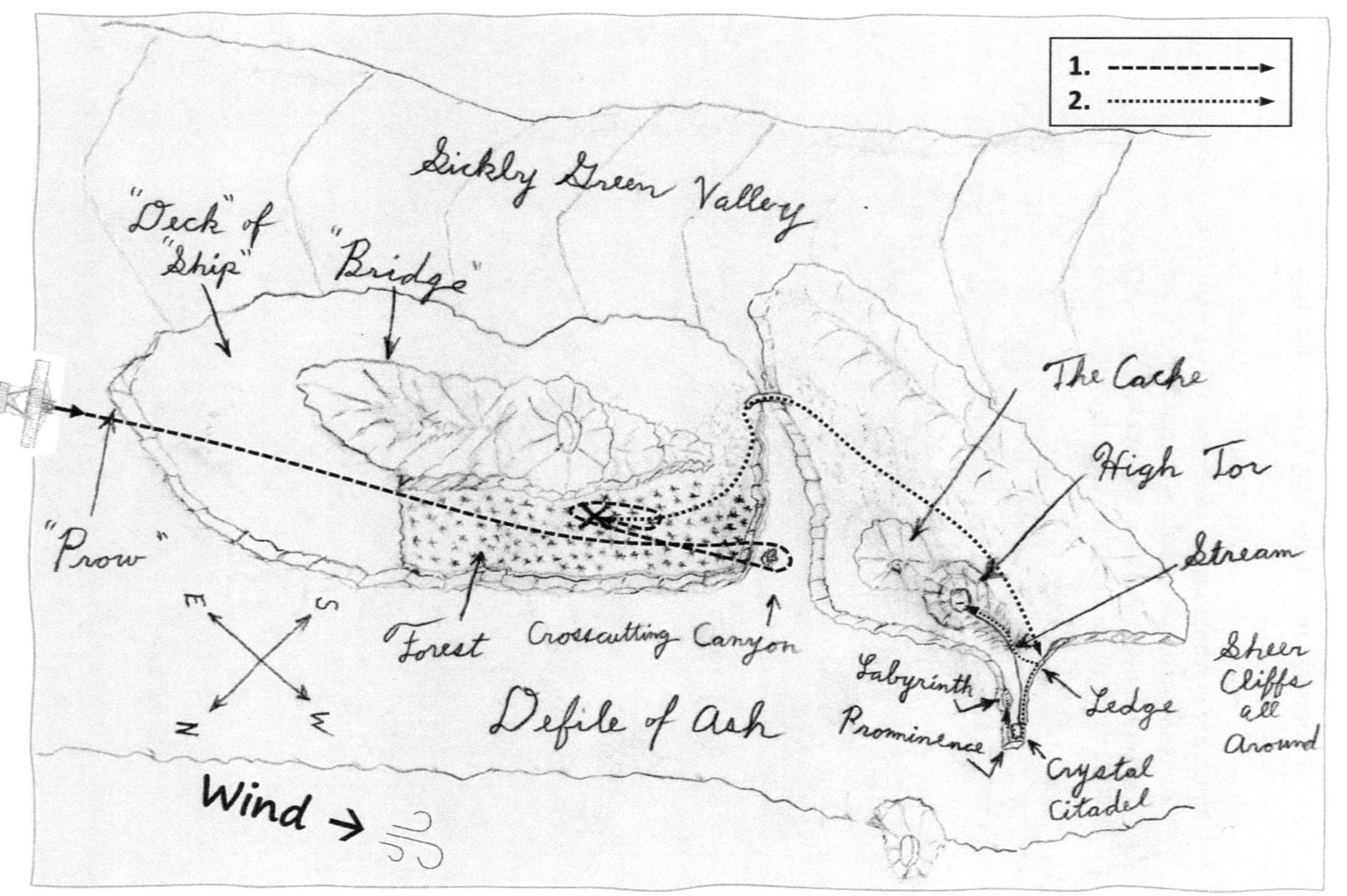
1.
2.
Sickly Green Valley
"Deck" of "Ship"
"Bridge"
"Prow"
The Cache
High Tor
Stream
Forest
Crosscutting Canyon
Defile of Ash
Labyrinth
Prominence
Ledge
Crystal Citadel
Sheer Cliffs all Around
E
S
N
W
Wind →

CHAPTER 7

Carried on the Wind
49-4-19

Colonel Sir Geoffrey had met all night with Dr. Wells, Mrs. Neville, and Reverend Towers—all the remaining members of his team except Mrs. Holliwell—and made no progress. The solution to *Beset Girl* seemed further from his grasp when he left Exeter at daybreak than when he had arrived the previous evening. Wells, a professor of Mesopotamian history, believed the drawing pointed to the final apocalypse. There were the horsemen, and the key verse involved the restoration of the nation of Israel—or so they thought. Wells hypothesized that a breakup of the Ottoman Empire after the war would allow the establishment of a Jewish state in Palestine—a precursor to the final events described in the Bible.

The colonel was frustrated. Sir Robert's drawings encoded a wealth of information but were not straightforward prophecies. Someone assigned a task by God always came to understand what was meant, but this time the Lord had revealed nothing to him.

He rode westward on the country road through rugged moorlands. Of all the number sequences that had to be guessed, he was bothered most by sixty-six, twenty-two, four. Book sixty-six—the Gospel of John—had only twenty-one chapters. What appeared to be sixty-*six* must be sixty-*five*. That meant the verse was actually *Luke* twenty-two, four: *And he went his way, and communed with the chief priests and captains, how he might betray him unto them.*

Who was the betrayer, and what was that person going to do?

The colonel had little hope now that *Beset Girl* would be of any use. The old soldier was weary and depressed. The cold made his joints stiff. His body was out of harmony with Thane's gait. He ignored a soft call from the Lord.

Not now, he thought irritably. *I'm trying to solve the puzzle you've given me.*

He began to doubt his abilities, the nature of God's plans, and his part in it all. Was his entire life a madman's fantasy? He sighed. *With all I've experienced and seen with my own eyes over a long lifetime,* he wondered, *how can this one frustration make me question everything?*

He let the horse guide itself, paying little attention to the world around him. Vigilance wasn't necessary. He was not anchored to the Primary World—he did not have to be ready to fight demonic spirits lying in wait. He was not at the battlefront in France—there was no need to hide from German snipers or jump into a foxhole at the sound of an incoming artillery shell.

Hearing a vehicle behind him, he nudged Thane to the side of the road. A truck slowed and passed. Sir Geoffrey did not even glance at it. One of the two men in the cab leaned out and looked back.

The truck stopped a little way ahead, beyond a turn. The colonel reached it a minute later.

They're having mechanical trouble, he assumed without a second thought. *Common enough.*

He steered around the blockage, but a man stood in his way. He noted with surprise that the fellow's face was hidden by a scarf. Then he felt a sharp blow to the back of his head and lost consciousness.

Patrick struggled to keep his airplane straight and level but had no problem flying it westward. Hurricane-force winds propelled it in that direction. An optimally trimmed F.B.5 Gunbus had a top speed of seventy miles per hour. This one was overloaded and had a petrified teenager clinging outside its fuselage. Patrick couldn't have fought the atmospheric riptide if he had wanted to.

Nor could he avoid the treacherous wind shear at Primary World boundaries. Some interstices extended from the ground to the stratosphere. The F.B.5 was kicked hard in the tail by a high-speed airstream at the shoreline of the interstitial sea. The plane corkscrewed violently and spiraled downward. Patrick thought he heard his passengers screaming, but the roar of the rotary engine was deafening, so it might have been his imagination.

While regaining control and bringing his battered craft back to a reasonable altitude, he was struck with sudden insight. The problem of fluid behavior at interstitial interfaces had been bothering him for some time. How did air and water move seamlessly throughout the fragmented silhouette world? The analogy of an electrical transformer occurred to him. The wires on one side of a transformer are not connected to the wires on the other side. Instead, current in the first side creates a magnetic field that induces current in the second side. Electrical power flows into one side and out the other even though there is no electrical connection between them. Perhaps movement of silhouette matter was induced or projected by interstitial matter—or maybe Primary matter was more than the sum of silhouette and interstitial matter.

He didn't have time to reflect. He was approaching the far shore of the sea.

He killed the engine so he could speak with the others. Wind whistled around the gliding plane's struts and wires in the comparative silence.

"What's wrong with the motor?" Gwen yelled.

"Nothing. We're about to hit another bump. Everyone hold on."

"Where are you going?" Jack clutched the strut beside Patrick's shoulder as if his life depended on it, which, in fact, it did.

"West." Patrick did not elaborate, assuming that mention of The Cache would not be helpful. He braced for the interstitial transition.

Crossing, it was as if a great gust blasted them backward. Actually, the plane had flown at high speed into a relatively stationary air mass.

This time, Patrick was ready and maintained control. He released the blip switch, and the windmilling engine backfired, shuddered, and returned to full power. He adjusted his course and studied the terrain. Flanked by fields of tall grass that fluttered and rippled wildly in high winds, the F.B.5 was cruising serenely in the still air above a narrow, northward-curving strip of Devonshire heather. It was as if the airplane was passing through the eye of a storm—but it was a cat's eye, and the winds in the eyewall roared perpendicular to the plane's heading. Unfortunately, the ribbon of calm ran smack into a mountainside.

Turn right or left? Into the gale and risk being batted backward, or run with the wind toward the interior of the mountain range? Once again, there wasn't a good choice.

Well, nothing for it. He banked hard left, leveled out, dove to gain speed, and plowed through the downwind boundary. The buffet was less violent than previous crossovers, but not by much.

In moments, there was no hope of returning to silhouette terrain. Patrick steered away from the mountains, turning almost completely around, but the wind raced northwest faster than his plane could fly southeast. Foothills rose below. A torrent of air carried the F.B.5 upslope toward crags, traveling backward.

Patrick suffered a crisis of confidence. He had assumed he could follow the road they had ridden the previous day, find the conjoined peaks Colonel Sir Geoffrey said were above The Cache, and land nearby. But the road was nowhere in sight. The oily streamer of engine exhaust trailing behind his plane pointed deep into the mountains. The F.B.5 was being dragged there despite flying at full power in the opposite direction.

Presently, mountains rose on all sides. Looking unhappily over his shoulder, Patrick steered toward a valley to miss a crest.

He had never landed an airplane. His father had taken control for that part of his lesson in the Avro trainer. Crashing backward would add insult to injury. What was he doing? What had he been thinking?

The immense mountains were like broken teeth formed of rock strata that had been twisted, tilted, and snapped. The upper slopes of pinnacles and ridges were too steep for snow to cling, their naked rock as gray as the overcast spread over the range. Pockets of slush deepened the gloom, save for the few places where sunbeams broke through the clouds, glinted off snow, and dazzled the eyes. But the gleaming patches made the shadowed recesses appear even deeper and darker.

Soon, Patrick was at his physical and mental limits. There was no room between the rock walls to turn around, and controlling an airplane being dragged backward through a mountain range by a hurricane-force wind was remarkably hard. He had to bend unnaturally to see rearward while he fought the air currents. And he found it difficult to estimate the heights of looming features.

Upon being pulled into one valley, as best he could tell, his airplane would have to gain another thousand feet to clear the ridge at its far end. That was going to be a problem. The F.B.5 could climb no higher than nine thousand feet and was already at that altitude.

Just when Patrick thought they were doomed, a powerful updraft blew them skyward, making his airplane shudder and twist from wingtip to wingtip. It was frightening, but Patrick was glad for the boost—or was until the engine started running so erratically he thought his plane would shake itself to pieces. He adjusted the fuel mixture ratio, and that helped.

Ears popped. The temperature plummeted.

They cleared the crest of the ridge and sailed into the gloomy dale beyond.

Jack was petrified, and not only because he was perched on the wing of a flimsy contraption flown by an untrained teenager with a powerful slipstream trying to blow him into spinning propeller blades. What *really* terrified him was being drawn deeper and deeper into a shadowy, demon-infested world.

Patrick was fed up with going backward. Seizing an opportunity afforded by a broad valley, he banked steeply left and turned his plane around. That put it on a bearing more or less with the wind. The groundspeed became scary, but at least he could see where he was going—which was not to say he had any idea where to steer.

Gwen knew exactly where they were going regardless of where Patrick steered. She gazed at the tarsia mounted to the side of the gunner's cockpit. The fish was taking her to a place she didn't want to go to do something she didn't want to do. She huddled against her little brother. Christopher smiled bravely as if everything was going according to plan.

Patrick nursed the F.B.5 up and over the next mountain ridge. His goggles fogged. He didn't like to think how cold Jack's hands might be. On impulse, he removed his flying gloves and held them out to the other boy. Jack stared at Patrick with hatred—his grip was precarious, even with all his fingers rigidly clamped. However, when Patrick was about to pull back, Jack chanced letting go one hand, hooked his arm around the strut, and grabbed the gloves. He fumbled twice, almost losing them to the slipstream. But eventually, he worked them onto his frozen hands.

It was perhaps best that Jack had to concentrate on clinging to the airplane. It meant he didn't see the flying spirit. Thrusting itself through a squall line a few miles to the north, the thing looked like an oversized bat or enormous spider with webbing between its legs. Patrick had not imagined that a demon could fly. Those he had fought at Maham House had been quite heavy.

Whatever the spirit was and whatever its errand, it was moving away and soon out of sight.

But there remained any number of problems. Patrick wanted to land as quickly as possible. Unfortunately, he couldn't get his airplane to go where he wanted, and the wind wasn't the only difficulty. Aim as he might toward clearings wide and flat enough to serve as a landing field, he ended up over slopes crisscrossed by gullies and strewn with boulders. He was probably misestimating distances, as he had done when passing the mountains on the way to Buckton.

The mysterious crags and forests were disturbingly familiar to Gwen. They triggered elusive and fragmented recollections of dreams. She was returning to a bad place. The first time, she had gone there deliberately, grimly determined to have her way. Now, she was going there to pay for what she had done.

It had begun with the book *Wisdom and Knowledge of Salamanca.* She had found it lying in plain sight in Miss Harkless's sitting room. The binding and pages were new, but the words were old. *Invocations and rites conferring power over spirits and men,* said the forward. Among other things, it contained spells purported to open the barrier between life and death.

Her first reaction had been revulsion, but she kept sneaking back to read more. What she recognized at first to be twisted and immoral became, over time, familiar, and familiarity formed a cocoon of normalcy around things that were not normal at all.

Then Freddie died in the Somme. Gwen told God she wanted nothing more to do with Him. The book became her hope, and in late September 1916, she performed the rite.

As much as he loathed the whole business, Jack did what she asked. He took her on horseback to High Tor and helped her climb to the top. That tall pile of rocks was somewhere in this range.

Patrick cut the engine. "There's a lot of smoke up ahead," he said in the temporary quiet, speaking loudly because everyone was half deaf by that time. "I'll find a place to land once we're past it."

"No!" Jack yelled. "Get us out of here! Go back!"

"This is where the prism is," Patrick protested.

"We don't know that! Take us back, I tell you!"

Patrick didn't want to be insubordinate, but there was no way to carry out the order. "I'm sorry, m'lord, but it's not possible. The wind is too strong." He let go of the blip switch, and resurgent engine noise drowned out Jack's probably obscene reply.

In truth, Patrick had no idea how to locate the prism. He was hoping Gwen would spot something like the contrail she had seen the previous day. If only she would give him a bearing to fly!

Just then, Gwen turned to stare southwest at a plateau resembling the prow of a monstrous battleship. Beyond that, heights loomed like the warship's bridge and superstructure. Smoke puffed from a volcanic stack. Valleys ran to either side. The gulch off the formation's starboard beam was moldy green. Its vegetation appeared entirely unwholesome. But it was the fractured obsidian canyon on the ship's port side that held Gwen spellbound: a vertical-walled phantasmagoria of slag and angular shadows. She was staring at the Defile of Ash. Dun-colored vapor seeped from its depths.

Gwen was willing to die, just not in *that* place. Were it not for the small hope that she could somehow help the boys, she would have climbed over the cockpit coaming and thrown herself from the airplane.

She thrust out her arm and pointed at the amphitheater-like feature where the angel had told her to go, emphasizing to God where she *didn't* want to go.

Almost immediately, the F.B.5 turned in that direction. Stunned, Gwen looked back at Patrick. He nodded. She had no idea what was in his mind. She felt more lost and powerless than ever. Sagging forward, she put her face in her hands and began to cry.

Christopher wanted to comfort his sister but was airsick, and it is hard to be encouraging when your stomach is frothing like a broken soda fountain. And even he was afraid of the evil that lay ahead.

None of them knew that something evil was already in the airplane with them. Right before they lifted off the field behind Patrick's house, it had sprung out of the grass and wrapped itself around the plane's undercarriage. Somewhere over the interstitial sea, it had wormed through a hole in the fuselage into the stowage compartment beneath the gunner's seat. There, it had wriggled inside a canvas bag with tools and a roll of wire left over from Patrick's repairs. The evil spirit was delighted with developments.

Patrick, on the other hand, was at wit's end. Converging airflows near the ship-like highland funneled the F.B.5 inexorably toward its mountainous prow. He coaxed his airplane higher, but the engine skipped and sputtered in the rarefied atmosphere.

They were too low. They were going to crash head-on into the face of a cliff.

"Please, Lord…help!" Patrick prayed.

He yanked back on the control stick at the last possible instant, raising the nose to gain altitude. It worked. He cleared the bluff—barely—but the maneuver bled away precious airspeed. Next, inevitably, the airplane was going to stall and auger into the plateau at one hundred and thirty miles per hour.

But it didn't happen. The lower wing was so close to the ground that it skimmed on a cushion of air. The F.B.5 flew on, straight and level, six feet above the deck. Patrick couldn't set down—the undercarriage would catch in a gully or on an outcrop, and the plane would disintegrate. The terrain was a blur—the airplane was running at full power, and the ferocious tailwind doubled its groundspeed. Trapped between a mountainside on the left and a thunderhead on the right, Patrick felt like meat being fed into a grinder.

His passengers weren't doing any better. Jack's skin was a deathly pallor. Gwen was not visible. She had pulled her head down like a turtle. Christopher peered bravely forward, but his face was greenish-gray. Patrick didn't want to see that. He was somewhat queasy himself. He was elated when a smooth, grassy meadow appeared ahead. He prepared to cut the engine.

But it wasn't a field. It was the canopy of an evergreen forest nestled below the ship-like formation's main deck.

Patrick flew over it for a few minutes, watching for a clearing. Then he had to turn to avoid the crown of an exceptionally tall tree, and the wings lost lift. That triggered a terminal oscillation. Each time Patrick raised the nose, the airplane gained a few yards altitude, only to lose airspeed and dip again. The floundering plane settled among the treetops. He clenched his jaw.

They were saved by a cross-cutting canyon. Suddenly, there was a deep, wide space with no obstacles. There was also plenty of wind. Patrick let the nose drop to gain airspeed and banked right, reasoning that flying through a thunderstorm would be better—even if only marginally—than crashing into trees. Unhappily, as they came around a granite pinnacle, the wind whistling through the pass caught a wing and tipped the plane up on its side. Patrick could not stop the rotation. Instead of fighting it, he barrel-rolled the F.B.5 upside-down and on around until it was right-side up again. This time he was sure his passengers were screaming. Happily, Jack remained fastened in place, having found new strength in the middle of the startling maneuver.

But the plane had dropped over two hundred fifty feet and was aimed back at the trees.

There was nothing Patrick could do. He flew into the forest.

He had misjudged the size of the trees. They were larger than giant sequoias, towering well over five hundred feet into the air. Spaced at wide vertical intervals, their limbs spread horizontally like spokes of wheels.

Patrick threaded his way through the open space between wildly swaying branches. He would not have been able to avoid the trunks if the F.B.5 had been moving any faster than a jogging pace with respect to the trees. Fortunately, the plane was pushing directly into the sixty-mile-per-hour headwind so its ground speed was only five miles per hour. But it would drift sideways at frightening speed whenever it pointed more than a few degrees from the wind.

Patrick thought he could land without a runway if he could work his way to the ground. But his heart sank when he saw, not far ahead, a rock wall at the eastern edge of the forest. He had few options. He was sure to smack into something if he turned from the wind, but if he did not, he would hit the mountainside. While he pondered what to do, the decision was taken out of his hands. A vicious, swirling gust snap-rolled his plane. Jack lost his grip. He cartwheeled the length of the wing and flew off into space.

Christopher nearly jumped after his brother. "Jack! Jack!"

Patrick saw it happen out of the corner of his eye. He did not have time to agonize. He fought to control his bucking airplane. The wings fluttered and bent. Turned from the wind, the F.B.5 careened through the trees at one hundred twenty miles per hour—precisely what he had been desperate to avoid. He maneuvered wholly on instinct, unable to think even a second ahead, steering so violently he was amazed his spruce-and-wire airplane held together.

Gwen rose up in the forward cockpit, looking frantically about for her brother.

God save us, Patrick thought. *God save us!*

He banked his airplane all the way on its side to evade a trunk. He held the turn, starboard wing pointed straight at the ground, to miss another tree.

And abruptly, they stopped in midair—or nearly stopped. Having come back into the wind, their speed through the forest returned to a walking pace.

"Where's Jack?" Gwen screamed hysterically, turning around backward, kneeling on the gunner's seat, and leaning over the cockpit coaming so that her face was inches from Patrick's. Her wind-blown hair streamed around his head. She looked deranged. "What's happened to Jack?!"

"I can't see!" Patrick hollered. "Sit down, Gwen, sit down!" Some obscure recess of his mind registered that he had not only omitted the honorific *Lady* but also used the diminutive of her name. So much of his brain was focused on survival that he had no neurons available to be appalled at his indiscretion.

Christopher pulled on Gwen's arm and pointed.

Jack dangled from a limb three hundred yards ahead, two hundred feet from the ground. They had come full circle to where he had fallen off.

Animated by the high wind, the tree swung the boy back and forth.

Patrick worked his way toward Jack. He pulsed the blip switch to match the velocity of the headwind. They were practically hovering. Of course, it was a backward and forward surging hover.

The motion was finally too much for Christopher. Overcome by nausea, he grabbed the only container he could find—the canvas bag under his seat—and threw up into it.

It was terrible luck that Jack was on the windward side of the tree. Patrick side-slipped around its enormous girth and inched forward behind the hanging boy. The maneuver would have been an extreme test of skill for the most experienced pilot. A particularly powerful gust might blow the F.B.5 backward into the trunk. The fragile airplane would crumple, and everyone onboard would perish. Or, if the wind slackened, the plane would surge ahead, hit Jack, and knock him off the branch.

Sure enough, the wind died, and the plane flew at Jack. Patrick cut the engine and dove.

Then the wind picked up again, and the F.B.5 lurched backward.

Patrick let the engine go to full power. The rudder brushed the tree trunk.

However, luck was finally with them. The headwind remained strong and steady long enough for Patrick to ease the forward cockpit into position beneath Jack.

Gwen clutched her brother's ankles.

Jack did not understand what was happening and held tightly to the branch.

"Let go!" Gwen cried.

Christopher could barely contain himself. "Let go, you idiot!"

Jack was too far gone to listen, even if he could have heard anything above the engine's noise.

Patrick lost control. The plane dropped.

But then he had it back. He eased the F.B.5 upward until Jack's legs dangled into the front cockpit. Gwen wrapped her arms around her brother's legs. That gave Patrick a bad turn—he might lose them both if Jack didn't let go.

Christopher grabbed on.

Jack fell into the plane.

"Well done!" Patrick cried in jubilation. Then he realized that the extra hundred and thirty-five pounds in the front cockpit seriously unbalanced his airplane.

The nose dropped.

Patrick hauled back on the control stick, but it was no good. The center of gravity was too far forward. He barely had time to curse his stupidity before they hit the ground.

CHAPTER 8

Confusion

48-50-6

At the same time Patrick's F.B.5 was plowing into a gigantic mound of decaying pine needles, Lord Buckleigh was backing away from the telegram his wife was waving in his face. Somehow, Miss Harkless had learned that the earl and countess were in London and had sent the missive to their Mayfair townhome.

```
Return to Devonshire at once. Gwendolyn must
not be left in her great-uncle's hands.
```

Thankfully, none of those concerned were aware of recent developments. News of the children's disappearance would have caused pandemonium.

Lord Buckleigh said, "I won't have a servant ordering us about. That Rasputinina has some sort of hold on you, Ceil."

"How dare you, George!" The countess brandished the sheet of paper as if it were a weapon. "This only says what I've known all along. We shouldn't have left."

"For heaven's sake! We've been gone less than twenty-four hours. We'll be back tomorrow evening. We have a dinner engagement with Lord Milner, and by Jove, we're going to keep it."

Lady Buckleigh flung a hand straight up. "You stay, then. I'm going home." Whereupon she turned on the ball of her foot and marched toward the door.

Belatedly, the earl realized he was in trouble. It was as if he had woken up and discovered that something had gone horribly wrong while he had been sleeping. He had been so engrossed in developing the right arguments to convince Milner to back his proposal that he had entirely failed to pay attention to his wife's expressions and gestures. She was not being melodramatic. Reasonable or not, she was frightened for her daughter's life.

Ordinarily, he shied away from emotional or illogical situations and, when forced to deal with them, did not handle them well. This time, however, he acted decisively and got it right.

He blocked the door. "I'm going to wire Mrs. Nellis and tell her to keep Gwendolyn in her room even if it means locking her there. If Uncle Geoff pulls any more of his shenanigans, he'll be banned from Maham House."

The earl paused.

"I'll arrange for Doctor Foley to visit Gwendolyn and give her a full checkup next week."

He looked unblinking into his wife's eyes. "I've been as worried about her as you have. Nothing is more important to me than our children. That's precisely why…" He paused. "Jack is sixteen…I have to do something about this war before he goes into the army." He looked at the floor. "And to do it, I need Milner's support. He's…well, whatever you think of him, he's the sort of man to take bold action in difficult situations, and I think he'll back me. But I can't manage him without you."

They both knew what the earl meant. Countess Buckleigh could charm a constipated rhinoceros. Her husband, on the other hand, was animated and glib only when discussing topics like the use of amphiprotic solvents in nonaqueous titration—in other words, highly technical subjects. He had the logical arguments laid out to make his case to Viscount Milner but needed his wife's sparkle to secure the deal.

He ran his hand through his hair and looked lost. He would have been ashamed to know how pathetic he appeared at that moment, but it caused Lady Buckleigh to hesitate.

"I need you there, Ceil," the earl said in a small voice.

It was a masterful performance. It was completely unintentional. It worked beautifully.

The countess stayed.

Christopher was scrunched like a wad of dirty clothes into the front of the gunner's compartment, where he had served as a crash bag for his sister. The airplane was standing nearly on its nose. Gwen was inert. The little boy wriggled and pushed to squeeze past her. Exiting the aircraft was easy. The front of the forward cockpit was practically flush with the ground. He had only to flop out.

"Gwen? Gwen?" He pulled her arm.

"Yes, I'm here…Where *is* here?"

"Are you all right?"

In answer, she crawled out of the wreck, hampered somewhat by her heavy overcoat and long skirt.

"Did Jack go somewhere?"

Christopher gazed up at the system of roots arching down from the trunk of the immense tree beside them. Jack was caught in a fork of roots ten feet above the ground. He had never gotten more than half his body into the plane, and the violent updraft that arrested the F.B.5's dive at the last moment had slung him out.

"Jack!" Gwen called. "Jack?"

He didn't move.

"Patrick! Go help Jack!" Gwen looked about. "Patrick?"

"Here," said a voice from within the airplane.

The F.B.5 was flexing and swaying in the wind. Were it not in the lee of the giant tree, it would have cartwheeled through the forest. Christopher stood on tiptoes to peer into the aft cockpit.

"I'm stuck." Patrick's foot was jammed between a rudder pedal and the floorboard.

He worked it free, climbed out of the cockpit, and eased himself to the ground, keeping a hand on the plane until he had his balance. "Lady Gwendolyn, are you injured?"

"No, but Jack…" She pointed upward. "I think he's unconscious."

"I'll help him." Patrick scrambled up an arching root and took hold of the inert boy's arm.

Jack twitched spasmodically, gasped, fell, and screamed when he hit the spongy ground. He rocked back and forth, cradling his right arm with his left, alternately gasping and moaning.

Patrick dropped and landed in a crouch. "Your arm is broken."

"It's not broken." Gwen stared at Jack's gnarled shoulder. "It's dislocated."

"Oh. I guess that's not as bad?"

Jack swore.

Gwen turned to Patrick. "You'll have to pull it out."

"Er…" Patrick looked back and forth between Gwen and Jack. "Pardon?"

"You know—reseat his arm in its shoulder socket."

Patrick's conception of the procedure was somewhat vague.

"Tug on his arm until his shoulder snaps back into place." Gwen explained.

"Get it over with," Jack hissed between clenched teeth.

Gingerly, Patrick took Jack's wrist and pulled.

"*Aiii!*"

"Sorry!"

"You have to yank hard," Gwen instructed.

Patrick pulled again, with the same result as before.

"You're making it *worse!*" Jack roared.

"I can't get enough leverage."

"Put your foot on his side," Christopher suggested.

Patrick was going to respectfully decline to do that, but upon reflection, decided it was actually a good idea. He braced the sole of his shoe on Jack's ribcage and pulled on the arm with both hands.

Jack screamed and nearly fainted, but the ball slipped into the socket. He slumped to the ground and lay panting.

"How did you know how to do that?" Patrick asked Gwen.

"She's spent a lot of time with doctors," Christopher noted.

"Mother did it for Lord Chesterfield's son. He tried to jump our old mare Buttercup over a hedge. Buttercup was not inclined."

Patrick offered Jack a hand and was shoved for his trouble.

"Get away from me!"

Gwen glowered at her brother. "Let him help you."

"Nothing can help me or any of us. He's gotten us all killed."

"He saved our lives. He saved you."

"Oh really? He brought us to this godforsaken place and crashed us here." Jack turned on the other boy. "Why didn't you take us back to Dartmoor? Are you daft?"

"The wind was too strong," Patrick said weakly.

"Now we *can't* go back. We're going to be hunted down and—" Jack covered his face with his hands.

Patrick gazed through the forest. There were wide, clear corridors between the tree trunks—wide enough, perhaps, for a take-off run if they could haul the F.B.5 to a sufficiently long strip of hard ground. "I think I can fix the airplane…" He meant to sound confident but failed.

"Fix *that*?"

A powerful gust rocked and twisted the nose-planted craft from end to end. A brace wire snapped, and the tail sagged.

"We'll pray. God will show us what to do." Christopher placed his hands together and bowed his head. "Please, God, show us what to do."

A great light shone off to the west, inside a dark cloud.

"There. That was a sign. "That's where we should go."

"Um, it might have been lightning," Patrick said diplomatically. Thunder rumbled over the dismal countryside.

"That doesn't mean it wasn't *also* a sign."

"It's rather desolate in that direction."

"Christopher's right," Gwen said despondently. "The prism is over that way in a canyon called Defile of Ash."

"How do you know that, m'lady?" Patrick took special care to address her appropriately. In-flight emergency or not, he should not have called her Gwen. It was too much to hope she hadn't heard him.

"An angel showed it to me in a dream." Gwen screwed up her face. It was the sort of thing a madwoman might say. She did not want Patrick to think she was crazy. She hoped that, in light of present circumstances, he would give her the benefit of the doubt.

Christopher said adamantly, "If an angel showed Gwen where to find the prism, we have to go there."

No one spoke for a time. Jack massaged his injured shoulder.

Horror, something whispered into their minds. *Horror.* Voracious supernatural assassins prowled the shadowy, steep-walled Defile of Ash. All four children shared the same vision.

Jack shook his head. "We are not going there. God can get someone else to do His dirty work."

Gwen would have done anything to avoid the place, but now that she was here, she wanted to get the ordeal over with, whatever her end might be. Jack's resistance, formerly comforting, was now galling. "You need the prism, Jack."

Brother turned on sister. "How are we supposed to deal with the demons guarding it? There are sure to be some. My arm is useless. Do you expect McCray to fight them all by himself? And with what? Your dagger?"

Christopher pointed at the airplane. "We have a machine gun."

"Do you think I *want* to go?" Gwen sobbed, inhaling air in great whoops. "I *don't.* That's why I didn't tell you before!"

Christopher touched her hand. "God will help us."

She wished she could believe it. She was persuaded that God did not care what happened to them. They were pawns in a supernatural game, and she was going to be sacrificed.

No one said anything for almost a minute.

Patrick went to inspect his airplane. The wind had slackened somewhat. He wrestled the tail down until the vehicle was repositioned on its undercarriage. Miraculously, none of the struts were broken. Everything was out of alignment, but tightening and bracing might make it serviceable for one flight. The crumpled nose was inconsequential. The engine mount was sound. Luckily, the propeller was in the rear—it would have been smashed to splinters if it had been in front. Then again, he realized with a shudder, it was amazing that the spinning engine hadn't ripped loose and minced everyone aboard.

"Thank you, God," Patrick said softly, making a mental note to thank Him more frequently.

He was pretty sure he could get his plane back into the air. If the engine ran. If the control linkages weren't bent. If any number of things weren't broken. Some fuel had leaked, but the tank appeared to be sound. Now, where was the satchel with his tools? It had been under the gunner's seat.

The canvas bag was one of the few things that had stayed put when they hit the ground. Patrick pulled it from its place and lifted it from the plane. It smelled awful; it appeared to be oozing vomit.

Just then, the dense clouds overhead opened and poured rain. Everyone scrambled into a hollow space under the tree's roots. Patrick left the bag out in the rain to be doused by a torrent of water gushing down a gutter-like groove in a root.

For the duration of the shower, everyone huddled cold and miserable in the shelter of the tree. Gwen began shivering and coughing again. Christopher put his arms around her. Patrick longed to do the same but wouldn't have dared.

Jack, deep in a private hell, rubbed his injured shoulder incessantly. He and the others could not get to Maham House on foot. Even if they could, what would they do when they got there? There was no escaping the Primary World. What would it be like to be killed by a demon? Consumed body and soul? Could a demon keep his soul? Drag it to Hell?

Gwen gazed unfocused in the direction of the Defile of Ash. She was thinking about nothing because she had no future to think about. But then her eyes drifted to Christopher's, and that jolted her out of her stupor. The little boy was holding her tightly and staring intently, his forehead almost touching hers. He didn't want anything bad to happen to her. He was going to be terribly hurt.

I'm sorry," she whispered.

The storm increased in intensity for a quarter of an hour. At its crescendo, the downpour looked like a waterfall. Then, within the span of two minutes, the air stilled, and the rain dwindled away. Drops continued to fall from drenched tree limbs but not the sky.

The canvas sack was sopping wet and, thankfully, stinking less. Patrick fished it from a big puddle and hooked his fingers into its cinched mouth to work it open. The drawstring wouldn't slip through the wet piping. He pulled harder.

Then the bag snarled, writhed, and kicked as if filled with a dozen snakes and a mongoose.

Patrick jumped, screamed, stumbled, and fell to the ground.

The drawstring caught around his wrist, yanking the bag toward him.

A long, thin snout shot through the cinched opening. Needlelike teeth nipped the air in front of his face.

"Help!" He shoved the bag to arm's length.

The nasty little mouth snapped at his nose.

Jack grabbed for Gwen's dagger, but his injured arm was numb. He fumbled and dropped the weapon.

Patrick tried to hurl the bag away, but the loop in the drawstring pulled tight around his wrist. The vicious snout stretched toward him. Patrick leapt to his feet. He swung the sack over his head and slammed it on the ground.

"Ooff!" The grunt was accompanied by the jangle of metal tools.

Encouraged by the result, Patrick swung the satchel back over his head and down on his other side.

"Ow!"

Patrick kept up the arcing, side-to-side pummeling until the thing inside yelled, "STOP IT!"

Patrick did not stop.

Whatever was in the bag began cursing in some unintelligible language. *"Cragg friss,"* it sputtered after being whomped on one side.

"Holoth gol cracken," it said as it thunked on the other. *"Garic tagth!"*

Whomp…Thunk…Whomp…Thunk…Whomp…Thunk.

Gwen, Jack, and Christopher watched, powerless to help.

Tiring, Patrick slung the bag beneath the airplane's undercarriage and rolled a wheel over the cinched end, squashing the still protruding mouth.

"You're going to regret that," said the run-over mouth in a nasally, run-over voice.

Christopher cheered. "We've caught a demon!"

Jack seized Gwen's dagger—this time with his good hand—and advanced on the sack.

"Don't cut the bag!" Gwen warned. "The spirit will escape."

"I'm going to kill it," Jack proclaimed.

"I don't think you can," Gwen said quickly. "It's the pseustee. The one that was whispering to Mother."

"Let me out of this bag, or *I'll* kill *you*," the thing growled.

Hastily, Patrick worked the drawstring off his wrist. "Can a canvas sack hold a demon?"

Christopher shouted at it, "Demon! In Jesus's name, I command you to stay in that sack and not come out."

Everyone held their breath. The sack stopped moving.

"Do you think that worked?" Jack asked doubtfully.

"Of course it didn't." The thing in the sack wriggled slightly. "However, now that I think about it, I may stay here. Hmm. Yes, I believe I will."

Jack set his jaw. "I may not be able to kill it, but I can cut it to pieces. That should set it back."

"I can't help you if you do."

The tone was so rational and calm that Jack paused. "What do you mean?"

"We have a common cause. Several, in fact. Let's declare a truce. We can help each other."

"We don't believe you," Gwen said.

"The ghoulies down in the Defile of Ash"—the proboscis protruding from the sack pointed westward—"are particularly foul and ravenous: machirai and carnalots. They're hunters. They saw your airplane. They know you're here. They're on their way."

The children looked at each other.

"How do you know that?" Jack demanded.

"Trust me. I know."

"Why would you help us? You want us to die."

"It doesn't matter to me if you die or live. I'll be just as happy if you live, so long as I get what I want."

Patrick's eyes narrowed. "What is it you want?"

The thing licked its lips. "Robert Maham's book."

Gwen scowled. "You can't have it."

"I only want to look at it. I won't take it."

"Why do you need us for that?"

"It's anchored to shadow, and I'm anchored to the Primary World. I can't open it, can I?"

Gwen shook her head. "We're not going to make that deal."

But Jack's eyes shifted between his sister and the bag, and from then on, the pseustee focused on him.

"No sense denying I want power," the demon said. "But I don't particularly care who my allies are—they might as well be you. Honestly, I'd rather they be you. I trust you a lot more than a bunch of demons. Let's help each other."

Gwen said, "Devils always lie."

"Not when it's in our interest to tell the truth."

"Sometimes the best deception is the truth told in a way that is completely misleading."

"I have told you no lies."

"Hah! That's the biggest fib of all," Christopher yelled. "Let's get rid of this baggage. It's not going to help us. It's confusing us, and even if it's telling the truth, it's distracting us from what's important—praying and asking God for help."

"You're hemmed in by mountains," the pseustee said. "Don't delude yourselves—your airplane will never fly again. Eventually, you'll go into the Defile of Ash because it appears to be the only way out. You have no idea what infests the cracks and holes in that place. You won't survive by yourselves."

In their minds, they saw twisted creatures rising out of the smog. Shadows that moved. Things with smoldering eyes and fanged mouths. Things coming to suck out their blood and their souls.

"There's another way, but you'll never find it, and you'd be ambushed if you did." The pseustee became perfectly still. "But I can get you safely through it."

"There's a cliff not far from here," Christopher said. "Let's throw the bag off it."

"Yes," the pseustee said sadly. "That's what I would expect of children too stupid to make an alliance. Well, if that's your decision, go ahead."

"It wants us to throw it off the cliff," Patrick observed. "Like Brer Rabbit. It must believe it will survive."

"Correct," said the demon.

The airplane shifted, and the wheel rolled, letting the bag open a little more. An eye appeared. It was yellow with a glistening black pupil like a tiny tainted egg yolk. Christopher refused to look at it, but the others couldn't look away.

"We've already established that you can't kill me."

Jack brandished Gwen's dagger. "We've also established that we *can* cut you to pieces."

The eye rotated to look at the blade.

"I'd rather you didn't do that. It does hurt. But I'll reconstitute unless you eat me, and I don't think you're prepared to do that."

Gwen gagged. "Ugh!"

"Even then, I'd still exist—diminished, but enough to give you some pretty bad stomach aches. I'd be *in* you." The eye brightened. "Say, yes, on second thought, that would be excellent. Please eat me!"

Jack pointed Gwen's dagger at the bag. "We can't let it go—it would bring others. And we can't kill it." He thought a minute before saying, "We've no choice. We'll have to take it with us."

"What a sensible lad," the demon said. "That is the logical conclusion. Take me with you in this bag. Carry me along. I won't be any trouble at all. And you'll see—I'll help you."

"Just what it wants," Gwen said, frustrated to tears.

Jack turned on her. "We don't know what it wants. It wants to be thrown off the cliff. No, it wants to be eaten. No, it wants to be carried along in the stinking sack!" He waved his arms. Rather, he waved his left arm and winced at the pain in his right shoulder. He was terrified, ashamed of his fear, and wanted to do anything, even if it was hopeless, so long as he could be in motion. "We're taking it with us. If it gets us home, we'll let it look at the blasted book. Come on. We're going."

Gwen held up a hand. "The prism! We have to find it first."

"Oh," the demon said. "I completely forgot about that. Are you sure?"

"We can't stay anchored to the Primary World."

"Hmm…I suppose you have a point," the spirit conceded. "Very well. We'll get your trinket first. It will take a couple of hours."

Surprised, Patrick looked at the eye protruding from the sack. "You know where it is?"

"Of course. You came here and you *don't*? You're even stupider than I thought."

"We don't know *exactly* where it is," Jack said defensively. "It's over that way." He pointed toward the Defile of Ash.

"Well, you're warm," said the demon.

"Then tell us precisely where to find it," Jack commanded.

"Certainly. See that peak?" The mouth pointed to a dark summit visible between trees. "To the right of that, down in the wall of the defile."

"How do you know?"

The thing laughed, a spine-chilling combination of an animal's growl and a little child's giggle. "We demons see far and wide."

"Is the taraph there?"

"No. Long gone. Flung the nasty thing into a shaft and got away as fast as he could."

"Why?"

The pseustee grunted. "It disgusts us. That taraph couldn't get rid of it fast enough."

"What is the prism, exactly?" Patrick asked.

"What am I, your personal professor? Make up your mind. Are you going after it or not? Now is your chance. All you have to do is pick it up." The demon began ejecting Patrick's tools from the bag: wrenches, pliers, hammer, wire cutter.

Christopher still wanted to chuck the demon off the nearest cliff, but Jack was in control. The pseustee would guide them to the prism and the secret way through the mountains back to Maham House.

Patrick had no choice but to leave his airplane behind. He consoled himself that it had flown and he had done a passable job piloting it, even if he had crashed in the end.

Jack glanced at the machine gun mounted to the mangled front of the plane. He sighed. It was an awesome weapon, but too heavy and bulky to take with them. "All right. Let's go."

To carry the demon, Patrick tied the sack's drawstring to a long, straight stick and set the stick on his shoulder so the bag hung away from him. Christopher fetched the canteen that had been in the gunner's compartment. Then they began the trek southwest.

This diagram might be helpful. I'm pretty sure Patrick drew it. I added the dashed lines.

Kirk

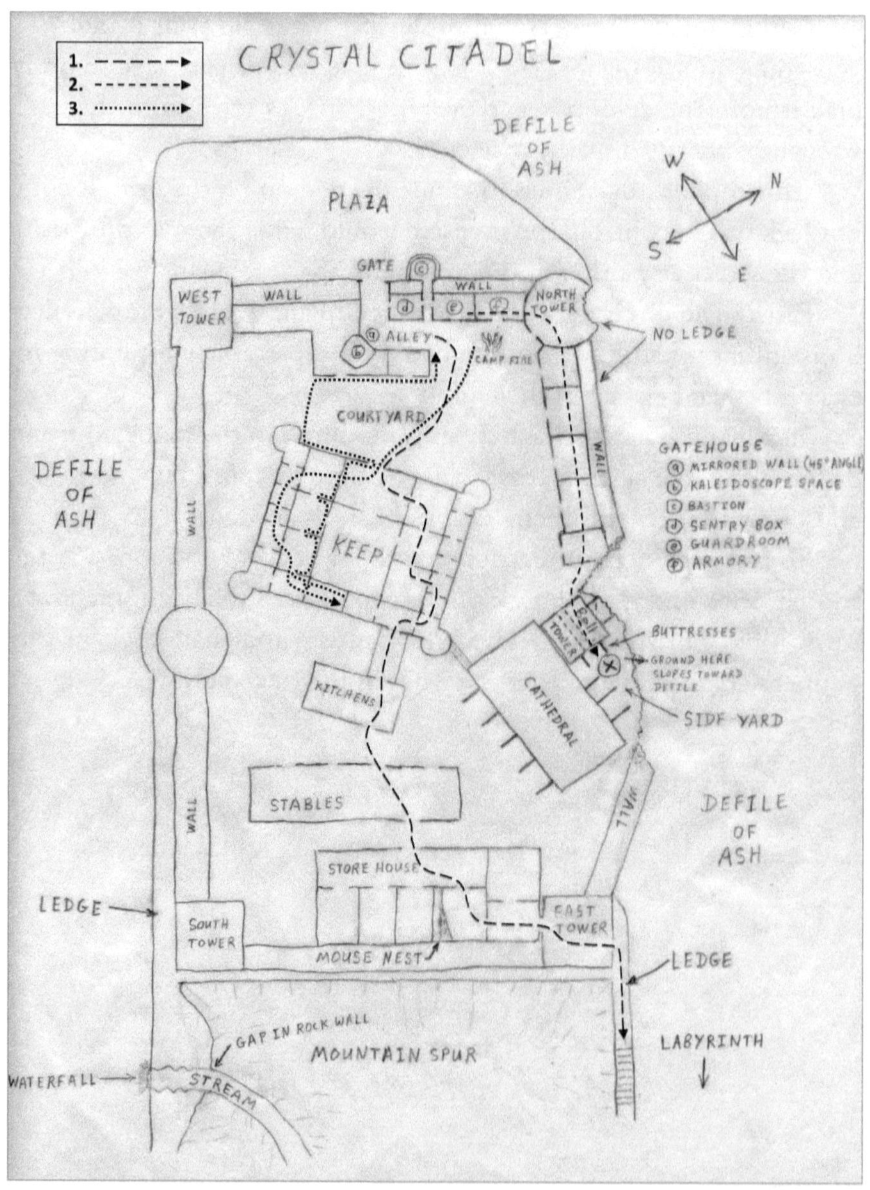

CHAPTER 9

Strike Slip

1-8-44

At the outset, the demon in the bag weighed about as much as a small dog, but it somehow varied its mass, becoming randomly heavier and lighter, so Patrick had difficulty keeping his balance. He wanted to smack the thing.

Jack stumbled over the uneven terrain with his injured arm cradled in his good one. He gripped the dagger so tightly that his hand cramped. Holding a weapon was the only thing that gave him any comfort.

Christopher felt lost and strangely numb.

Gwen was freezing. She trembled, and her chest ached with every breath. This was her death march.

They trudged through the dusky world of giant trees, shoes sinking into the soggy, frigid forest floor. No one talked except the demon, who nattered on and on about alliances and bonds between those with a common cause. Its name was Nozmantis, and it spoke in a low, even monotone as metered as a metronome.

Patrick paid little attention to the voice coming out of the bag, concentrating on keeping his footing despite the swinging weight. He became alert and alarmed when he looked at his watch and realized he had no clear memory of anything that had happened for the previous fifteen minutes.

The demon was talking about "the Foe," whom he called a callous master of manipulation. Before that, there had been something about the nobility of giving one's life—not merely to save others but as a general practice for its own sake.

"Shut up!" Patrick growled at the bag. "We're not listening."

Gwen did not think she was listening. Her conscious mind might as well have been anesthetized. But her subconscious was operating at full capacity. She and the boys were being hunted, and it was her doing. She would be the death of them all. The thought looped over and over. She kept walking because she didn't know what else to do. It would be better to lie down and die sooner rather than later. Enter the sleep of death. It couldn't be any other way, and anything was preferable to this agonizing march.

Death is rest, whispered the wind as it swept through branches high above. *Lie down and rest forever. Save your brothers and Patrick. Save them by dying.*

Why had Uncle Geoffrey told her that she mustn't die?

The trees were so huge she felt like an ant with no significance in the world. She was spiraling headlong into a trap. There was no escape for the boys while she was with them.

Christopher sensed something was wrong with his sister and was afraid for her. He suspected the devil in the bag was responsible, and he was determined to get rid of the thing as soon as possible. He tried to pray but couldn't concentrate because the path was difficult and Jack forged ahead mercilessly.

The children had to zigzag around colossal roots running half below and half above ground. They happened upon a narrow but deep gully cutting like a tunnel under the roughest region and took the shortcut beneath the spreading roots.

In the beginning, the forest canopy had been as far away as the sky, and the underbrush light. As the children progressed, everything shrank and tightened, becoming cramped, thorny, twisted, and dark. More and more, they had to contend with tangled branches infested with hairy lichens that dangled like shabby, wet beards. Things in the shadows watched the humans go by.

Jack shivered. *Not good,* he thought. *Not good. We're being allowed to pass. We're going where they want us. It's like crawling down the throat of a carnivorous plant.*

The children came to the canyon where Patrick's airplane had barrel-rolled. It cut all the way through the highland.

"How do we get across?" Jack asked.

The pseustee pointed with its snout. "There's a bridge."

Jack didn't see anything he would have called a bridge. He supposed the demon meant the granite arch a quarter mile to the southeast. It spanned the narrow part of the canyon. "What are our other options?"

"There aren't any."

Jack sighed. "Come on, everyone."

They pushed through thickets of waist-high ferns. Gwen tried not to think about what might be hidden in the sea of green fronds. She imagined that the spongy ground was eating her shoes. She frowned when she saw the so-called bridge up close. It was more than fifteen feet wide, but water and wind had worn down its shoulders. And the canyon floor was a long way below.

Jack studied the smooth, rounded surface. "Keep to the middle," he advised.

Gwen followed Jack onto the arch, moving slowly and deliberately. The solid rock felt slick underfoot, and the cruel wind seemed to be deliberately shoving her. But she reached the other side without incident. So did Christopher.

Patrick was last to cross. He stared fixedly at the stone below his feet, never once looking to the side, and took very small steps. But he made it safely over, and his face relaxed when he was on flat ground.

Jack pressed westward through dark woods. The children passed a mud pit where brown bubbles swelled and popped, releasing noxious volcanic steam. Vapor misted everything in the vicinity, nourishing the scruffy fungi that coated fallen and living trees alike. Gwen brushed limp, damp hair out of her face. Airborne spores and ash made breathing awful. Nearly every one of Gwen's exhales was a cough.

The trees became thicker and more gnarled. Black, tumorous knots grew like boils on the slimy trunks and branches. Jack watched them out of the corners of his eyes. He kept imagining that the growths were sliding deviously along the limbs.

Gwen's skirt caught on a bramble and ripped to several inches above her knee. She didn't care.

Finally, they emerged from the western edge of the forest and blinked in the light. Gray and cheerless, the spot was bright compared with the cave-like dusk of the woods.

The Defile of Ash opened before them. The rim to their right curved and jutted like a promontory out into the gorge. But gauging distance was impossible; neither the cracked facets of the canyon's obsidian walls nor the rivulets of charcoal-gray sludge in its bottom provided visual cues for scale.

With mountains rising at their backs, the land seemed to Gwen and the three boys to be nudging them into the chasm. They saw no path the way they had come—as if none had ever existed.

"Stop," Jack said. But when he opened his mouth to give the next order, he found he had nothing to say.

Gwen's legs gave out. She fell at the lip of the abyss and didn't have the strength to get back up. Jack helped her to a sitting position. She slumped against a boulder. There wasn't any reason for her to move anywhere else; no place was dry, and every place was frigid.

Patrick dropped the canvas bag and leaned on his carry pole while he surveyed the defile.

"You were clever to bring the little boy," Nozmantis commented, "though you didn't know it. He's the only one of you who can worm down to your trinket."

"What's that supposed to mean?" Jack couldn't help but stare at the eye looking out of the sack.

"It's in a shaft. You'll have to form a human chain to reach it. None of the rest of you are light enough, except maybe the girl there, and I don't expect you want to send her. The shaft is hundreds of feet deep." Nozmantis smacked his lips. "Happily for you, the prism landed by chance on a shelf near the top. Master Christopher should be able to get it if one of you Gorton boys holds his ankles and the other keeps his mates from slipping. Be a pity if someone slipped. It's a long, long drop. But I think you can pull it off if you work together."

"Where is this hole?" Patrick asked warily.

The snout slithered out of the neck of the bag and pointed north. "Down that path."

Jack looked this way and that. "What path?"

"Right in front of you."

Jack leaned cautiously over the edge of the cliff. "That's not a path! It's a ledge!"

"Well, it's the way you have to go. Take it, or leave the prism behind. I don't care either way, but you better make up your minds quickly. See that storm coming up the gorge? It's not just natural elements."

Jack shuddered. "How far are we from Maham House?"

"Ten hours march, assuming you keep a brisk pace."

"We've no chance!"

"No. Not much. Fortunately, you have me. I'll get you home— stealth and deception, decoys and false trails for the hunters. You can count on me. Hurry now, or it will be too late."

"The thing is lying," Christopher said. "It's leading us astray."

"Ask your sister," suggested the pseustee. "She knows."

"It's true. The prism is down there somewhere." Gwen pointed northward. "On the other side of that prominence." She closed her eyes and hugged herself. "I can't negotiate the path. Go without me."

"We won't leave you here by yourself, m'lady," Patrick declared.

The snout turned toward Jack. "We'll be coming right back."

"We won't go without her," Christopher said firmly.

"Then forget the prism."

"One of us will stay with Gwen," Jack decided.

"That won't work," countered the thing in the bag. "I told you— two alone will plummet to their deaths. There has to be a third to hold them. You have a fine and logical option: The girl stays here; the boys go grab the prism and hike back, quick as quick."

Jack hesitated.

"Time's running down," the pseustee said casually, as if it didn't really care.

"All right, all right!" Jack cried. "The three of us go. Gwen stays."

Patrick drew a breath. "I don't like this."

"Am I the only one feeling the urgency here?" The pseustee directed its snout toward Patrick, but its words were aimed at Jack. "Do you want to deal with an army of raving devils? Because that's what you've got coming at you."

Jack's knees might have buckled then and there had not a sunbeam found a hole in the clouds and fallen in full brilliance on a crystalline formation at the end of the prominence. Every wavelength of the spectrum blazed out of the minerals in a dazzling display. For a moment, his fear lifted, and he felt as if he were flying—not like in the airplane but soaring in the sunlight above clouds, lighter than air, safe and watched over.

The sunburst lasted only seconds. Then the light winked out, and the world was gray again. But it was enough.

Jack rushed to Gwen and whispered in her ear, "God is here!"

The eye in the sack swiveled, but the demon was too far away to hear what had been said.

Jack hopped down onto the ledge. It was about four feet wide. He beckoned to the other boys. "We're going." He didn't look back.

Patrick set the canteen at Gwen's side. "We'll hurry, m'lady."

She returned no emotion.

Reluctantly, Patrick picked up the bag with the demon and followed Jack.

Christopher hugged his sister and wouldn't let go.

"Get on with you." Gwen pushed him roughly away.

The little boy stood up, stung. But he did as he was told, turning and working his way down after the others, glancing over his shoulder until his head was out of sight.

The boys progressed well enough along the ledge for the first hundred yards. Patrick avoided looking into the chasm a footstep to his left, keeping his eyes fixed on the line between the narrow footpath and the cliff wall. He glanced up only when necessary to check what lay ahead. He repositioned the carry stick on his shoulder so the bag swung over the canyon. The demon inside remained still and felt lighter than before.

The ledge curved with the prominence out into the Defile of Ash. The angles and projections of the terrain confused Patrick's sense of true up and down. He wobbled. Walking beside a sheer drop was entirely different than looking out of an airplane. On the ground, Patrick was afraid of heights.

In contrast to the murky canyon, the towering mineral formation at the end of the prominence was beautiful. To the subconscious, it suggested a crystal citadel. Even in low ambient light, it scintillated.

Nearing the south corner of the citadel, the boys came to a place where the ledge widened and water issued from a crack in the cliff. A stream flowed across their path and fell into the canyon. Jack stepped cautiously into the water. It was icy but not much more than ankle-deep. He slogged across.

Crossing next, Patrick glanced at the stormfront to the southwest. A downpour would turn the stream into a raging torrent. He examined the wall to his right. "Quartz."

A hundred yards on, the boys rounded the west corner of the fortress and found themselves on a broad, flat plaza. They were at the end of the prominence, far into the Defile of Ash.

Jack walked to the edge of the plaza. *This is what it is like to be a rat on an open field with hungry owls circling overhead.*

He studied the crystal formation. Towers—two round, four square—rose asymmetrically around its periphery. The spire in the middle of the northeast side was the grandest. It looked like the bell tower of a cathedral and was half again taller than any other. However, the turret farthest east drew his eye higher, upward along the mountain spur to the summit of a steep hill in the misty background. He would have been horrified if he had known that Gwen was at that very moment starting to climb it.

Christopher went to the far corner of the plaza. Looking along the side of the prominence, he saw a conical depression like an amphitheater a few hundred yards from where he stood. But the place couldn't be reached. There was no ledge on this side of the castle; there was a sheer drop from the citadel's wall into the darkest depths of the Defile of Ash. "We can't go any farther," he called.

Jack joined Patrick in front of what appeared to be the citadel's main gate.

"That way." Nozmantis waved his proboscis at the entryway.

Jack looked inside, considering. "Very well." He strode into an alley that appeared to run straight ahead. But fifteen steps in, he was knocked sideways by something rock-hard.

Stumbling, he cursed loudly.

"What is it?" Christopher cried.

Jack grimaced. "An invisible corner! I ran into a mirror."

Patrick looked carefully. "There's a very flat, clear quartz wall at a forty-five-degree angle. It creates a perfect grazing reflection. Makes it look like the way runs straight when it actually runs off to the left."

Jack cursed again.

"You are rather stupid, even for a human boy," Nozmantis told Jack.

"Shut up, you! Where do we go now?"

The eye peering out of the sack contemplated Jack with silent disdain.

"Well?" Jack demanded.

"You told me to shut up," Nozmantis said. "I'm a very accommodating person."

Jack punched the sack. "Just tell us where to go!"

The demon did not say where it would have liked Jack to go. Instead, it said, "Continue down the alley."

Jack stomped off warily but determinedly.

The internal architecture of the formation was, like its outside, similar to a citadel. Walking to the end of the short alley, the boys stepped out into a courtyard. After turning and crossing it, they followed Nozmantis's directions through a series of interconnected chambers, most of which had no roof. Some walls were nearly transparent and absolutely smooth—as polished as gemstones. The ground was hard stone in some places but soft turf in others.

In a corridor, the boys watched something like a small rodent materialize out of solid rock, dart across their path, and disappear into the opposite wall.

"What was that?" Jack gasped.

"It looked like…" Patrick began.

"Haven't you ever seen a mouse?" sneered the demon.

"It ran through stone!" Jack said.

Christopher pointed. "There's another one!"

"Keep moving," Nozmantis commanded.

"Mice can't run through rock," Jack said.

"Maybe not where you come from. Don't dawdle."

Patrick had the answer. "The open space here is silhouette. The walls are interstitial."

"Obviously." The pseustee's tone implied that anyone who hadn't figured it out was a complete moron.

Jack was too cold, too tired, and too on edge to care if he sounded stupid. "How is that?"

Patrick explained. "The mice are anchored to silhouette, so they're running through the interstitial rock the way we rode horseback through the interstitial ridge across the road to Buckton."

Jack and Christopher were still baffled.

Patrick tried again. "These walls don't exist in silhouette. It's as if blocks and strips of interstitial rock have been laid out on a silhouette field. Have you ever been in the ruins of an ancient building where nothing remains but the foundations? You can walk directly across spaces that someone couldn't a thousand years ago. To the mice, this is all open Dartmoor. They aren't moving through walls. They're crossing a lattice of rock-filled interstices without knowing it."

"Less talking, more marching!" insisted the demon. "The girl is waiting, and an army approaches!"

Patrick ran his fingers along a wall. "This place is a fossil."

Jack paused in a doorway. "What?"

"Interstitial quartz has filled in voids to create an echo of a castle."

Jack frowned. "There has never been a castle like this in Devonshire."

"Left," directed Nozmantis.

Were they doubling back? Patrick had stopped paying attention. "Isn't that a mistake? Don't you mean right?"

"No, Irish. I don't make mistakes."

"Do as it says," Jack directed.

The next room had a semi-transparent wall as thin as film. Seeing what looked like a pickaxe behind the glaze, Patrick pressed his fingers to the quartz membrane. It shattered. He jumped backward, evading the mirrored shards.

"That's seven years bad luck for you," jeered the demon.

"I'm not superstitious," Patrick countered.

The yellow eye looked up at him. "We'll see about that."

Jack bent down and picked up the tool.

"Mislaid rock axe," Patrick declared. "We may be near one of the old tin mines."

Jack weighed the axe in his good hand. Solid, if a little rusty, it was similar to a large carpenter's hammer, except that there was a long, sharp pick opposite the head. Twice, he swung it in an arc. "This might come in handy." He slipped the axe handle through his belt.

"Keep moving!" growled the demon.

They forged on.

Christopher stopped at an interstitial boundary that cut right through a mouse nest. He could have reached right into the burrow. The mice had no idea they were vulnerable.

Patrick was unsettled. How many times had evil spirits been as close to him as he was to these mice, and he had never known? Then, even more unsettled, he wondered what would happen if he gave in to the temptation to reach across the interstitial boundary and touch a mouse. Would his entire body be pulled across the boundary and compressed into the nest? After all, contact with the mortal creature would instantly anchor him to silhouette, and he would no longer be able to occupy interstitial space. He had no desire to experiment and find out.

"Move!" Nozmantis bellowed.

They did.

When the boys were beginning to suspect that the demon was leading them in circles, Jack stepped through a breezy doorway and stopped. He was outside the castle, on the northeast side of the prominence, where there was another ledge.

"Oh!" Patrick muttered.

"How much farther?" Jack asked sullenly.

"Down there." Nozmantis indicated the amphitheater-like formation that Christopher had seen from the plaza. From where they stood, it resembled a sloping labyrinth of deep trenches.

Faster than was safe, Jack set off along the side of the cliff. Patrick followed, and Christopher brought up the rear.

The narrow ledge angled precipitously downward. For quite a way, it was saw-toothed and broken—more like a dreadfully steep, crazy stair than a trail.

The boys descended through the dark world, fighting to keep their balance in the gusting wind, traveling as swiftly as they could without slipping and falling into the abyss on their left.

Eventually, the track leveled and they thought they were home free. But then the ledge vanished for a span of six feet.

Jack lunged and cleared the gap.

Patrick hesitated. He hefted the bag with the demon, testing its weight. He looked at Jack.

"M'lord…perhaps I could toss you the sack?"

Jack hissed. "If you must." He held out his hands.

Patrick stepped to the brink of the gap. He swung the sack and let go. But the bag's drawstring snagged on his right coat sleeve button, and the demon inside suddenly had the inertia of a locomotive.

"Ai!"

Yanked forward by the bag and completely off balance, Patrick attempted at the last second to jump to the opposite ledge.

He missed it and plunged.

He caught a lip of rock and clung to it, but his scrabbling feet found no purchase. The bag swung outward and back, thumping against his hip. "Help!" he cried automatically.

He was too far below the ledge for Jack to reach.

"Hold on!" Christopher yelled.

Patrick got a toehold in a tiny niche. If he was lucky, his sleeve button would rip off, and the heavy sack would drop away. Otherwise, he couldn't possibly move his right hand. The cliff face was nearly smooth.

He was not lucky. Incredibly, the button held.

Jack stared down, appalled.

"Let me out of the bag," Nozmantis suggested. "I'll help you."

"No!" Patrick screamed.

"Why haven't you come out already?" Jack yelled.

"Master Christopher commanded me to stay inside, remember?"

"You said you could escape any time you wanted!"

"True, but I decided to do everything you asked. Do you want me to come out now?"

Trembling, Patrick scanned the rock wall. A glaze of moisture made the surface treacherously slippery.

"Don't want my help?" Nozmantis inquired.

Patrick could not resist glancing at the jagged canyon floor hundreds of feet below. "I…"

"All right, demon," Jack ordered, "come out!"

"The little boy told me to stay in."

"Come out!" Christopher shouted.

"The name. Use the *name*," demanded Nozmantis.

"In *Jesus's* name, come out of the bag, demon," Christopher commanded.

The pseustee laughed—an eerie atonal warble of off-pitch whistles and guffaws. "Very well." It worked open the mouth of the sack, extended three sets of arms, and emerged. The evil spirit looked like a monstrous tick with a human head and tubular proboscis.

It placed the lips of its long, fleshy mouth to Patrick's ear and, in a moist, smelly breath, whispered, "Step *there*"—it pointed with a claw to a horizontal crack—"and pull yourself up using that knot of rock"—it extended a long finger toward a small protuberance two feet above Patrick's head. Then it sprang onto the ledge.

Jack backed away from it.

"Don't waste time, stupid boy," the demon chided. "Give the Irish a hand."

"You said *you* would help me!" Patrick shouted.

"I just did. I told you where to find steps and holds. You thought I was going to haul you up? Do I look like I could do that? Follow my instructions, and your comrades will assist."

"Try to climb, McCray," Jack urged.

Patrick stared up at the knot of rock the pseustee said to grab. Then he looked down, put the toe of his shoe in the recommended crack, and extended his left arm upward. "Nothing for it." He breathed and lunged for the handhold.

A lightning flash lit the defile; harsh light glinted off ten thousand fractured obsidian facets. Thunder rolled up and down the canyon, reverberating wall-to-wall.

Patrick's sweaty fingers slipped off the knot, but he scrambled until he caught it and had a firm grip on the wall. He was three feet below the ledge.

Jack reached down as far as he could. "Keep coming."

"I—"

Gusting wind raked the cliff face.

"Here goes."

Patrick thrust with his left leg, pulled himself upward with his left hand, and grabbed for another crack with his right.

He slipped and lost all hold on the wall.

Jack caught Patrick's wrist. For a moment, the Irish boy hung in midair. Then, empowered by a surge of adrenalin, Jack hauled him onto the ledge.

Patrick banged his knees hard on the stone but couldn't have been more relieved. He scrambled up and clasped Jack's hand. "You saved me, m'lord! You saved me! I've never been so scared. I'm not good with heights."

Jack shrugged, embarrassed. "I couldn't let you fall, of course."

"Touching," Nozmantis said snidely. "Such a tender moment. But time's ticking."

"We know. We know!" Jack looked at Christopher. "Can you manage the distance?"

In answer, Christopher took a running start and had no trouble leaping the gap in the ledge. Jack caught him.

"Keep up!" Nozmantis yelled as he scuttled off. It was a taunt, not useful instruction.

"Hang that thing!" Jack sprinted after the demon.

At the far end of the ledge, Nozmantis darted between two pillars and disappeared into the upper corridors of the labyrinth. The boys reached the spot seconds later, only to watch their guide vanish around a corner.

From above, the area looked like an amphitheater. It was, in fact, a complex system of deep trenches. Its winding, intersecting switchbacks ascended and descended haphazardly.

The boys lost all sense of direction as they chased the demon around the conical hillside. Having a partial view of the sky didn't help. The shifting black clouds were false references.

Nozmantis continued to disappear. Losing sight of the demon for the ninth time, Jack ground his teeth in frustration. "Where the devil did it go?"

Finally, the pseustee halted, and the boys caught up.

"We've arrived," Nozmantis announced.

Panting, the boys stopped and stared. They were at the center of the labyrinth. The semicircular floor sloped downward to an opening in the ground not too far from the edge of the defile.

The demon pointed at the hole. "Your bauble is in that shaft. Go get it."

Jack hesitated. He sidled step-by-step down the steep slope until he could peer into the shaft. The prism lay on a tiny rock shelf several feet below the mouth of the otherwise smooth-walled chute.

He thought for a while, then looked up at the demon. "You seem to be able to cling to rock. Bring the prism here."

"I have no intention of touching that thing."

Jack scowled at the demon but didn't waste time arguing. He looked at his brother. "Christopher—you'll have to get it." He turned and beckoned to Patrick. "McCray, lie on your stomach and lower Christopher by his ankles. I'll hold your legs to keep you from slipping."

"Good plan," said the pseustee, "since it is exactly what I told you to do."

"Stay back, demon."

"Of course."

Christopher knelt at the mouth of the shaft.

Patrick lay down and took hold of Christopher's ankles. Something was not right. The demon had implied that the prism had landed on the shelf by chance. But if the artifact had been flung, why hadn't it ricocheted or skipped off the shelf? Or shattered?

Jack pressed down on Patrick's legs, anchoring the human chain. Christopher went into the hole headfirst, arms stretched toward the prize.

"I'm not close enough," the boy reported.

Patrick wriggled inch by inch down the slope until his head and shoulders were over the shaft.

Nozmantis came alongside, put a clawed foot at the edge of the hole, and bent over it. "Yes, very good. Just a little farther."

"Can you get it now?" Jack called to his brother, who was out of his sight.

"Almost…"

"Down," ordered the demon.

Jack let the other boys slip a couple of inches.

"Stop!" Patrick yelled. "No farther! We'll all slide in!"

Christopher stretched. He could brush the top of the prism with a fingertip but not get hold of it.

Taking the empty canvas bag, Nozmantis sidled like a spider into the shaft and squeezed past the boys to get below the shelf. Holding the bag open, the demon said, "Nudge the thing in here."

When Christopher hesitated, Nozmantis explained reasonably, "I'll carry it up for you."

The little boy managed enough contact with the tip of his middle finger to knock the prism off the shelf. It dropped into the bag.

The pseustee grinned triumphantly. It shot upward, scrambled over Christopher and Patrick, and scooted on its many legs up the conical slope. It was out of Jack's field of view in seconds.

Jack cursed. Not thinking, he twisted to look over his shoulder. The movement was a grave mistake. Without his full weight on Patrick's legs, the human chain began to slide.

In Gwen's mind, her craggy perch emptied of existence when the boys left. The only sound of life was her wheezy, rattling breathing. She raised the canteen in trembling hands and took a sip of water. Sputtering and coughing, she spilled more than she swallowed. Poignant regrets pulled her down with many times the force of gravity. She had not said proper farewells to Christopher or Jack. Or Patrick.

The wind was an inorganic spirit emphasizing the hollowness of existence. Why had Jack said *God is here!* like that? Of course God was there—but His presence was meaningless. God was as detached and aloof as the air. He was like a silent stranger sharing a train compartment. Right now, she feared Him not in the biblical sense of awed respect but in the more mundane meaning—dread.

Yet, inexplicably, she also longed to call to Him. Here, at the end, whatever she had been and whatever she might become, she found herself wanting forgiveness.

Then defiance seethed within her. She may have done things He detested, but He had driven her to those things. He had taken Freddie from her. She had every right to blame Him.

She looked up, and her gaze happened on the summit above the ridge to the east. There seemed to be battlements. Something about them was odd. Perverse curiosity drove her to stand. She wobbled, a fall of several hundred feet a misstep away, but caught her balance. The great grim vista of the Defile of Ash opened before her. Drawn against her will toward the formation on the ridge, she took a step, and then another, and then kept going despite her exhaustion.

It was farther away than it looked. After five minutes, she was above the gnarled trees choking the north end of the forest. She continued upward. She didn't need to save strength to go back. She would not be going back.

There was no path. For nearly fifteen minutes, she picked and toiled her way across loose gravel and around a succession of waist-high rocks, pushing off them to help support herself. Her skirt ripped again, almost to her waist, allowing her legs full range of motion. Every so often, the sky would course with lightning, accentuating the harshness of the stark land. Thunder passed through her body as if she were no more than air.

The curving hillside blocked her view of the battlements until she emerged onto a little plateau. The crenelations weren't battlements. They were standing stones. Now she recognized the place. She dropped to her hands and knees, then lay down on her side and curled up into a ball.

This was High Tor.

CHAPTER 10

High Tor
1-3-16

Miss Harkless once declared that Christian clergymen were insanely jealous of anyone who controlled spirits. The hypocritical Church, she told Gwen, preached prejudice. But strong men and women with secret knowledge could do wondrous things if they were willing to step beyond pedestrian strictures of pretend morality.

And Miss Harkless's book of spells promised Gwen that a life could be exchanged for a life.

Jack had refused a dozen times before throwing up his hands and giving in. He trapped a rabbit.

The two of them rode to High Tor on the autumnal equinox, the date that night overtook day. The journey exhausted Gwen; determination sustained her. They left their horses at the base of the rocky hill. There were no mountains on mundane Dartmoor, but the ascent to the top of the tor was steep. Gwen did not look at the rabbit in the wire cage. She laid out articles on the stone slab she selected to be the altar: Freddie's uniform, a lock of his hair, and the medal he received posthumously.

The night was murky dark. Gwen scraped a pentagram into the ground next to the altar using a chunk of hematite and performed the ritual by lantern light.

She used Freddie's shaving razor.

The killing was very messy. The animal nearly got away from her. It thrashed desperately. She had never heard a rabbit scream. The high-pitched shriek was shocking—like that of a terrified human child.

Disgusted with herself the moment she began, Gwen nevertheless followed the spell's instructions precisely. She had practiced the complicated Latin incantations so many times that she was able to speak them swiftly and unerringly. As the rite progressed, she was increasingly conscious of the wickedness of her actions. Yet she was impelled by her overwhelming desire to have her brother back.

Halfway through the conjuring, Gwen found herself swept along as an observer rather than the priestess.

Freddie did not emerge from the pentagram, of course. But something had. And suddenly she was immensely powerful and achingly beautiful—indeed, the strongest and most desirable woman in the world. Her strength and stamina were limitless. She could have lifted the stone altar and hurled it across the moor. She could have run to Land's End. If she had commanded the generals of Europe, they would have jumped to execute her orders.

She drank in the sensations. Filled with terrible glee, she raised her arms to command the winds to roar and the clouds to burst.

Wait—why had she done that? Had *she* intended to raise her arms?

Blue-white lightning dazzled her eyes, and she was shocked to see, in the photonegative afterimage burned on her retinas, something like a pit viper coiled and knotted around her torso, arms, and legs. She wasn't controlling a wondrous power of earth and air—something dreadful was operating her as if she were a puppet. The exhilaration she felt was not her own; her thoughts were not her own.

The thing's body widened and flattened; its coils merged and contracted, becoming like her skin, constricting tighter and tighter. And the inky darkness was snaking *inside* her, also.

Panicking, she resisted. But she couldn't even slow it down.

The suffocating skin flowed up her neck to her chin. Memories of the Lord flashed in her mind—triggered by a survival instinct, not a yearning for Him—but those memories were rubbed out by a syrupy, anesthetizing fog that soothed away fear. She lost focus.

I'm here, the Lord called.

All she saw was a crowd adoring her, the people of the world worshiping her.

But as the darkness closed over her face and wormed toward her brain, another lightning bolt struck nearby. She never knew exactly what final, desperate train of thought led her to do it, but in the moment of clarity that followed the thunderclap, she cried out to God and gave Him control.

The Lord ripped the evil thing from her. It was like being turned inside out. In that instant, she saw the full horror of the thing that had entered her.

She screamed and screamed. The lock of Freddie's hair blew away in the wind.

Ice-cold rain fell throughout the long, muddy ride back to Maham House. She lay in bed for a month, feverish. In the black nights, she dreamt of rivers of blood. The dead invaded her nightmares.

Sin is sin, no matter the form it takes, but some sins are more obvious and poignant than others. Gwen could shrug off gossip, lies, and mean remarks—all sins she had committed at one time or another—pretending they weren't so bad. But butchering an animal in a dark rite was blatantly, undeniably evil. It forced her to realize her true nature.

She pushed God even further away. This time, she did it out of shame more than anger.

A year and six months later, Gwen struggled to her feet. She leaned on the stone slab. The bloodstains were still there. She slumped. Now she, not a rabbit, was lying on the altar. Her wasted body was featherlight, but utter exhaustion pinned it down. Whether or not demons found her, she would die. She was hollow, with no substance, no insides at all. She dreaded what was to come. The place beyond death was impenetrable darkness and pain.

"Save me, God," Gwen suddenly pleaded. "Save me."

But why would He? What had she done for Him? Nothing. Could she claim credit for any good things she had done? Of course not. No one is given a reward for doing what he or she was supposed to have done anyway. Instead, she had done what she knew she should not. She was, at heart, no different than a demon.

A thought was placed into her mind that it was ignoble, even wrong, to plead for mercy. But she was so sorry and scared that she was ready to give in to Him.

"I found you!"

Gwen would have jumped if she had not been so exhausted. Instead, she convulsed and pulled up on one elbow.

It was Christopher. Rather, on second examination, Patrick. Or… no, it wasn't either.

"Things have gone horribly wrong!" exclaimed the boy. "The others need your help!"

"What?"

"They found the prism, but they slipped on the slope!"

The boy held a canvas sack. He carefully emptied the contents onto the altar.

"You have to destroy it!"

Apprehension gave Gwen energy to rise. She stood and stared at the prism. Raindrops began splattering around it.

"I don't understand."

Urgency, fear, and bewilderment—she felt them in equal measure. Who was this person? Her first impulse was to do whatever he said. Nevertheless, she hesitated.

He spoke again. "When the prism is broken, you and the boys will revert to your normal state anchored to silhouette. Your brothers and Patrick will be safe."

His face was not quite right. The left eye was as green as Patrick's and larger than the right one, which was brown like Christopher's. His forehead was too high and slightly concave on one side. Ironically, the urgency of the situation paralyzed Gwen. Her mind whirled.

"You're the demon in the bag."

"Well, I *was* in the bag, in the form your God cursed me to assume except when I try very hard to show my *real* self. You've been told that God is good, but He is *not*. He starves and disfigures anyone who isn't his slave. What you see now is more like my real essence."

Gwen wanted to believe. She wanted to be able to do something to save the boys and end her agony. She felt inclined to do as the demon said. His eyes became more alike, and the deformity in his face smoothed so that he was beautiful. But a part of Gwen clung to Jack's last words: *God is here!*

She wavered. "Why didn't you tell us before? That all we had to do was destroy the prism?"

"I wanted to be able to enforce your promise to show me Sir Robert's book."

"Why are you telling me now?"

"I won't have any hope of getting what I want if the boys are dead. And…" Nozmantis seemed to search for words.

"And what?" Gwen prompted.

The pseustee shrugged apologetically. "I didn't tell you before because there is one other"—again, he paused—"*technical* requirement that you might find disagreeable."

Icy rain fell harder and harder. Gwen registered the dampness but not the temperature. Her body was shutting down. She was not even shivering anymore. If not for her concern for the boys, she would have lain down on the rain-splashed alter and gone to sleep.

"What will I find disagreeable?"

"Well…"

"Hurry up!"

"Now *you're* the one in a hurry?" Nozmantis rubbed the altar idly with his fingertips. Then he looked penetratingly into Gwen's eyes. "Here it is, then. Blood. You've read your Bible, haven't you? Atonement always requires blood."

"A sacrifice? We don't have anything to sacrifice."

"Actually…we do."

Injured right arm hooked tightly around Patrick's legs, Jack scratched frantically for a handhold. He yanked the rock axe from his belt and hammered the pick into the slope. It went into a crack and held firm. The boys stopped slipping and jerked to a stop. Jack winced but ignored the pain shooting through his shoulder.

Christopher swung below Patrick like a pendulum.

"What do we do?" Patrick called, his voice quavering badly. The upper half of his body dangled down the shaft.

"Please, God," Christopher prayed, eyes closed, "don't let us fall!"

"No one move!" Jack gripped the axe handle so tightly his fingers ached. His shoulder burned. "Now listen. Christopher—reach backward so McCray can take your hand. McCray—let go of one of Christopher's ankles and catch his wrist. Tell me when you've done that."

After a moment, Christopher yelled, "He's got my hand!"

"Good. Good. Now, McCray, let go of Christopher's other ankle so he can turn around. Then pull him higher so he can get onto your back. Christopher—grab McCray's coat and climb up."

The little boy did as he was instructed.

"My coat is slipping," Patrick announced.

Christopher wedged his toe into Patrick's belt. Patrick grunted. "Sorry!"

Christopher clambered out of the hole.

Jack held tightly to the rock axe. "All right, McCray, push yourself backward."

Patrick couldn't rely on more than token friction against the smooth stone, but with Jack's help, inched upward. He wriggled until his shoulders were clear of the shaft. Once he had carefully turned himself around, he and Jack crawled upslope to join Christopher on level ground.

Jack was trembling, but he smirked grimly when he saw that Patrick was also shaking.

"Where's the demon?" Jack asked.

Christopher didn't bother to check. "Long gone."

Jack scrambled to his feet. "We have to catch it!" He dashed into the system of trenches, the others hard on his heels.

The three boys made turn after turn, thinking they had caught a glimpse of the devil, but they were chasing shadows and figments. If not for the changing colors of the walls, they would have suspected they were going in circles. The hues varied between red, orange, yellow, green, blue, and violet.

The pattern nagged Patrick, but he was too tired and preoccupied with following Jack to think about the implications of the color sequence.

Every time they reached a dead end, Jack cursed and doubled back, pushing past his companions. Dead ends became more frequent.

Eventually, Jack stopped. There was no sign of the demon.

"I think we should return to Lady Gwendolyn," Patrick said quietly.

Jack stood still for a long time. "Yeah." He looked around dejectedly. "I don't know the way. You lead."

Patrick worked his way back through the labyrinth. However, the three boys had reversed direction so often that, even though he recognized places, Patrick couldn't be sure when he had seen them. They were on a bowl-shaped hillside and needed to proceed upslope. Navigation should have been straightforward, but passages that started upward often curved back downward, and it was impossible to guess the points of the compass. Converging and diverging walls and shadows made the corridors hopelessly confusing.

It began to rain. Jack tapped Patrick's shoulder. "It's late. We have to get to Gwen before dark."

"We should be out soon," Patrick said, but his declaration lacked conviction.

The trench walls brightened momentarily. Christopher tilted his face skyward. Cold raindrops wet his face. "At least the sun is breaking through. There's a rainbow of colors."

Jack pointed to a triangular mark on a wall. "We've been by here before."

"Yes…I think this way will take us west and—" Patrick inhaled sharply and breathed out through his teeth. "We keep turning and…" He took a step in one direction but then stopped. "It's impossible to tell which way we're going in these trenches."

He reversed course twice. It was no good. He stood still. "I don't know how to get out of this place."

Gwen stared at the demon. "You want me to sacrifice myself?"

"I'll put it plainly: The prism has to be smashed and its fragments submerged in a gallon of blood."

She would do anything to save the boys and was going to die anyway, but the demon's statement was so unexpected and shocking it immobilized her.

Nozmantis sensed an odd nuance and became concerned. The girl's hesitation was fully expected. But something else he couldn't identify was at work, and there was nothing a demon couldn't identify unless God was involved. "If you don't hurry, it will be too late. Grab a rock and smash the prism. Christopher, Jack, and Patrick—their lives are in your hands. Quickly now!"

"If I do what you say…"

"Do it. Delay will kill them."

Nozmantis misread what was occurring because he could not accept two possibilities: first, that Gwen's willingness to die for her brothers and Patrick amounted to anything more than perverse and hysterical fear of bereavement, and second, that God would refrain from manipulating the girl. Demons are tremendously skilled at injecting thoughts and beliefs into human minds. They cannot, however, assume direct control of a person without his or her permission. God, being omnipotent, could seize control but never does. Nozmantis assumed that God must be slyly working the girl to achieve His purpose and so focused his attention on the wrong thing. He concentrated on breaking God's control. And because he didn't understand self-sacrifice, he miscalculated the effects of his inducements.

Demons grasp the concept of altruism but have never experienced it; it is entirely contrary to their nature. That is why the powers of Hell labored with all their skill and cunning to persuade men to kill Jesus of Nazareth. Up until the instant of Jesus's death, they believed it would achieve their every hope—a rift between mankind and God that could never be repaired. Instead, to their utter shock and everlasting horror, it did the opposite. Evil spirits may have an academic understanding of self-sacrifice, but they have no understanding whatsoever of love.

Gwen was capable of both love and sacrifice. But what the pseustee was telling her to do did not feel like an act that had anything to do with love. Her great-uncle's words resounded in her mind—she mustn't die. She must be strong in faith.

"God always demands blood," the demon said, misconstruing her thoughts. "He's like that. Cut your wrists."

"I don't have a knife."

"There's a woman's compact in the mud at your feet. Break the mirror. The jagged pieces will have sharp edges."

Gwen bent down, her drenched hair falling over her face and sticking to her cheeks. The compact was hers. She must have lost it the night she slaughtered the rabbit. She held it up, and the pouring rain washed it clean.

"I haven't lied to you," said the devil. "You know that."

She did *not* know it. What should she believe?

God is here! Jack had whispered. She believed *that.* But what help was He? He had afflicted her with a wasting disease and then taken Freddie—good, brave Freddie. What was her family being punished for? God had sent horrible Miss Harkless to control her, deprive her of decent human company, and torment her day and night. Was it a twisted test?

Have I killed anyone? Am I an adulterer or thief? I'm not mean. I don't curse, and I've never disobeyed my parents in any significant way.

Suddenly she was very angry. God was supposed to be good. Was He? He filled the world with wars and pestilence. Across the globe, life was nothing more than dread, pain, and suffering. It would be better if no one had ever been born.

Why do you require blood? she demanded of Him bitterly. *You are* not *a good God.*

She opened the compact and held it up, meaning to see the haggard, wet face of the new sacrifice God demanded.

Instead, her eyes were drawn beyond the mirror to the blasted and poisonous Defile of Ash.

And abruptly, inside her thoughts, God answered her.

WHO DO YOU THINK YOU ARE?

All at once, she was caught up in a vision. She saw all of creation as it was meant to be, perfect and radiantly beautiful—eclectic symmetry and elegance realized in endless variety, harmony, and grandeur. Everywhere, the Earth was magnificent and delightful, alive and healthy. Men and women had extraordinary experiences and made joyful discoveries. Everyone gave thanks. There was no death.

Into this perfection fell a drop of corruption: a sin—the one recorded in the book of Genesis.

Ripples spread backward as well as forward in time because, as her great-uncle had pointed out, time is merely a property of the cosmos. Murder, disease, and famine were conceived and loosed upon the world. Demons issued from behind the broken barriers of the prison in which they had been sealed. They tempted men and encouraged pride so that everyone did his or her own will rather than God's. Every sin begot more and greater sins, multiplying until the whole universe rang with pain and anger. Every kind of animal and plant was changed, and the damage spread to the inanimate. Storms, earthquakes, fires, and floods ravaged land and sea. Creation vibrated with a horrid noise.

Her sins—the rite on High Tor and others—had created the Defile of Ash. Immediately she knew the truth: Every trivial lie, unkind word, and inconsiderate action spawned accelerating damage. She felt her heart stop. Any man who thinks himself good, any woman who believes herself virtuous and worthy of no punishment, is horribly mistaken. No one can face God and survive. The only way to reverse the damage is to utterly and permanently eliminate all sin.

Gwen withdrew deep into herself, into a claustrophobic well of despair so intense she would have cried out if there had been any air in her lungs. Her skin was a thick, crusty shroud of sordidness.

She had to die. It must be complete and eternal. To heal God's creation, her sin and everyone else's—*every* sin, no matter how tiny— had to be completely erased.

She saw the Lord standing on the opposite rim of the Defile of Ash, in form like the essence of lightning. Before Him were laid out the vast, blasted battlefields of France, Belgium, and Russia—of Austria, Italy, Palestine, and Gallipoli. Watery graves of ships and sailors fouled the Atlantic and North Sea. The world was a verminous ecosystem built on dead bodies. It was unendurable—all because of human sin.

Gwen had thought God didn't care about Freddie. The truth was that God loved Freddie immeasurably—even more than she did. He was heartbroken by Freddie's pointless suffering and death. She might have been angry at the injustice in the world, but He was *furious*. Furious that sin not only continued but escalated. He hated sin with an intensity beyond human comprehension.

She fell face down and covered her head with her hands, terrified out of her mind.

"Forgive me!" she moaned, nearly senseless, knowing justice would be served. It would be a total cleansing.

God's terrible wrath came at her like a blast wave. She pressed her face to the ground and waited to be obliterated.

I'm guilty with no defense. Her last thought was *I surrender.*

It hit, and there was no describing the force of God's vengeance upon the Earth. She grabbed blindly to hold herself down, hands gripping what might have been the base of a small tree. She knew her body was dead; she wondered how she could still think.

Opening her eyes, she saw she was in a stony, cheerless place below a walled city. The sky was nearly black, coloring the scenery the same gray as the Defile of Ash. A few women and men stood nearby with eyes downcast; Roman soldiers watched them. Other people walked past, some staring curiously, some leering and jeering. It was not a tree that Gwen was holding but the upright post of a cross fixed in the ground. She gazed upward, knowing in advance what she would see.

Jesus of Nazareth was nailed there.

A drop of his blood fell on her head. He had taken the annihilating wrath. God was holy and righteous; He would not and could not forgo justice, but to save Gwendolyn Europa Maham, He had Himself taken the full force of the punishment for her sins, completely erasing them and their effects.

At that moment Gwen finally understood how unimaginably good God is and how fiercely, absolutely, and wholly He loved her. And for the first time in her life, she truly loved Him back, for He is a God entirely worthy of love.

Her vision ended, and she stood exactly where she had been, blinking rain out of her eyes, looking past her compact at the defile. No time had passed—not even a fraction of a second. The demon was unaware that anything had happened.

Gwen knew with complete certainty that killing herself was not what the Lord wanted. Not at all. She was not to be sacrificed. The sacrifice had already been made. God had never rejected her—He had always done everything He could to draw her to Him except use force. She must *not* destroy the prism.

"I haven't lied to you," repeated the devil. "Not a single time." He now appeared to Gwen as skin stretched over a ramshackle anthropoid frame, his cheekbones protruding and his teeth much too sharp. His clothes had the texture of a mangy pelt.

"All right," she told the demon. "Here goes." She reached for the prism.

"Don't touch it!" Nozmantis shrieked. He flung out an arm. His clawed hand hovered near her wrist. "Smash it with the rock." He meant a large rock resting beside the prism.

She hesitated, unsure she could move her hand faster than the monster could react. The demon would rip into her if she did not follow instructions—of that she was certain. But now she had a purpose. She had to protect the prism.

Give me the ability, Lord, she thought. Then she felt Him by her side. Then her thoughts became continuous prayers.

"What are you waiting for?" hissed the demon.

An ocean of rain poured down. Water flowed everywhere. A hundred tributaries gushed into a channel alongside the trail down the mountain.

The demon was muddled. Not drastically, but Gwen's prayers were having a marked effect. He couldn't see her connection with the Lord. Still, he knew something was amiss.

Gwen moved as if to pick up the rock on the altar but then darted her hand at the prism instead.

Nozmantis was a fraction of a second too late.

Gwen's fingers closed around the glass.

The demon was *not* too late to sink his claws into her wrist. She cried out in agony; it was as if fire were shooting up her arm. She almost lost her hold. But the Holy Spirit that filled her gave her the ability to ignore the pain and bend her wrist, forcing the prism toward the demon's misshapen hand.

The glass touched his skin.

Nozmantis screamed and recoiled. He dropped to a crouch.

Now Gwen saw him as a twisted human torso with multiple legs and a tooth-filled face drawn from the demented imagination of an evil artist. She was no physical match for him.

The Lord commanded, *RUN!*

She broke and dashed toward the steep trail down the mountain.

The demon lunged. However, he was confused, and the inertia of his misdirected jump carried him sideways. He splashed in the deep rainwater and skidded.

But he didn't lose his balance, and he reoriented.

Gwen could hardly see through the rain. It didn't matter. Her body knew where to go, and gravity accelerated her escape. She gripped the prism and raced downhill almost as fast as the torrent of water in the wide channel alongside her.

But the demon was on her heels in no time.

Then Gwen slipped and fell into the raging stream.

The demon howled in frustration. It dove after its prey.

Gwen was at the mercy of the freezing flood. It swept her down the mountain at terrific speed. She was practically falling. She expected to go over a cliff any moment. Then perhaps she did go over a cliff, because everything went black.

"Maybe there's a pattern," Christopher repeated. "Like our hedge maze."

Patrick shook his head doubtfully. "This is a natural formation. Not planned."

"God made nature, and He always has a plan."

"Unfortunately, in this case—" Patrick stared at the upper few inches of the trench wall: a bright ribbon of deep blue light. The rest of the wall was lifeless gray. "In this case…" Some distance away to the right, the ribbon transitioned to green. "Wait a minute…hold on…"

Immediately, Patrick set off, motioning for the others to follow. "Blue to green, then yellow, then orange, and on to red. That will get us out."

"How's that?" Jack asked, hurrying to catch up.

"The crystal citadel is casting a spectrum on this maze," Patrick said. "Christopher was right. There *is* a pattern to guide us. Blue is north; red is south. And south is up." He led swiftly. Each time they came to a lengthy run, he chose the direction that shifted toward the longer wavelengths.

"The sun is setting." Jack glanced at the fading color around them. "What happens if we're still in here when it gets dark?"

"We're almost out. We've made it to red."

"*All* the light is red now. The sun is setting."

Something large and solid swept overhead.

"What was that?!" Jack croaked.

"I hope we don't find out," Christopher muttered.

Patrick stopped. "Here's the exit." If the hair on his neck were not sopping wet, it would have been standing up.

Jack edged alongside. "What do you see?"

Patrick leaned out. "Nothing, I guess."

Jack stepped onto the ledge, rock axe in hand. The wind was much stronger outside the protection of the trenches. "Here." He handed Patrick Gwen's dagger. "Let's go on. It's not as if we have a choice."

The Defile of Ash was uniformly black and nearly featureless in the low light. The footpath was indistinct. Other than a single spot where the last rays of the sun filtered down from the west, the clouds were impenetrable. There would be no moon or stars visible that night. After sunset, the boys would be traveling blind.

First Jack, then Christopher leapt the gap in the ledge. Patrick took a breath, ran, and jumped. This time, he cleared the void with several feet to spare.

The boys labored up the crazy natural staircase toward the castle, using their hands as much as their feet, continually looking over their shoulders. The rain had become a deluge. The tilt of the haphazard steps into the defile was disconcerting, but it directed most of the rainwater into the canyon so there wasn't a cascade roaring tread-to-tread down the staircase.

All three boys were praying continuously without entirely realizing it—not monologues, but deep communications. And they were allowing the Holy Spirit within them to formulate the messages. Even Jack's prayers had progressed beyond stark pleas for deliverance, maturing into a genuine desire that God's will be done because the Lord's plan was ultimately the best one.

Their devotions did more than keep them from mental breakdown. Their prayers permitted God to continually alter their reality, hampering the six evil spirits prowling the citadel. Prayer dulled the demons' ability to strategize, detect, track, and attack.

But the boys were at their limits, and by the time they reached the citadel, the intense lightning was frightening them as much as the supernatural undercurrents. More than one jagged bolt arced so close to them that its flash and nerve-annihilating report were nearly simultaneous. Thunder reverberated the length of the defile.

Exposed and soaked, the boys were nonetheless hesitant to enter the castle. The blackness in the first room was as deep as India ink.

A pale rectangle defined the doorway on the far side of the chamber.

Jack steeled himself and marched across, holding the rock axe in his good hand, ready to swing, eyes darting side to side though he couldn't have seen an enemy an inch from his face.

They made it through the room without trouble.

A minute later, a carnalot picked up their scent. It was not hampered by low light. On the contrary, its lean and powerful body was optimized for quick, savage strikes in utter darkness. Moving silently atop the castle ruins, it slipped ahead of its prey. It planned to spring down and crush the first boy's skull, then pivot and claw through the second's throat before either knew what was happening. It would munch the third at its leisure.

Jack, Patrick, and Christopher came to a room with no roof. The last dying daylight revealed the chamber's south corner to be a steep silhouette embankment. The embankment and a few feet of the ground out from it were soggy Dartmoor dirt and grass, but the rest of the walls and floor were hard interstitial stone.

A cluster of mice on the silhouette slope nibbled on what appeared to be overripe berries. The animals knew nothing of the interstitial space concealing the boys.

Patrick walked to the corner and studied the unsuspecting rodents. "We need those mice."

Jack shot him an incredulous look.

"I'll get them," Christopher volunteered. "How many?"

"At least three, but more is better. Spares would be prudent."

Jack was flabbergasted. "We're in a hurry! What on earth do you intend to do with mice? Eat them?"

"They'll give us an advantage in a fight."

Christopher crept to the edge of the silhouette corner but kept to the interstitial side of the boundary so the mice wouldn't know he was there. "Why are they staggering and falling over like that?"

"I don't know, but stay off the grass until you're ready to grab them," Patrick cautioned. "They'll see you the moment you cross from interstitial to silhouette space."

"I'm ready."

"This is ridiculous. Keep moving." Jack reached for Patrick's arm to drag him away from the mice.

But Christopher was already poised. He lunged and snatched up several of the little animals. As a consequence of touching them, he became anchored to silhouette. Then he slipped on the slick, uneven slope.

Patrick stepped forward to steady Christopher and became anchored to silhouette through his contact with the little boy.

Reaching from across the interstitial boundary, Jack clasped Patrick's arm and also became anchored to silhouette—and consequently could no longer occupy interstitial space. He was instantly displaced two feet toward the embankment. If he had not been to Patrick's side, the two boys would have collided like billiard balls.

It was at the precise instant of Jack's displacement that the carnalot, having launched itself from the top of the northwest wall, reached the spot Jack had occupied a nanosecond before. Instead of being cushioned by its soft prey, it crunched into the southeast wall headfirst.

Jack responded entirely on instinct. He spun and swung his rock axe into the demon's skull. Patrick acted just as reflexively, letting go of Christopher and plunging Gwen's dagger into the carnalot's scabby torso. The blade went in up to the hilt.

The creature screeched. Hot, sticky fluid spurted out of its wounds. Half dazed, the demon shot a razor-clawed hand at Patrick, but Patrick bumped against Christopher and was ejected from the interstice into adjacent silhouette space. The carnalot's swipe missed by an inch. That put the demon even more off-balance.

Jack landed a blow that carried away a chunk of the carnalot's head.

Patrick, stepping away from Christopher, slashed so violently that Gwen's dagger severed its hand.

The boys were now beyond fear; they thrust and hacked in a frenzy.

The demon had endured enough. Its assault had gone horrifically wrong. God was clearly involved. It snatched its detached hand and fled. Sundry severed lumps wriggled after it, leaving only goo and disoriented fragments quivering on the floor.

The boys no longer noticed the howling wind or splashing rain.

Patrick sank to his knees and put a hand on the floor to support himself, trying not to touch any of the foul sludge swirling in the rainwater. "Rabid, jackal-jawed thing," he gasped.

"Cat-eyed, I would have said." Jack sagged against the wall, trembling.

"It had an evil man's face," whispered Christopher.

Patrick rinsed the ichor off his dagger and stood up. He stumbled, weak on his feet.

"How did it not kill us?" Jack asked.

"The mice," Patrick said. "When Christopher grabbed them, they anchored him to silhouette. I grabbed Christopher, and you grabbed me. This space"—he pointed at the stone floor beneath his and Jack's feet—"doesn't exist in silhouette, so you were thrown out of the demon's way." Patrick stared at the mice. "I haven't made complete sense of how anchoring works. Apparently, we don't have to be carried or riding an animal. Simply being in contact works. Which makes me wonder why insects landing on our skin or microbes entering our bodies don't do the same thing. I guess we don't know all the rules."

Jack did not have the time or inclination to try to understand; he accepted the fact. "How many mice do we have?"

Christopher looked at the furry creatures cupped in his palms. "Four." The boy made a sour face. "They relieved themselves on me."

"What's wrong with them? Why are they so docile?" Jack wondered.

"They're drunk," Patrick guessed. "They've been eating fermented berries."

"Where did the berries come from? This is March."

Patrick did not have the answer to that particular mystery, but he did have a recommendation. "We should each put a mouse in a pocket."

Jack didn't argue. They divided up the rodents. Christopher kept the spare.

"Watch this." Staying on the strip of silhouette Dartmoor grass, Patrick walked toward the doorway. But instead of turning to go through it, he walked straight into the stone wall.

And bounced off, nearly knocking himself out.

"Ow!"

He rubbed his head contemplatively.

"Exactly what did you expect to happen?" Jack asked, dumbfounded.

Patrick stared at the wall. "It's interstitial. I thought that if I were anchored to silhouette…" he stopped rubbing his head. "Oh. Maybe…"

He put his hand in his pocket and stepped cautiously forward. This time, he vanished into the wall. He reappeared out of it a moment later and waved to the others. "You have to have direct contact with your mouse. Anchoring doesn't work through clothing." Except that it *had* worked without direct contact with the horses. Perhaps because he and the others had been riding? Or the animals were bigger? What about when he merely bumped into Christopher a few minutes earlier? He'd have to think about it later.

"We can walk through these walls," Jack said in wonder. Then he laughed, drew a sharp breath, and laughed twice more. Or maybe it was a series of weird coughs. "That's convenient because, in another minute, we won't be able to *see* the walls."

As if responding to Jack's pronouncement, the last light dwindled away.

The boys' collective sense of purpose faltered. Getting to Gwen before dark had been critical. They had failed. Now, as much as they were afraid for her and still wanted to find her, they were preoccupied with their own situation.

"Keep moving. Hold onto the mice," Jack ordered. "Demons can't follow us through walls, right? Maybe we can stay ahead of them."

Chilled to the core, exhausted, apprehensive, and shivering, the boys stumbled across silhouette Dartmoor, more confused than guided by glimpses they got of the fossilized fortress when lightning flashed. Only Patrick had any idea where they were. He offered a suggestion when he thought they had drifted too far northeast. Otherwise, he slogged along behind Jack.

Jack had a very strong feeling that there were demons nearby. The evil things were getting closer.

Then the boys came to an open space.

"Is this the courtyard near the main gate?" Patrick asked. "Or are we lost?" The mouse in his pocket had stopped trembling. It was either playing dead or had fainted. Between lightning flares, the darkness was so absolute it seemed solid.

"We need light." Christopher meant to phrase the sentence as a prayer. It sounded more like a statement because he was too mixed up to think straight. No matter, God knew what he intended—had known from the beginning of time.

Moments later, the courtyard was ablaze. Half a dozen beings bright as the noontime sun strode out of the alleyway that led to the fortress's main gate.

Jack shrank backward. He was in the presence of thrumming dynamos radiating wild energy.

"Lieutenant—we've found the boys," proclaimed one of the beings.

"Yes. Very good," said the lieutenant.

When Jack had recovered from his fright, he saw tall, stern English soldiers with powerful flashlights.

Four of the men continued purposefully toward the interior of the citadel. The lieutenant—two pips on his uniform—and a corporal—two chevrons—stopped in the courtyard.

The officer addressed the boys. "You three—you dealt with one of the devils, eh?"

"Yes, sir," Jack replied, trembling.

"Are you Yanks?" Christopher asked in awe.

"British uniforms," Jack managed to say. His stomach was a knot, his legs wooden. In the soldiers' presence, he felt inadequate and oddly guilty.

The lieutenant turned to his subordinate. "Give the boys torches."

"Yes, sir." The corporal set his pack on the ground and opened a pouch. He handed Patrick a flashlight.

It looked ordinary but had an exceptionally strong beam. Remarkably, it didn't blind Patrick when he pointed it at his own face.

Jack reached for the next flashlight the corporal produced, but flinched. His injured shoulder had gotten worse after the fight with the demon.

The corporal placed his hands on Jack's shoulder. "Allow me." He kneaded the joint.

Jack cried out. But then he relaxed. "It…it's better." He moved his arm, marveling.

The corporal winked. "A little trick."

Thunder or gunshots—Jack could not determine which—echoed throughout the castle.

The corporal lit a campfire in the courtyard near the north tower. It grew into a cheerful blaze. The lieutenant motioned for the boys to warm themselves.

Christopher looked up at the officer. "Sir? We need to find our sister. She's all alone."

The lieutenant shook his head. "I'm afraid you can't reach her."

Jack's stomach twisted. "What do you mean, sir?"

"The south rim is occupied."

The boys were still trying to absorb this information when the lieutenant continued. "Our battalion is approaching from the west. This fortress overlooks our right flank." He looked around, assessing the citadel architecture up and down. "Post a watch in the gatehouse bastion."

Patrick signaled the lieutenant. "Excuse me, sir, but by 'gatehouse,' do you mean the rooms at the entrance to this formation?"

"Correct, Mr. McCray. That's where you can fight most effectively."

"Fight?" Jack twitched. "Sir, I'm afraid you've made a mistake. We're not soldiers."

The lieutenant's stare pierced Jack like a white-hot lance. "Are you with God," he asked, "or are you with the evil ones?"

Jack gulped. There was latent power in the officer that, unleashed, would crush him.

"Either you are with us, or your actions encumber, obstruct, and oppose ours. There *is no* neutral. Do you understand? Which side are you on?"

"Yours," Jack squeaked.

The lieutenant nodded in satisfaction and looked around one last time. "Much of this place is fragile." His gaze lingered on the structure that resembled a bell tower. "If you damage the buttresses, something could collapse on you."

The four soldiers who had dispersed throughout the castle returned.

"Cleaned 'em out, sir. Five total."

Pleased, the lieutenant acknowledged the report with a nod. "No casualties?"

"No, sir. Bebeas and Tharsal were injured, but neither has requested to be withdrawn."

"Excellent. You sealed off southern and eastern access?"

"Yes, sir. Nothing will be coming in from those directions."

The lieutenant turned to Jack. "You heard? We've blocked all entrances on the other side of the citadel, so you don't have to worry about anything getting in behind you."

He had a final piece of advice. "Take care of the mice in your pockets. With luck, they'll remain passive until morning." The lieutenant glanced at the stormy sky. "We have to be going."

"Why are you leaving?" Jack asked. The truth had sunk in. He had been rescued only to be abandoned and put in an even worse predicament.

"You'll have a couple of hours' peace. Then be ready."

The corporal waved. "Good luck to you."

"What about Gwen?" Christopher called, in tears.

But the angels had already passed out of the gate.

Hi Lara,

To answer your question, a Cambridge "college" is a department or subdivision of the university. It's not a stand-alone institution like an American college. Mine, Trinity College, is one of thirty-one colleges at Cambridge.

And to answer your other question, I'm looking because I want to know truth. I want to search and learn—not blindly accept what society and governments tell me I have to believe. Sometimes I'm tempted to agree with whatever my friends say because I don't want to be scorned, shunned, and canceled. Go with what's self-indulgent and popular.

But I hate it when I do that. I want to meet Him in person.

Kirk

CHAPTER 11

Kyrios

12-6-12

Nozmantis and many other demons called to Gwen through the darkness, vowing they would make her a goddess if she released the prism. She refused. Instead, she clung to it even tighter. The last of the anger and shame that had prevented her from asking for help was either scraped off by the rocky riverbed or torn away by claws.

Jesus! The cry burst out of her.

It wasn't a combination of sounds. It wasn't a group of letters visualized in her mind. It was the true Name. No other thought accompanied it.

Gwen saw God in all his majesty and power coming for her with a mighty host at His back. She didn't know or care if she was conscious, her body being tossed and spun in a raging river, or fantasizing, her brain already having been smashed against a boulder. The Lord was so beautiful that the yearning welling in her heart was nearly unbearable. She watched Him fling away the evil spirits.

All motion ceased.

Straightaway, Gwen found herself floating somewhere warm. She was at peace. She had done what was required of her. She had kept the prism.

She opened her eyes. What struck her first was the light. Specifically, it was the way the light made the world solid and real, as if, instead of photons, the true, actual essence of everything she saw was entering her pupils.

The stream's terminus was a wide stone-lined pool in a spacious glass building. The warm water was as clear as flawless crystal. She splashed it. Flying droplets sparked like diamonds lit by internal stars. Arms outstretched, she propelled handfuls into the air; an entire galaxy shimmered around her.

She slipped away from the tatters of her clothes. The wonderful water cleaned her body in a way she couldn't define. Her skin was entirely smooth and perfect. Her hair smelled fragrant.

For a time, she could not be sure of anything that had happened in the past. It was as if her history had been edited. She had memories, complete and specific, but they might have belonged to another person. Her entire life, past and future, had been rolled up and reconstituted. Her sins were gone—each and every one. Their consequences had not disappeared—the immediate damage could never be undone—but the eternal effects had been unscrambled and reassembled into the perfection that was before and would be again.

She dove underwater, glided to a flight of steps, and climbed out of the pool. Finding towels and clothes on a table, she dried herself and dressed. The soft, fresh fabric pleased her very much. The simple but elegant white dress was trimmed at its collar, cuffs, and hem with rose point lace of exceptional quality. She picked up shoes that had been set beside the table but did not put them on because the thick grass felt silky underfoot.

She walked outside.

There had been so much light around the pool that she hadn't noticed it was nighttime. The moon hung huge and silver above snow-covered heights to the west. The black firmament was spangled with stars. As she watched, however, the sky gradually lightened to pale blue. Then, it took on a golden-red hue. A bird sang. Reluctantly, Gwen put on the shoes.

"Hello, Gwennie."

Only one person called her that.

She spun around. "Freddie!" She threw herself into his arms and buried her face in his chest.

"You've come a long way!" he said happily.

It occurred to her that she had been longing to talk with him, but now that they were together, she didn't know what to say. Oddly, what came to her mind was, "Where do you live?"

He laughed and took her hand. "Come. I'll show you."

Freddie led her along a stone walkway to a road that followed the curve of a mountainside. A sprawling city came into view on the plain below. She was looking down on magnificent copper roofs and gilt domes: a sea of green patina flecked with gold. There were grand buildings with towers and spires of every design. She loved the rich textures of the alabaster and ebony facades, red and brown brick walls, and colored awnings. Bright flags and pennants fluttered everywhere. She thought of her visits to London and Paris during national celebrations, and the city was immediately reminiscent of them. The place felt increasingly familiar, but then again, increasingly new and exciting.

There was an odd effect: When she tilted her head or looked out of the corner of her eye, she saw the tall skyline of an American city… or curving Japanese roofs…or rural villages…or even the architecture of ancient Egypt or Persia.

She was sure she could touch the buildings if she merely extended her arm. She raised her hand and ran her fingers along the horizon, feeling the boundary between sky and ground.

Just then, the entire east flamed red and gold like a visual trumpet blast. The intensely bright light did not hurt Gwen's eyes or make her blink. It made everything she saw sumptuous and vibrant.

Freddie said, "Let's go down, shall we?"

He set a brisk pace, and Gwen loved it. Every part of her body felt energetic; she could walk—even run—all day. Movement was pleasure.

Freddie described the fantastic things he and his friends did in the King's service. He spoke so excitedly that Gwen was convinced her brother had the best job in the world. It was quite important and a continuous joy. While she was listening, for a fraction of a second, Gwen asked herself how she could be with Freddie, who had died, but the question evaporated before it was fully formulated in her mind.

Entering the city, they traversed parks and gardens resplendent with color. Gwen adored the picturesque houses with ivy-covered walls and luxuriant window boxes.

They came to a district with impressive buildings and proceeded down wide boulevards. Light streamed everywhere. The sounds of life and vitality possessed a musical quality that made her happy. She felt confident that every one of her favorite places was just around a corner.

Along their way, Freddie introduced her to dozens of delightful people, several of whom were apparently relatives, though Gwen couldn't remember ever having met them. Her brother was particularly eager for her to meet two Mahams: John and Robert.

"*Sir* Robert," Freddie announced.

"My! You seem too young to have been dubbed," Gwen told Sir Robert.

Freddie laughed cheerfully. Gwen did not know what was amusing but laughed with him.

Everyone greeted her with such warmth and joy that she felt enveloped in friendship. She was lucid…her mind was working perfectly, but it never occurred to her to question or analyze anything she was seeing or feeling or doing.

She, Freddie, John, and Sir Robert passed elegant examples of Gothic, Georgian, and neobaroque architecture. The quarter appeared very English to her, but for no clear reason, she believed it would have looked equally familiar to someone who had grown up in India, China, or Peru. Continually distracted by new attractions, she wasn't able to refine the thought. She felt a growing sense of expectation.

At last, they stood before the grandest palace Gwen could have imagined.

"Well, Gwennie"—Freddie looked thoughtfully at the splendid entrance—"you've gotten yourself a special invitation. Not many people get an advance visit, you know."

Before she could ask what he meant, her brother led her past the uniformed doorkeepers and through the great entryway. They strolled down exquisitely furnished corridors. There was life everywhere. The way exotic flowers flourished in vases and water-filled bowls, they might still have been growing.

After progressing quite a distance and climbing numerous flights of stairs, Gwen and Freddie were ushered into an expansive, high-ceilinged, well-appointed room. A dozen tall French doors in the rear wall opened to a balcony overlooking a broad plaza. She and Freddie were escorted by someone she first took to be a footman but then decided was a powerful officer or official.

There were further introductions, which seemed more like happy reunions than first meetings. Bountiful trays of food and drinks were available for the guests. Gwen could have eaten that food all day. The air was suffused with music and the happy hubbub of conversation. All her senses were in a state of delight.

Then, a wave of energy passed through the room. She became aware of a beautiful and awe-inspiring presence. The man drew all attention. He approached her.

He greeted her brother. "Hello, Freddie. Thank you for bringing her."

Freddie bowed. "Yes, Sire."

Gwen recognized the Lord. Suddenly, in her mind's eye, the wooden cross was above her, and she saw him hanging, infused with her sins. Then she saw him sweeping away the foul spirits that pursued her. Then she was back in the present, standing before him.

She dropped to her knees and bent her head. "Lord!"

It was all she could say. There were no words to describe what she felt. She was kneeling before someone of such power that her mind could not process the sensation. The entire universe was in him. She did not fear rebuke or punishment—all the damage she had caused had been swept away, and she was clean. But she was immobilized by intense awe. She could hardly breathe. The elation was so extreme and unusual that she thought she would explode.

Though her head was still bowed, she knew the Lord was pleased with her. She looked up and felt love for him unlike anything she could have imagined. It was adoration. It was worship.

Spontaneously, without prompt, Gwen said, "What should I do?"

The Lord smiled, but there was deep seriousness in it.

"Will you do what I ask?"

"I will."

"Will you set aside your own plans?"

"I will."

"Will you persevere in my purpose?"

"I will."

"Without reservation or condition?"

"Yes, Lord."

"Though it be difficult?"

"Yes, Lord."

The Lord placed his hand on Gwen's head. She felt his strength.

"Then, Gwendolyn Europa Maham, I commission you in my service. I command you to be steadfast in faith. Hold to what is true and right, and keep yourself uncorrupted. Hate what is evil; cling to what is good. Be resolute. Be humble. Be devoted to your brethren. Be joyful in hope, patient in affliction, and faithful in prayer. Bless and do not curse."

"Yes, Your Majesty."

"Do not be proud or conceited. Do not take revenge."

"I won't."

He took her hand and drew her to her feet.

Dr. John Maham stepped forward with a gleaming shield. He guided Gwen's left arm through the straps. Sir Robert put a sword into her right hand.

For a brief moment, she perceived the three aspects of the one single God: the infinite power and holiness of the Father, who is the substance of all things; the creating agency of the Son whose sacrifice saved the world; and the all-pervading and indwelling Spirit empowering those made in God's image to do His will. She was as ecstatic as if she had been swept up and carried into the air. Any other happiness was nothing compared to this. *This* was the job she was designed for: to love God and enjoy Him forever. She had once heard a vicar say that in heaven Christians could worship God without end. Sitting in the hard church pew, wishing she was out riding or playing with her brothers, she had thought that would be a dry, dreary existence indeed. Finally, she understood what worship really was.

"You have been presented this shield and sword so you may carry out your duties," proclaimed Sir Robert.

What duties? It was too late, but she wondered what she had signed up for.

The knight took the shield and sword from her and put them on a table. Somehow it felt as if she were still carrying them.

She was congratulated all around, though she didn't know why.

Later, she could not recall many details of what she had seen, heard, or felt that day. How could she remember experiences that her mind had no ability to process? The memories dissolved into tenuous bits and pieces of image, sound, smell, texture, and flavor. Feelings became difficult to reconstruct. But she remembered the intense joy, and that she had her heart's desire, and that every moment was somehow more wonderful than the last.

But what was it He wanted her to do?

CHAPTER 12

Fray

24-17-14

"Do you want the dagger?" Patrick asked.

"No, I rather like the axe." Jack swung it side to side experimentally.

Christopher sulked. "I need a weapon. What about my pocketknife? It's a big one."

Jack shook his head. "You have to hold a torch for us, and you have to keep your other hand on a mouse."

"Just a torch," Christopher grumbled.

"These aren't simple torches." Patrick directed the beam of his flashlight at the nearest wall. "Look."

Christopher knit his brows. "What is it? I don't see anything."

Patrick turned the beam parallel to the surface.

"How about now?"

"You mean the blue glow?"

"It's the boundary between silhouette and interstitial space."

Jack stood up and examined the effect. He slowly swept the beam of his own flashlight around the mineralized walls. "This place is like a jigsaw puzzle. With the mice, we'll be able to pop in and out of reach."

Patrick nodded. "Most of the interstices are filled with rock."

Jack stared at the walls. "We just might…not die." To his brother, he said, "You shine light. It's an essential job. We have to be able to see what's around us. Without you, we'd be blind." He looked at the campfire illuminating the courtyard. "Let's shut off our torches until we need them. We don't want to drain the batteries."

"Should we map the citadel first?" Patrick asked. "Make sure we're familiar with the terrain?"

"Oh," Jack said. "Of course. I meant we should shut off our torches *after* we scout around."

The rain had slackened to a mist. With their hands on the drunken mice squirming in their pockets, the boys explored the passages and rooms adjacent to the main gate, memorizing the layout and location of interstitial boundaries. Walking through walls was unnatural, and none of the three were entirely comfortable doing it. They began to call the feat *vaulting*.

"Remember to hold your mouse whenever you're near an interstice," Patrick cautioned. "If you enter an interstice without maintaining contact, the animal will vault without you."

Jack learned the lesson the hard way. He wandered across an interstitial boundary without his hand on his mouse, and the animal disappeared from his pocket, never to be seen again.

Christopher gave his brother the spare.

Jack named places to simplify communication. Gatehouse rooms included the sentry box, guardroom, and armory.

The boys crisscrossed the grounds until they knew them by heart. They identified the keep, kitchens, storehouses, and smithy. There was also the fossilized cathedral.

Virtually all structures, quartz or otherwise, were interstitial except for a narrow, vertical-sided tor at the front of the cathedral. The majority of open space was silhouette.

Quite by accident, they discovered a twenty-foot cube of interstitial stone riddled with small silhouette volumes; the trio vaulted through a gatehouse wall and found themselves in chaos. Their bodies appeared to have been chopped into pieces that slid, darted, and shifted about. Jack gasped but felt no pain—only a vibrating sensation.

"We're inside a kaleidoscope!" Christopher cried.

"Don't worry—we haven't been cut to pieces," Patrick said, after the initial shock had worn off. "Our bodies are distributed throughout bubbles of silhouette in a block of interstitial quartz. If we saw only silhouette, we'd see ourselves standing perfectly whole somewhere on Dartmoor."

The astonishing place was behind the mirrored wall that had fooled Jack when the boys first entered the fortress.

"We can hide in this kaleidoscope space!" Jack said, pleased with himself. For once he had worked out something Patrick hadn't. "There's no way for spirits to get in!"

He was exceedingly annoyed when Patrick argued against the idea.

"All the interstitial volume here is filled with quartz," Patrick said. "If one of us were to lose contact with his mouse and become anchored to Primary, he would be minced and all his parts entombed in stone."

Jack scowled. "Blast it all." He blew out an annoyed breath.

Patrick quickly added, "But that was very clever thinking, and we can use this kaleidoscope space as a temporary refuge if things get bad. Good idea, m'lord."

Jack felt patronized. He was more irritated than if he had been insulted. He turned on Patrick. "We've got to take some risks if we're going to survive. Don't we?"

Patrick nodded somberly.

Jack stomped off. "Let's make one last survey of the cathedral. If we have to fall back, it will be in that direction."

They hiked to the northeastern bulge of the fortress, where the massive glass cathedral overlooked the Defile of Ash. The moon was hidden. Still, the sky was pale enough to reveal the entire outline of the Gothic church and its soaring bell tower.

Patrick studied the eroded edifice and its flying buttresses. "I can see why the lieutenant warned us to stay away from here. That tower should have collapsed long ago."

"What's on the other side?" Christopher asked.

The boys vaulted through the tower into the cathedral's side yard, which sloped steeply downhill to the canyon's rim. The treacherous ground was strewn with granite rocks.

Patrick could not shake the impression that the leaning bell tower was gradually toppling into the Defile of Ash. He was afraid to touch the colossal but brittle quartz buttresses bracing its walls. Cold wind whistled eerily through the skeletal structure.

The boys stood shivering in the desolate yard for several minutes. Jack contemplated the fantastical cathedral and its crazy leaning tower. Then he turned and stared into the seemingly bottomless Defile of Ash. Finally, he gazed up at the half-seen mountain spur looming in the darkness above the citadel's southeastern perimeter. "Let's go." He led the way back to the gatehouse.

They took turns watching through the arrow slits in the bastion adjacent to the front gate. During Patrick's shift, Jack and Christopher loitered by the fire in the muddy courtyard.

"I can't believe the soldiers abandoned us," Jack grumbled. "They could have at least left us something to eat."

"They did." Christopher pointed at a haversack that had been set in a corner.

"What's inside?"

Christopher went and rummaged through the pack. He took out three paper-wrapped parcels and opened one. "Meat pies."

In other pouches, Christopher found cloth bandages, tubes of oint-ment, and bottles of ginger ale. He gave his brother a pie and a bottle.

Jack's stomach was a knotted ball; a few sips of ginger ale settled it a little. He nibbled on his meat pie and did what he could to hide his trembling. "I'm cold," he said, as if that were the cause of his shaking.

Christopher chewed mechanically and glanced nervously at the black, angular shadows in the gatehouse alleyway. Jack supposed he should say something to encourage his brother but couldn't think of anything that *was* encouraging. He rewrapped the remaining two-thirds of his meat pie and went to the bastion to take a turn as sentry.

When Jack arrived, Patrick was gazing forlornly through an arrow slit out into the plaza.

"Go get some food," Jack said.

Patrick sighed. "I don't feel much like eating."

"Neither did I. But you need something in your stomach—nourishment, you know. For the long night."

Patrick nodded reluctantly. "Very well." After glancing one more time out the arrow slit, he turned and stepped past Jack.

"Hey, McCray?"

Patrick looked back.

"You're all right."

It sounded like a farewell.

Patrick nodded. "You too, m'lord."

Alone in the bastion, Jack let himself shiver freely and began to pray in earnest. The living darkness was closing in. He was ashamed to be thinking about himself and his troubles rather than Gwen and little Christopher, but there was no helping it. Each second grew longer and longer. Nothing stretches time like waiting for something certain to be dreadful.

Just after ten o'clock, the air became very still. Jack clenched his jaw to silence his chattering teeth. The breeze picked up again, coming from the southwest, and a nauseating reek wafted in through the arrow slits. Nearly invisible in the dark, two cat-eyed carnalots slunk through the front gate.

Jack rushed through the corridor to the courtyard and gestured frantically. "They're here! They're here!"

The carnalots were inside the fortress before the boys could get to their preplanned positions. However, Christopher's flashlight blinded and disoriented the demons. They sprang at a specular reflection in the mirrored wall of the gatehouse and did not heed the axe and dagger coming from their sides.

Jack connected, dealing a crippling axe blow to a demon's shoulder.

Patrick extended Gwen's dagger but hardly had to move his hand to gore his opponent. The snarling carnalot lunged indiscriminately and ran into the blade, doing more damage to itself than Patrick could have.

The boys prayed fervently; that had become ingrained. But they failed to make good use of the mice. They were too preoccupied with surviving each moment to think ahead, let alone vault strategically.

How to describe the demons? They were dripping fangs and jagged claws half seen in the darkness. They were jointed appendages that shot out, their skin rough and diseased. They had eyes peering backward as well as forward. Their motions were rabid random frenzy. It was as if bits of madly whirling air solidified to become cutting tools. When the two demons attacked simultaneously, it was impossible to track which part belonged to which being.

The boys backed from the alley into the courtyard. However, by giving up what they wanted and praying sincerely that *God's* will be done instead of their own, they gave God leave to control their movements.

The demons lost.

One of the battered carnalots grabbed the exposed spine of the other and dragged its thrashing, biting, and screeching meal back the way the pair had come.

"To the gate!" Jack yelled.

The boys charged into the gatehouse alleyway.

But Jack stopped abruptly before they reached the mirrored wall.

"More of them are already inside!"

He didn't need to see the evil spirits. Their presence felt like cold, slimy sludge creeping on his skin.

"Where?" Christopher asked.

"Sentry box." Jack pointed at a wall. The sentry box was on the other side.

Patrick looked for a crack or hole to peer through. "Are you sure?" He couldn't move any closer to the wall because there was an interstitial boundary two feet from it.

Christopher did not realize the open-space interstice was there. He stepped toward the wall.

"Watch out!" Patrick yelled.

It was too late.

Christopher went through the boundary and, since he was holding his mouse, vaulted beyond the wall into the room with the demons.

"No!" Jack jumped to save his brother.

Patrick followed immediately behind.

The three machirai, their eyes startled by Christopher's brilliant flashlight beam and their minds dulled by God's response to the boys' prayers, were slow to react. Machirai specialize in grasping and consuming with surgical precision; they plan carefully and waste none of the substance of their prey. They are almost never surprised, so are especially vulnerable when they *are* surprised.

Jack saw the demons as many-armed apes with fang-filled skulls. Swinging his axe instinctively, he smashed the eyes and teeth of a machirai reaching for Christopher.

Patrick thought the demons' limbs were like snakes with human mouths. He slashed one.

"Retreat!" Jack flung his arm around Christopher and hauled the little boy through the northeast wall, across the corridor, and through the next wall into the guardroom.

Patrick came right after.

"Get ready!" Jack ordered.

Across the corridor, the sentry box reverberated with snarls, screams, scrambling, and crunching noises.

Axe at the ready, Jack crept into the corridor. Cautiously, apprehensively, he peeked into the sentry box.

The two machirai he and Patrick had wounded were preemptively consuming the third demon. Like snakes, the two feeding devils unhinged their jaws and devoured their thrashing comrade. But when their mouths met in the middle, each tried to expand its gullet around the other.

Jack darted back to report. "They're feeding."

The boys waited anxiously.

"Demons can move in both silhouette and interstitial space," Patrick muttered. "And they can attack us even when we're proxy-anchored to silhouette." His eyes narrowed. "But they're blocked by interstitial walls, whereas we vault right through."

He pondered.

"On the whole, we have the advantage."

The vicious snarls and frantic squeals coming from the guardroom evolved little by little into sucking and belching sounds. Finally, scraping and shuffling noises painted an auditory picture of something bloated and lethargic—the ultimate victor—dragging itself away to digest its meal.

Jack turned on Christopher. "Don't ever do that again!" He listened intently for another minute. "Actually..." his brow furrowed deeply. "Let's do that again." He looked southward and stiffened. "Do you feel them?"

Patrick and Christopher shook their heads, confused.

"They're inside the gate," Jack said, a distant look in his eyes. He stared intently at the room's southeast wall. "They'll be in the courtyard soon."

He thought for a while.

"We'll do the same thing as last time. Surprise the demons, wound one or two, and vault away." He drew his sleeve across his forehead to wipe away the sweat beading there. "Then we'll wait while they eat each other." Jack looked at Christopher and Patrick. They both nodded. "Our point of demarcation is...uh..." Jack looked left and right, at a loss.

"The interstitial boundary is two feet from the wall," Patrick said.

"Yes, of course." Jack pressed his elbows to his sides to keep his arms from trembling quite so badly. "All right. The demons are in the courtyard."

Patrick hesitated. "M'lord...are you sure?"

"Don't you *feel* them? This is it. Ready...set..." Jack swallowed. "GO!"

It worked—more or less.

The instant they vaulted into the courtyard, Jack and Patrick chopped and stabbed two of the five surprised carnalots lurking there. Then, together with Christopher, they vaulted back into the guardroom. The boys suffered minor scratches to their faces.

But contrary to Jack's expectations, one of the five carnalots did not linger in the courtyard to feed. Instead, it dashed into the gatehouse.

"On your guard!" Jack screamed, sensing the approaching monster.

The three boys jumped into formation in time to meet the carnalot as it sprang into the guardroom. Jack and Patrick hacked savagely, but the demon slashed Patrick's arm, clawed Jack's hip, and continued to press its attack, oblivious of its own injuries.

"Retreat!" Jack shrieked, "Armory!"

This time, Patrick shoved Christopher through the wall and Jack followed.

"Don't stop!" Jack yelled. "Keep going!"

Hands on their mice, the boys vaulted into the base of the north tower.

"Mind the drop!" Patrick cried. The tower's outer wall had crumbled into the Defile of Ash. The round room's floor was a broken platform a thousand feet above the deepest part of the abyss. "Stay on silhouette ground!"

Jack stared across the blackness to the opposite rim of the defile. "Do you think we could vault that way?"

"We have no way of knowing what's there," Patrick said, pulling his coat sleeve around his bleeding forearm. "It might be worse than here."

Jack grunted.

Patrick waited nervously by the door. "The injured demon has to go through the courtyard to get to us. Do you think it can get past the others?"

"Only a matter of time before *something* comes," Jack said, his voice cracking. He limped to the edge of the floor and peered down into the Defile of Ash.

And gasped.

Two hundred feet below, a line of demons—more than two dozen jackal-like carnalots and ape-like machirai—were scaling the canyon wall. They were led by something lithe and liquid gray—Colonel Sir Geoffrey would have called it an apok.

Sensing itself observed, the apok turned its head upward and locked eyes with Jack. The thing had terrible, penetrating eyes within eyes. Each oculus had multiple pupils, and the pupils had pupils.

To Jack, the demon's gaze was as paralyzing as a physical blow to his gut. He reeled—he didn't even realize he was falling toward the canyon until he felt himself swung sideways and around and realized Patrick had his arm and was pulling him from the precipice.

"I…" Overcome by nausea, Jack fought to keep his legs from buckling.

The apok yapped a series of earsplitting shrieks downward into the defile.

Jack dropped his axe, let go of the mouse in his pocket, and covered his ears to block the horrible sounds.

The demonic call was repeated and answered by howls and baying in the abyss.

Jack got on his knees. He leaned outward so that he could see what was happening below.

The demons were scrambling upward at breakneck speed.

Jack grabbed his axe, lurched to his feet, and shoved his trembling left hand into his coat pocket to make contact with his mouse. "Run!"

He sprinted pell-mell through the tower's eastern wall and continued blindly through several more interstitial walls after that.

Suddenly, the three boys were outdoors, standing in front of the cathedral. Jack hesitated only a moment before continuing on, vaulting through the bell tower into the side yard. The place was scattered with black shadows so absolute that anything could have hidden in them.

Jack looked back the way they had come and held up a hand. "Stop. They're too fast. We'll have to make a stand here." He indicated the archway at the base of the bell tower. "They're going to come through there."

Patrick stared at the soaring tower. "That's interstitial stone," he said slowly. His gaze wandered from the structure's canted top to the fragile quartz buttresses supporting it. "Falling interstitial rock should pass right through anyone anchored to silhouette." He took a long, deep breath. He looked scared but determined.

"The demons are gathering underneath the tower now," Jack said, hardly able to form words because his body was shaking so violently.

Patrick pulled his mouse from his pocket. "Master Christopher—keep this little fellow for me, will you?"

Confused, Christopher accepted Patrick's mouse.

Without the animal, Patrick was anchored to the Primary World. "Well," he said, "here goes." The yard was littered with heavy granite rocks. He scooped one up and marched to the nearest glass buttress.

"What are you doing?" Jack asked.

"I'm going to bring the tower down."

"*What?*"

"On the demons."

"Are you insane?" Jack yelled, diverted momentarily from his inward-looking fear by Patrick's irrational behavior.

"You're anchored to silhouette," Patrick called. "Falling interstitial stone won't hurt you." He slammed the granite rock against the flying buttress. The support was as thick as a large tree trunk but extraordinarily fragile. A big chunk of quartz splintered off.

"You're anchored to Primary, you idiot! Everything's going to come down on *you!*"

"Have my mouse ready for me."

"You *are* insane!"

There was no time to argue. The entire platoon of demons—condensed fear grown in the paralysis of nightmares spawned after blackest midnight—was in the bell tower.

Patrick struck the buttress again. It cracked all the way through. The tower shuddered and slouched. Patrick darted to another pillar. One blow with the granite rock completely shattered the buttress. Giant shards rained down. He barely dodged them.

The tower settled and swayed.

"Get out of there!" Jack screamed.

Patrick sprinted for the patch of silhouette where Jack and Christopher stood gaping upward at the swaying structure.

Demons emerged from the tower. Sensing something amiss, they also looked up.

The top of the tower crumbled. A chunk struck Patrick on the head, and he fell unconscious three feet from silhouette space.

Jack reached into the interstice—and vaulted to the other side of the tower. Anchored to silhouette, he couldn't reach Patrick. He jumped back to where he had started and let go of his mouse. Anchored to the Primary World, he dropped to his hands and knees, dove the front half of his body into the interstice, and seized Patrick's wrist. His legs remained in silhouette space at Christopher's feet.

"Christopher! Grab my ankle," Jack yelled. "And *don't* let go of your mouse!"

When Christopher made contact with Jack's ankle, all three boys became anchored to silhouette.

Jack and Patrick were thrown backward out of the interstice.

"Christopher—keep hold of my ankle!" Jack shouted. He gripped Patrick's wrist so tightly that the Irish boy would have cried out if he had been conscious.

The base of the bell tower burst entirely apart, and the whole structure crumbled. Fifty thousand tons of stone tumbled in a roaring avalanche down the steeply sloping yard and cascaded off the cliff into the Defile of Ash, sweeping all the mangled demons with it.

But the skipping, spinning quartz blocks passed through the boys as though they were ghosts. When the dust had settled, the three humans were completely untouched.

Hi Paige,

Tell Lara she really cheered me up. I'm glad you two are there for me.

I've attached the final pages of the first diary. The other photos in this message are of a guest list, room assignments, menus, servant instructions, and schedule of weekend activities. I found those papers in Lady Buckleigh's records. That woman organized and kept everything. Notice the dates—they're from March, 1918. You'll probably recognize a couple of names on the guest list: David Lloyd George and Winston Churchill. You know Churchill, at least.

Something odd happened at the party, and I think it affected the outcome of World War I. You can expect more on that thread after the holidays.

Kirk

CHAPTER 13

Taraph

43-34-4

Faintly discernible clouds above the jagged eastern mountains gave the horizon a bruised appearance. The harsh wind blew cold and cheerless. Everywhere, the ashen landscape was sharp and hard. But the canyon wasn't lifeless. It crawled with demons. They scuttled among monstrous stone barricades and spikes. Opposing them, approaching from the southwest, came the Army of Light.

From the debris-strewn cathedral yard by the cliff, all three boys saw the same thing: Even as darkness spread and absorbed whatever it touched, a wave of light swept into the Defile of Ash. The darkness tried to cling within crevices and holes in the canyon floor, but the light found and dispelled it.

However, the demons regrouped and attacked, driving back the angelic host. The boys were dismayed. Surely good was more powerful than evil? It seemed that the fortune of war was balanced. Beings of titanic power fought in the defile and on the mountainsides.

"What do you think is actually happening?" Jack asked after a time. No one considered the question odd.

Patrick spread his hands on the ground to steady himself. He had never felt so dizzy. "I don't even know when or where it's actually happening."

The boys began to think the outcome would go against the Lord's

Army. The pivotal factor turned out to be the crystal citadel on the cliff. If the demons had controlled it, they could have launched attacks from the east, downward on the angels' unprotected right flank. It would have been catastrophic. Why hadn't the angelic commanders placed troops to defend the citadel?

In the end, the demons could not outmaneuver the angels. The Army of Light breached their lines. Radiance entered every jagged fissure in the canyon's floor and every recess in its walls; no demon could hide.

The soldiers of God triumphed.

Jack, Patrick, and Christopher stumbled to the courtyard. Amazingly, the fire was still burning. They did not post a guard. The battle was over. Anyway, they were too weary to fight anymore.

"Patrick, your mouse died," Christopher said sadly. He laid the little body gently on the ground.

Patrick gazed at the dead mouse. Its mouth hung open pitifully. "We manhandled the poor things wretchedly. I feel sorry for them."

"Not very honorable of us," Jack said, "but we couldn't have survived without them." He sighed. "Mine's gone, so we have only one left." He looked at Patrick. "McCray, you have a nasty bruise where that rock hit you, and your wrist is oozing."

Jack opened the haversack and hunted until he had found disinfectant, salve, and bandages. "Christopher—help McCray with his arm, will you?"

Christopher cleaned and bandaged the deep scratches on Patrick's forearm. Next, he took care of Jack's wounded hip. After that, he dressed the rest of the nicks and cuts they all had.

Jack opened a bottle of ginger ale and took a sip. He wished he had not lost his axe; it was buried in the rubble that had tumbled into the canyon.

Christopher pulled the remaining mouse from his pocket and stroked its gray fur.

"Mordecai. I'm going to call you Mordecai. You're a hero, you know. Your brothers were heroes, too."

The little boy put Mordecai and some pie crust into a side pocket of the rucksack and carefully folded the pocket's flap so the mouse couldn't escape. Next, he used a shell-shaped stone to dig a grave for Patrick's mouse. After burying the dead animal, he solemnly placed the stone to mark the site.

The three boys sat silently for a time. There is a strange kind of relief that follows escape from death in battle. It is not necessarily joyful. It is frequently accompanied by feelings of insecurity and sometimes guilt, and it is quickly succeeded by depression and fears that rush in to fill the emotional vacuum. That is especially true if you are utterly exhausted, a person you love is missing, and you have no idea what to do or where to go next.

They lay down on the warm ground near the fire. None of them said anything. They were drained and aching. They had lost the prism. They didn't know where to search for it. They were wondering if they would ever see Gwen again.

They slept.

Jack opened his eyes. After he had gazed for a minute, he decided that the sky had a red tinge. It was near dawn. They could finally take action. But where should they look for Gwen? As he pondered, his eyes settled on a motionless, bird-shaped darkness perched on the tor poking out of the cathedral. He had a sudden, almost overpowering urge to flee.

Patrick stirred, followed Jack's line of sight, and tensed. "What is that?"

Jack fought to make his lips move. "A gargoyle."

Ordinary statues blocked light. This one absorbed it.

"That tor is silhouette," Patrick said apprehensively.

Jack missed the significance of Patrick's remark—that even a creature anchored to silhouette could perch in that place. The more Jack stared, the more he saw a raptor with ragged feathers, scimitar talons, and a hooked beak filled with rows of teeth. The apparition was much, much larger than any normal bird because it had a mutant skull and torso, plus muscular arms and legs merged like biological interstices into its avian body. The thing was fifty yards away. Even at that distance, Jack saw eyes within its eyes. "Cormorant," he squeaked.

Shadows on the west side of the cathedral grew darker as if the dawn had tipped backward. The freakish bird-shape leapt into the air and dissolved. Was it an illusion? Was what Jack had taken for eyes only red sunlight glinting off the tor?

No. The demon cormorant streaked overhead, flying out of sight beyond the gatehouse.

Jack and Patrick sprang up simultaneously. Each of them seized one of Christopher's arms, yanking the sleeping boy from where he lay.

"Aii!" Christopher yelped.

Neither Jack nor Patrick could explain why he did it, but it saved Christopher's life. The monster burst from nowhere and struck the ground where the little boy had been sleeping.

Missing its intended victim, the demon reared on its hind legs and pivoted, wings churning the air.

"The keep!" Jack commanded, meaning they should take refuge there.

The three boys bolted across the courtyard. They reached the entry hall of the mineralized keep a few steps ahead of their enemy. Jack cut to the right, pulling Christopher into a room. He was so focused on escape that he hardly noticed the pain in his injured hip.

The boys fled through the quartz-walled ruins, scrambling, slipping, and skipping wildly over the patchwork mix of soggy Devonshire moorland and slick citadel stone, barely evading the demon's snapping jaws and slashing claws. Time after time, the thing nearly caught them, only to vanish before making contact. It went through walls; it blinked in and out of existence, disappearing in one place and reappearing in another.

But room after room, the boys managed to dodge it. They turned left, right, left.

Then their luck ran out. They came to a room without an exit.

Backs to the far wall, panting, wide-eyed, they faced the demon. They had no weapons. They had left everything in the courtyard.

The nearly six-foot-tall raptor-demon sauntered closer. Pieces of the cormorant's body shifted among the demon parts. In addition to wings, the monster had long muscular arms and hands with needle-pointed fingers. What appeared to be shocks of hairs sprouting from its armpits were, in fact, feathers. The demon's blood-red eyes stared out from above the cormorant's. The lower half of its face curved forward in jagged, ripping jaws—that was what Jack had previously thought was a beak full of teeth.

The thing slowly spread its wings. The boys pressed their backs against the wall.

The demon lunged and disappeared, only to come at them from the side.

"Don't move!" Patrick yelled, holding Christopher to keep him from dodging. "Don't move! Don't move!"

The demon screamed and fluttered its motley wings in frustration. It thrust its face a foot from Jack's and growled: an extraordinary sound coming from an organism with the overall form of a bird.

Jack stood mesmerized by the demon's eyes. It was as if flaming spikes were being driven into his head. His legs lost all strength. The thing's breath was rancid.

"We're in an interstice, and you're across the threshold," Patrick said as calmly as he could. He addressed the demon but was speaking mainly for the benefit of his friends. "You can't touch us, can you? Your bird parts have you anchored to silhouette. You can't get into interstices." Privately, Patrick was thinking that he, Jack, and Christopher were about to die.

The demon slowly extended its jagged claws toward Patrick's throat. But it couldn't get any part of itself across the interstitial boundary. It screeched a succession of shrill and discordant sounds. While the words were unintelligible, the message was clear: *I am going to eat you.*

"We know who you are," Patrick said. "You're the taraph that stole the prism."

Jack tottered on trembling legs. "Father God," he said feebly, "I don't care about glory anymore. Just keep me standing."

"You're ugly, and you stink!" Christopher screamed at the demon. His voice quavered badly, spoiling his attempt to sound brave.

Patrick slid sideways along the wall. "Let's go. We'll be all right if we keep to interstices."

Jack didn't move. "How can we tell what's interstitial and what's not? Do either of you have your torch?"

"We don't need one," Patrick said. "I can see the boundaries." He was exaggerating to confuse the demon and calm his companions. He had some sense of where the boundaries might be, but that was all. Quietly, he prayed, "God, lead me, give me discernment."

The demon grinned. None of the boys had ever seen a creature with a beak grin. It made their skins crawl. The thing uttered an odd cackling noise: a smug, mocking snicker.

Patrick picked his way from room to room, doing his best to ignore the taraph's feints. He hugged the rough rock walls, keeping to narrow strips of interstice.

The increasingly frustrated demon crept alongside, never more than three feet away. Sometimes, the taraph thrust a clawed arm at the boys like a cat pawing at lizards it couldn't quite reach.

The boys prayed continuously, and God steadied them. The situation was roughly the inverse of the previous night when, anchored by contact with their mice, they had vaulted through interstices. Today, it was the demon predator, anchored to silhouette by its mortal cormorant parts, that vaulted through interstices, winking in and out of view. So long as the boys remained in interstitial space, they couldn't be touched.

Luckily, all the doorways in the keep were interstitial—all but the exit, which was fractured vertically so that only the lowest two feet were safe. Patrick wriggled through it on his back while the infuriated demon slashed the air above him. Once outside, Patrick climbed cautiously to his feet.

Jack and Christopher imitated Patrick's moves and made it safely out of the fossilized building.

"Where do we go from here?" Jack wondered.

Patrick studied the courtyard. After some reckoning, he pointed westward. "That thin strip of interstice runs to the gatehouse." He glanced at the taraph. "Once we're out of the citadel, we're home free. The landscape is interstitial for miles."

The demon snarled menacingly.

"Lead the way," Jack commanded.

Patrick sidled along the wall to the corner of the keep and paused there. "The interstitial strip is narrow." When he set out across the courtyard, he moved slowly and carefully as if on a tightrope. Jack and Christopher followed exactly in his footsteps.

The demon crisscrossed the interstitial path, springing at the boys. When that failed to trip them up, the monster dove through a wall and vanished.

Once across the courtyard, Patrick continued alongside the building until he was around the corner and could see into the gatehouse alley.

"Where do you suppose the taraph went?" Jack asked.

"There." Christopher pointed upward.

The demon cormorant was circling overhead.

"Let's run for the gate," Christopher urged.

"No!" Jack grabbed his brother's coat and held him immobile. "That's exactly what the devil wants us to do. It can dive faster than we can dash. And we have to make a turn. The alley appears to run straight to the gate, but we're looking at the angled, mirrored wall, remember?"

"There are interstitial lanes on both sides of this alley," Patrick said. "But the corridor from the mirrored wall to the gate is entirely silhouette."

Jack sat on his haunches. "Even if we can get outside the citadel, we won't be safe. The taraph can dissociate itself from the bird by killing the cormorant. After that, it can attack us wherever we are." He stared straight ahead without seeing anything. "We have to incapacitate the demon."

Patrick squatted next to Jack and thought for a while. "Killing the cormorant would sever the taraph's anchor to silhouette. But I'm sure the demon doesn't want to do that except as a last resort. It's bound to the bird—remember what Colonel Sir Geoffrey said about animal possession?"

"All right. How do we get through the gate?"

"I've been thinking about that," Patrick said. "One way or another, we have to cross twenty-five feet of silhouette."

The brothers waited for Patrick to present the solution, but he had none.

"It's easier to fight a pack of them," Jack grumbled.

The taraph continued to circle.

"And this one is fear incarnate," Patrick murmured.

"Let's trick it into conking itself out," Christopher suggested.

Jack frowned. "How would we do that?"

"The reflection…" Christopher pointed to the angled wall at the end of the alley. "We'll run at that. When the demon dives on us, we'll jump out of the way at the last second. The demon will miss us and smash itself." He looked at his brother. "Like what happened to you yesterday, but a lot worse."

Patrick shook his head. "The taraph is too smart for that. And anyway, the mirrored wall is interstitial. The demon would vault through it unharmed. The thing would turn around in the kaleidoscope space and come at us out of nowhere."

Jack stared fixedly at the mirrored wall as if looking into the bizarre kaleidoscope space beyond it. In the long silence that followed, his eyes became unfocused. He glanced at his companions. He licked dry lips and took a long, very deep breath. His face was white, but his expression was resolute. "I need Gwen's dagger."

Patrick looked to his right. "It's next to the haversack."

Jack gazed at the haversack, which lay beside the cold remains of the campfire. "The mouse is in the pack?"

Christopher nodded. "Yes. Poor Mordecai."

"I'm going to create a diversion." It was a true statement—incomplete but true.

"What kind?" Christopher asked, suddenly suspicious and disturbed by something in Jack's voice.

"Both of you—make your way to the end of this strip of interstice so you have a straight shot to the gate. I'll go in the other direction—out into the courtyard to grab the haversack and dagger. I'll be in silhouette. The demon won't be able to resist coming after me. When it does, you two run out the gate."

Patrick frowned. "The taraph is quicker than you. You said so yourself."

"I'll get the dagger before the demon can get me."

"Even so, how will *you* get out the gate?"

Jack ignored the question. Instead, he said, "Wait until the taraph comes after me. Then run as fast as you can for the exit. Don't look back. I'll use the mouse to get out another way."

"The demon is too fast," Patrick repeated.

"Not as fast as the carnalots last night. Have you noticed? The thing's cormorant parts slow it down."

Jack pulled Patrick close and whispered, "Get my brother out of here. Get him home, do you understand?" Jack was shaking badly. "Now. Let's do it *now*."

He sprinted toward the haversack.

"Wait…" Patrick called.

"Move, blast it, MOVE!" Jack yelled over his shoulder.

The taraph dove at Jack.

Patrick, in a flash, guessed what Jack had in mind. Jack was going to do something stupid. But there was no way to stop him.

"Christopher! Come with me!" Patrick grabbed the little boy's hand. "Jack—!"

Patrick hauled Christopher to the end of the alley.

The taraph wheeled, no longer interested in Jack, its wings cracking like gunshots. It zoomed into the alley. But Patrick and Christopher stopped in interstitial space—out of its reach. The monster thumped to the ground and, snarling like a furious lion, clawed madly at the humans it couldn't touch.

Jack got to the haversack. He slid his left hand into the pocket with the mouse and closed his fingers around the wriggling animal. Then he grabbed Gwen's dagger with his right hand.

The taraph launched itself into the air and thrust toward Jack. But perhaps the move was a feint. The moment Patrick and Christopher sprinted into silhouette space on their way to the gate, the devil twisted its body in midair and came roaring back so fast that its change of direction seemed to defy the laws of physics.

Nonetheless, the taraph's reactions were slowed by God's answer to the boys' prayers. As supernaturally fast as the thing was, it was a fraction of a second too late. Patrick and Christopher crossed the interstitial threshold to safety outside the citadel.

The demon screamed in an unholy rage.

By now, Jack was halfway into the gatehouse alley, running straight at the mirrored wall.

The demon spun about-face and sprang.

Jack didn't turn. He plunged into the mirrored wall and, anchored by Mordecai the mouse, vaulted into the kaleidoscope space.

The taraph was right behind Jack. Whether it was the distracting reflection, the boys' prayers, a flaw in the union of demon and bird, or Jack's sudden twist to evade the claws reaching for his back, the taraph entered the kaleidoscope space off balance.

Jack, eyes closed to block out the bewildering multitude of fragmented images, pivoted and swung the dagger with all his strength.

As Patrick had surmised, the kaleidoscope space was composed of tiny pockets and slivers of silhouette entirely enclosed within porous interstitial stone. That was why, when Jack sliced cleanly through the cormorant's neck, the taraph was in serious trouble. The thing shrieked, which was astonishing since it no longer had a head. The headless demon tried to back out of the kaleidoscope but could not. The bird's dying body performed what could only be called a dance. For a moment, the possessor was at the mercy of the possessed.

In desperation, the demon grabbed at Jack for a connection to silhouette through the mouse. Jack hacked off its groping fingers.

The cormorant died. Jack vaulted out of the room as the demon, with one last scream, was crushed and squeezed throughout the lattice of interstitial rock—all except three severed fingers hooked in Jack's coat.

The fingers gripped and flexed with a will of their own until Jack yanked them off and flung them as far down the alley as he could.

"The demon—" Patrick called from the gate.

"Trapped in the kaleidoscope space. I killed the cormorant," Jack said, panting and quivering.

"That was brilliant," Patrick said, awed. "And incredibly brave."

"Says someone who collapsed a building on himself."

Patrick could only grin.

Christopher ran and hugged his brother tightly. "Well done, Jack!"

Jack held out his hand to Patrick. "I guess I've matched you."

Patrick shook it firmly.

The sun crested the ridge to the east, and the entire citadel lit up in golden light.

CHAPTER 14

Breath

64-11-28

After a short conference in the courtyard, the boys gathered their belongings. Christopher set Mordecai on the ground. The animal hesitated.

"Go ahead. You're free."

Mordecai looked up, unconvinced.

"We can't take you with us. We have to find Gwen, and you'll disappear when we walk into interstitial space." Saying *interstitial space* in a sentence made Christopher feel clever and grown up.

Mordecai bolted. In a flash, he vanished into a hole. Christopher was sad for a minute, after which his thoughts turned exclusively to Gwen.

The three boys emerged from the castle into the plaza outside the front gate.

Christopher prayed as he walked. "Please, Jesus…"

Yes?

Christopher didn't literally hear a voice. It was more like remembering a conversation that had happened another day.

"I'd like my sister back. I know it might not be possible, and I'll understand if you can't do it…but we want to see her again."

Look for her.

"That's what we're planning to do. But where?"

Simply look.

Christopher told himself not to be frustrated or impatient, but it was hard.

"Look!" Jack cried.

Christopher raised his eyes. "Gwen!"

She was sitting near the south corner of the fortress, where the stream emptied into the canyon. Seeing them, she stood up.

Christopher covered the fifty yards in seconds and threw his arms around her.

Jack abandoned all reserve and joined the embrace. "You're alive!"

Gwen appraised the boys' torn and bloody clothes, bruised heads, and scratched faces. "From the look of you, I'm the one who should be surprised." Her white blouse and navy skirt appeared to not only have been mended, but also cleaned and pressed.

Patrick gazed at her. Gwen couldn't quite decipher the meaning of the joy on his face, but she liked it a lot.

"We lost the prism," Jack blurted.

Gwen took his wrist, lifted his hand, and pressed the prism into it. "Yes, but *I* got it back."

Jack stared at the glass in amazement.

"Ah, there you are." It was the lieutenant and his men. "Lads. M'lady." He tipped his cap to Gwen.

Jack, still stunned by the turn of events, said, "Sir—we found our sister."

"So I see. We were wondering if you would like breakfast?"

Some of the soldiers unpacked a camp stove and food while others set up folding chairs and a table.

The corporal pried the boys away from Gwen and tended their injuries. He cleaned cuts, scrapes, bruises, and bites. Then he applied a salve with a nice floral smell and put on clean bandages. "You're all healing nicely."

A soldier named Bebeas handed out new clothes. The boys went around the corner to change. When they returned, the table was laden with food.

After Jack said a heartfelt blessing, they breakfasted on eggs, sausages, tomatoes, and thick slices of toast with butter and marmalade. The boys gorged themselves.

Gwen had only a cup of tea, explaining that she had just come from a banquet. She tried to tell them what had happened but was frustrated. Her memories were elusive, and she couldn't clearly relate what she had experienced. If not for the prism and her brand-new-looking clothes, the boys might have doubted that the disjointed scenes she described were more than hallucinations.

Likewise, the boys' story confused Gwen. Without having been there, she had difficulty understanding how they had maneuvered between different places in the various fights or why they could sometimes pass through walls and sometimes couldn't. They didn't think to explain what they meant by *vault* until halfway through their narrative.

"We have a lot to reflect upon," Gwen said.

"Look in your mirror," the lieutenant advised. "What you see will help you."

Gwen smiled, but the lieutenant kept a straight face.

Jack and Patrick drank coffee to stay awake. Nothing could stop Christopher from dozing.

After a time, they all became contemplative and stopped talking. Jack thought about Pamela Hamilton. How would she respond to someone who claimed to have fought demons hand-to-hand? It wasn't something to worry about—he would never find out.

The soldiers folded the table and chairs. They set Christopher on the ground. The boy complained; they chuckled.

The lieutenant came over. "Time to be off."

The officer led the children along the ledge, which seemed a wider, easier path than it had the previous day. Gwen hiked upward without trouble. Sunlight made the Defile of Ash less threatening. They saw grass and even wildflowers growing in places.

Upon reaching the rim, the lieutenant followed a trail to an open field. There, he turned and saluted. "Our thanks."

Jack said what Patrick was thinking, "All we did was stay alive."

"You did what you were asked to do," said the angel in all seriousness.

The lieutenant drew Patrick aside and pointed to the other side of the meadow. "We brought your airplane, Mr. McCray. Made a few repairs. Thought you might want it back."

Patrick tramped across the field and examined the machine. It was sturdy and sound. "Better than new!"

Bebeas joined him. "It should do."

Patrick nodded his thanks. He looked around the field and noticed ephemeral lines where the world on either side didn't quite line up. He studied the ground. "You've put it on a bit of silhouette Dartmoor."

"Right-O."

"So I'll be able to come back and get it even after the Mahams and I are reanchored to silhouette."

Bebeas winked. "Good luck to you." He saluted and went after his departing comrades.

Patrick returned to where the Mahams stood at the trailhead.

"What do we do now?" Christopher asked.

Gwen savored the fresh air. She took a deep breath and let the sun linger on her face. "Let's go home."

Meanwhile...

Colonel Sir Geoffrey ran down the rough, grassy hillside. More accurately, he limped and stumbled down the hillside. He moved as fast as his numb, stiff legs would allow. He believed the farmhouse where he had been held captive was on the outskirts of the defunct Whitebarrow tin mine. His original plan had been to escape into nearby Wolf's Tor Mire and lose his pursuers there. He didn't want to get into a fight. The small, thin knife he kept in the lining of his boot wasn't much of a weapon. But it had come in handy. His kidnappers hadn't found it, and he had used it to cut himself free when they left him alone for a few minutes. Unfortunately, they were already after him.

He came upon a horizontal tunnel into the hillside, which confirmed that he was near Whitebarrow or another of Dartmoor's tin mines. He made a spot decision. He grabbed some brush to use as a torch and hurried into the tunnel. He was in luck. A sledgehammer had been left inside. He took it and pounded a timber post supporting the roof, intending to collapse the tunnel's entrance. He didn't know if there was another way out, but he would be caught if he stayed in the open, and his abductors were not about to let him live.

The top of the timber moved an inch or two after each swing. On the seventh blow, it came out from under its lintel, as the colonel intended. Then things went wrong.

The second book in The Mirror and
the Prism series is *Point of Refraction*

About the Author

W. F. Rogers is a spacecraft systems engineer and program manager. He loves history, and he loves his two daughters. He wrote The Mirror and the Prism series for them.

W&P | WAYRIDGE PRESS

9 798988 174905